"KILL THE GENERAL is an exciting and suspenseful thriller. It is also a complex and detailed character study of an individual - a roller coaster ride through the transitions which have taken place over the last decades in Romanian history." (Mike Phillips)

BOGDAN HRIB was born in 1966, in Bucharest, Romania. He is the author of the Stelian Munteanu series which features a book editor with a sideline in international police work. *Kill the General* is the fourth book in the Stelian Munteanu series and Bogdan Hrib's first novel translated into English.

His other books to date are *The Greek Connection* (2006), *The Curse of the Manuscript* (2008), and *Somalia, Mon Amour* (2009).

Introduction

KILL THE GENERAL constitutes a bridge between several different phases of recent Romanian history, and outlines the differences and continuities between several different generations of Romanians over the last four decades.

By his own account, Bogdan Hrib set out to construct a psychological novel which would, in part, dissect and explore how the traumas of life under a dictatorship had determined individuals' attitudes and behaviour. In fact, *Kill the General* goes a long way beyond the merely 'psychological' and turns out to be a remarkable panorama encapsulating the pressures of a rapidly changing state, and their effect on individuals.

Hrib began writing his novel in 2010, partly as a response to the current debates across Europe about the after effects of former totalitarian regimes. In the process *Kill the General* developed as an exciting and suspenseful thriller, as well as a series of reflections about the Romanian way of life (and death) over the last four decades.

It is not only the novel's suspense, characterisation and intricate plotting which holds it together, however. There is also an acute feeling for the detail of 20th century history, based on the life story of Hrib's hero, Stelian Munteanu, who, as the novel progresses, inhabits the roles of schoolboy, student, army recruit, and craftsman. Finally, after the *Revolution* introduces new freedoms he becomes an entrepreneur, travelling in various European capitals – Vienna, Copenhagen, London.

From these vantage points Munteanu offers the reader a privileged view of some important, and sometimes unexpected, historical events – Nixon's tour of Bucharest, the apocalyptic explosion at Chernobyl, the chaos and street violence which ended the dictatorship.

The real point of this structure, however, is not a simple record of events. The important factor is the way that Stelian locates himself in the historical landscape. Stelian sees and understands no more and no less than would any other person in the same circumstances. This fact lends an outstanding credibility to his accounts, and immerses the reader in the matter of fact and routine reactions of the characters. This is, after all, the way that most of us experience great events, as powerless actors on a stage too enormous to comprehend, overwhelmed or swept along by irresistible currents, or too occupied with our own affairs to notice the world turning. With the knowledge of hindsight, however, Stelian reports on his experiences with a pokerfaced humour which makes them a delight to read. When Chernobyl explodes, for example, the boys in his army unit announce the start of a nuclear war, and after the real nature of the event becomes clear, they eventually locate a Geiger counter and are terrified by the flickering of the needle, because no one knows how to read the instructions which are written in Cyrillic script.

The incident shows the boys veering between adolescent panic and insouciant ignorance, in contrast to the sobering grief of the unit commander. The humour is also punctuated by telling asides – earlier on, during the American President's visit to the Titan neighbourhood of Bucharest, Stelian sits on his father's shoulders, screaming 'OK, Nixon'. He notes that he was not arrested or punished, then remarks – 'but these were Ceauşescu's good years.'

The crucial issue of the book, however is about the transitions between the periods before and after the

Revolution. We are accustomed to regarding similar changes in politics and society as if they divided a country's history into two distinct parts – *before* and *after*. In *Kill the General* the moment of revolution is deeply ambiguous, itself a fundamental part of the mysterious process of change and development affecting the Romanian state and the individuals within it. In this process, *before* and *after* are phases of the same historical continuum, in which the moment *after* is merely the period in which the unfinished business from *before* is carried on, achieved, and finalised.

In this sense, Hrib's intention, to explore and debate the country's recent history is beautifully and precisely executed. To read *Kill the General* is to be inducted into the complexity and excitement at the root of current discussions about the recent history of this 'unknown' half of Europe.

Translating Hrib's complex intentions presents similar difficulties to those outlined in the introduction to George Arion's *Attack in the Library*. Written 30 years later, however, *Kill the General* avoids Attack's riddling playfulness with linguistic genres. His intention is, in many ways, however, equally challenging.

Kill the General lampoons 'official' language, and illustrates the way that words could become the medium of resistance. For instance, the word *'pride'* features in many official pronouncements and songs. At the same time, in the soldiers' parlance, one's *'pride'* came to mean *penis* or *prick*. So the boys in Stelian's unit could march off singing about their 'pride', deliberately provoking the ineffectual fury of their officers. This is also a clue to *Kill the General*'s challenging approach to the restrictions imposed by the classical academicians of the language, an approach which raises interesting issues. Swearing, in our Anglo-Saxon inflected English, can be reduced to a single word, e.g. 'shit'. In the Romanian (and

Latinate) tradition, swearing makes use of metaphors, often centred around the idea of abusing one's mother. Simply to mention someone's mother, or his mother's genitals, is to launch a deadly insult. Retaining the metaphor in translation creates formulations which sound foreign to English ears. On the other hand, and more importantly, the metaphor offers readers an intriguing sense of discovery about the way that everyday speech (in particular the military slang of a militaristic society) encapsulates cultural values and beliefs.

Kill the General, therefore, does not only explore the broad sweep of recent Romanian history and its effect on individuals and institutions. In its use of language, the novel also investigates trends within the developing culture and their relationship to the political and social environment.

This first and only rendering of *Kill the General* in English, conserves and highlights the subtleties and modulations of Hrib's Romanian, and communicates the unique and authentic flavour of the author's vision of his country and his compatriots.

Mike Phillips

KILL THE GENERAL

Acknowledgements

There are many people the author should thank.

I will start with my beloved wife, Teodora, who tolerated my creative moods and especially my state of agitation when inspiration ran dry or I could not find the time to write. Then Iulia, my daughter – I think I told this story for her and her generation, the people born in the third millennium, people for whom the times of Nicolae Ceaușescu are on the same level of fantasy as those of Vlad the Impaler. My parents and parents in law, on the other hand, who lived through those years, will understand my book very well.

In addition to the above, there are many friends and colleagues who encouraged me to write, even if 2010 was not an easy year for Romanian society in general. George Arion and Alexandru Arion were, each in their own way, wonderful catalysts for the making of this volume.

All my heartfelt thanks go to my friends from Tritonic Publishing House, Crime Scene imprint, Romanian Crime Writers Club, and *Flacăra* Magazine.

I am indebted to the small Romanian-British team from Profusion for their desire to translate and publish this novel outside the Romanian area.

There are many whom I haven't mentioned and who, at some time or other, had a good word or advice for me, offered me an idea or a coffee, took me for a walk outside or brought their honest criticism. A good thought goes to all of you.

Copenhagen offered me the chance to write in peace

and quiet in a civilised – albeit a little cold – place, close to Nyhavn. My wife and I have found a wonderful place there, where I could gather my thoughts when necessary – the Brooklyn Caffe. Further north, in Hellerup, a stone's throw away from the longest street in the world, the Standvej, I found another place where I could write surrounded by books, and where I could drink a very tasty hot chocolate – the English bookstore Books & Company. Leif Davidsen and the coffee we drank at the BogForum book fair, and also reading his novel "Lime's Photograph", brought home the importance of the stories in a book, and highlighted the issue of the narrator's role…

I would also like to thank my past and present characters. The veterans Stelian, Misha, Sofia, Toni have once again done their duty.

I was overwhelmed by memories several times, but I somehow managed to go on setting my story down on paper.

A big thank you to all of you.

Major characters

Stelian Munteanu, Romanian, 45, former journalist, book editor at Trident Publishing House, collaborator of *Flacăra* Magazine, and an adventurer. Friends accuse him of being a Lothario. He is Sofia's lover. Stelian is 1.78 metres tall, chestnut brown hair streaked with grey, green eyes, short hair. He sometimes wears a moustache.

Gheorghe Simionescu, Romanian, 63, a retired army General. He met Stelian in '85 when Stelian was undergoing obligatory army training in the town of *Buzău*, central Romania. At the time, Simionescu was a captain. A friendly if capricious fellow. 1.85 metres tall, white hair and baldness going back to the time when he attended the Military Academy.

Diana Monica Simionescu, Romanian, 25, the General's daughter. A TV presenter for a second-rate station in Bucharest – Star TV, a former model and graduate in journalism. She's not stupid, but she is superficial. Not a snob, but a bonne viveuse. She runs off to *Telega* in the countryside whenever she finds the time. 1.72 metres tall, black hair – probably dyed, dark blue eyes – probably not tinted contact lenses, she wears glasses when she's not on the TV. Her very absent husband works in IT. She wants children and to be a celebrity.

Anton (Toni) Demetriade, Romanian, 39, police commissar in Bucharest, former investigation partner of Stelian's in the case of *The Greek Connection*. Married with a child in school. He's obsessed by the fear of getting fatter and keeps popping all sorts of pills to prevent it.

Sofia Matei, Romanian, 34, Stelian's lover, Professor of geopolitics, working in London. She featured in the book *Somalia, Mon Amour*.

Mikhail (Misha) Sergeyevich Pushkin, Russian, about 65, former FSB, KGB and maybe MI6, knows all and appears whenever he's not expected. A major character who puts in episodic appearances.

Steiner, Austrian, around 50, chief inspector in the Viennese police, he featured in *The Greek Connection*. Tall, white hair, doesn't speak much.

Prologue

Vienna, December 2010

I OPEN MY EYES AND I CAN'T SEE A THING. I shiver. In the room it's cold. This is the first sensation. Unpleasant. Then, in the silence of the room, I hear her deep, rhythmic breathing. I feel her hand on my right cheek. I start to feel calmer. This is the second sensation, a good one. My vision clears, and through the huge windows, I can see festive wreaths glowing with tiny bulbs. The glass is clean and the little points of light hurt my eyes. I sit up in bed and gaze at the view outside.

The sky is beginning to acquire a sombre dark violet tint. Five visibly freezing pedestrians hurry past, walking with long strides on the wet asphalt. It was raining during the night. I had been sunk in a deep sleep, so I hadn't heard it.

The weather seems quiet now. I try to work out if there's a wind. There are no trees out there, and nothing else seems to move. A car goes by and, braking sharply, turns to the right. The red stop lights invade my field of vision. Without realising it, I put a hand to my face, and groan. The bed shudders. She gives a start and sighs. My eyes still hurt and my vision is still hazy. My glasses. I stretch my arm out in the direction of the bedside table and search for them. I place them on my nose. They are filthy with the marks of my fingers. I have no inclination or handkerchief to wipe them clean. I give up.

It's quiet. I am glad of that. I keep staring at nothing. It's as if I want to stop time. A new sensation... as if I want to freeze it. The sky gains more colour. The violet transforms into reddish-orange. She stirs besides me and the rustle of the white sheets makes me feel dizzy. I lust for her. I long to run away. I think I am longing to run away from myself and my memories. Memories from my past and, most of all, memories from my future. I am very afraid of the memories which are still to come.

Time doesn't dissolve, though. It doesn't freeze either... *because* a black limo goes by, and then brakes suddenly with a brutal flashing of red lights; *because* two men dressed in heavy black overcoats and carrying huge briefcases, walk along the grey pavement with big, determined strides; *because* somewhere on the last floor of the store in front of my window, in the Japanese restaurant with all its lights on, a silhouette washes the floors, in between the deserted tables; *because* across the road, on the ground floor of the Mexx or the Zara or whatever store it is, a young man dresses the manikins in huge red paper sheets on which the word SALE is written; *because* the small wooden huts in front of the hotel open their shutters from the inside, as if they are haunted by ghosts; *because*...

"What's up, honey? Are you all right?"

I turn to face her. She looks at me with small, barely opened eyes, through the blonde dishevelled strands of hair. She's smiling.

"Are you feeling well? Is everything OK?"

I smile. I touch her pouting, baffled face with my fingers.

"Everything's fine. I was watching the street..."

My demons harass me. Fears and lost battles. All the dirt I've swam through for these past two years. And the years before that. My heart beats madly … I should take my hawthorn-berry pills. Why am I running all the time? Why can't I stop?

"I was watching the lights. The city is waking up."

"Do you want us to wake up too? To go and eat, to go out?"

I smile again and look around. On the little table near the door she has placed a bird cage. Inside it is a yellow Post It note marked S & S. Pff… If only I knew what I want. Actually, I know, but I lack the courage. I need a clear ending, a full stop, so that I can start over. Why am I fighting with myself? What for? Why? Who am I fighting?

"No. Go to sleep. I'll read a little."

"Fine."

She closes her eyes and falls asleep. I take her book and open it at the bookmark I left earlier. Page 9. Meaning only the third page of text. I can't read. I want… I want quiet. The type of quiet I don't know how to find in this world. Not right now.

When I wake up again it's a bright day. The clear skies are as blue as they are in postcards. She sleeps, sunshine on her face. Something pokes me under my left shoulder. It's the book. I pick it up with my right hand while I try to smooth its wrinkled covers. It's his memoirs. Red background with the picture of a general's cap. Thick, sharp, black letters say *My Revolution* by Gheorghe Simionescu. 516 pages, large format, paperback. An expensive-looking book.

On the back, Simionescu, wearing his general's uniform, looks at me with a sombre and solemn air. It's a good photo, he sent it to me himself, but it's too official, too *APV* (the first time I saw these initials I had no idea that they stood for the words, *Armată pe viață* - Army For Life), as if he had a stick up his arse. Now it's been published, I can't read it. It's a beautiful volume and I am proud of it, but I just can't read it. That general's hat and his photo stop me in my tracks … The official, half-hidden smile sends a covert message which says "I know everything". I first noticed this kind of smile on Misha every time he shook hands with someone he had just met for the first time.

The story of how this book came about also inhibits me from reading it. All books have a story, the one behind the printed words. Here it's different. I don't know if it's more dramatic or sadder or more profound. Normally, stories are either very sad, or nauseatingly beautiful and full of moral instruction.

In this case, I am part of the story too, and not simply as an editor. The truth is that this story can be told. Now. By me. Here it is!

Part One

We shouldn't be looking for heroes, we should be looking for good ideas.

Noam Chomsky

Chapter 1

Vienna, August 2010

MY FINGER IS ON THE TRIGGER. It's early. The city is sleeping. A grey-winged white gull, popping up out of nowhere, nosedives in front of the open window. I always loved Vienna, either as a tourist or on business. I always found something new, something pleasant here. A wine or a stew. A small café hidden in a side street, a good beer, a huge schnitzel, people smiling, a building, a tree, roses... I've seen pensioners holding hands in the park... I am enveloped by a nostalgia that clouds my eyes and relaxes my muscles...

I am looking for excuses for myself. I cannot pull the trigger. The time is flying. If I don't make a decision now... I have no guarantee that the General will still be here the following night. My finger is on the trigger guard. I am afraid to touch the trigger. The bullet may fly out accidentally, even though I know this is impossible...

I keep on thinking about money. About the money that will come in and the debts I'll need to cover. Also the launch of the book. Killing a man to pay back your debts to the state – it's mad, it's cynical! And we're not even talking about a lot of money. I should just take the money and disappear, like in the movies. That won't cover much of my debt either. They wrote me saying that, until I got my hand in, I would be paid less...

Oh god – until I got my hand in? I don't know if I want to go any further... I didn't think I would get this far... Shooting a bullet... killing. These were movie plots, a few of them good, and many of them very bad!

I know for a fact that, were I to be facing him, I could not fire. Because he would look me in the eye. What about shooting from a distance? From nearly 200 metres away, I see him only through the telescopic sight. It's as if he's not in this world, as if he's somewhere in another universe, like in a computer game. Actually, this is a game, I lie to myself.

Haydn Hotel is right on the corner of a street, on the first and second floors of a building in Maria Hilfer Strasse, close by the church and Haydn's statue. On the ground floor there is a rather expensive restaurant. I have been there a couple of times. Once, I went for breakfast. The other time I went in late one evening and had a large cognac to warm myself up. On the third floor there's another hotel, a bed and breakfast, and then the top two floors are occupied by private flats. A strange 19th century building.

At the corner of this building there is a big room with a double bed from where you can look at the street. I stayed in there. Room 128. When the bells toll, you feel as if you're right inside the church, near the altar... Lord, forgive me... I told Diana to book this room for him. I also suggested that she should tell him to sleep with the curtains open, so he could admire the wonderful panorama of the boulevard. All was premeditated. I had prepared my ground. In detail.

The gun is a very new one - that is, the model itself, not just the year when it was made. It's an Austrian gun, a Steyr-Mannlicher SSG 08, nearly 1.2 metres long, and weighing 6 kilos. The sites and blogs say this rifle is used by the mysterious special forces unit of the Austrian police, named Cobra. I could not find any other details about it. I didn't try too hard either. I only looked for it in open sources. It's rated with God knows how many stars in the lists made by nutcases who try out their guns in firing ranges across the world.

I got it as a present. From Misha. It wasn't exactly my birthday. It was February. A kind of idiotic gift for Valentine's Day. Of course, it was calculated. It was also he who pushed me into this trade. He convinced me. He manipulated me. I received the order directly and mysteriously, in an envelope shoved under my door, and through an email from an unknown address, but I am convinced it was Mikhail Sergeyevich Pushkin who found me this job. He wanted to transform me into a paid assassin. And he succeeded.

Sweat flows in big drops from my forehead to the floor. I have paper towels in my pocket, but this is not the moment. I look through the sight and the crosshairs are on the General's heart. I see him breathing in and out, deeply and rhythmically. He is peaceful. He sleeps on his back. I didn't convince him to do that. I couldn't have. I am a lucky man. I have a perfect shot. I just need to lower the trigger guard and then pull the trigger. One bullet is enough from this distance. I can't miss. He is too close. I am perfectly poised and I have been trained well enough. I have ten cartridges, but one will be enough. Straight through the heart.

Running through my memory, on fast forward and in short sequences, I see the people I love, the people I care for. My parents, Lulu, Sofia, life-time friends and drinking buddies. I am doing this for them! I deceive myself with excuses. I feel the mobile phone in the breast pocket on the right. It doesn't ring, although I want it to. It can't. I turned it off so that it can't give me away. But I would like it to ring, so that I could hear my girls' voices, either Sofia's or Little Lulu's. I feel like calling them. It's too early, and, paradoxically, it is also too late. Oh, mama, I am pathetic! Before becoming a killer I became pathetic.

A police car glides past silently, startling me. They are on patrol, rolling slowly, without the lights flashing. Five people on the street. Four men with briefcases and a young blonde with a red backpack. An overloaded white van. The noises of a city about to wake up begin to make themselves heard. The whirring of metal shutters being raised. Muffled voices. Brakes, engines...

I should get this job done and get the hell out of here!

The tension in my trigger finger is growing...

Chapter 2

Bucharest - Buzău, September 1985

I AM A BUCHAREST BOY. I was born in the *Titan* neighbourhood in those times when the park was still a deep hole filled with brownish, muddy water, where – so the legend had it – one of those army machines, which I would get to know by the name of TAB, years later, had sunk. This is a sort of armoured vehicle which has wheels and a propeller. It was supposed to float but it had sunk like a rock. Apparently they were still testing the thing. They tried for several hours to pull the soldiers out. They made it. With the whole neighbourhood watching. In fact, it wasn't such a big neighbourhood. There were some blocks of flats already built, but they weren't packed so densely and most of them were only four storeys high. Ours had ten floors, and we lived on the ground floor.

The park offered me numerous happy moments. Bike riding which invariably ended in my going back home with knees scraped and blood trickling down my legs to my Chinese-made tennis shoes. Another legend told by my parents says that I started to ride a bike when I was five. I simply started riding it and didn't want to get off. I have many memories connected to that park, such as wandering around by boat on the lake and escaping to the artificial islets, which were covered in tall green grasses and wavy willows, where we used to play at being Robinson Crusoe. Then, there were the snow slides in winter, and my wooden sleigh. And the very white, very clean snow.

My parents also say that some time in the '70s, when Nixon visited Romania, he also did a tour in *Titan* to see how the people lived. And I was sitting on my father's shoulders, screaming "OK, Nixon!" Nobody arrested us – maybe they didn't hear us, but, then again, those were Ceaușescu's good years.

I never went too far from my neighbourhood at the beginning. I attended School no. 199, behind the block of flats that everyone called the Horseshoe. The building curved, but it didn't look like a horseshoe in any way. The ground floor of this place was occupied by a local "commercial area"[1], which included an *Alimentara* store, where I have a vague memory that for one Leu[2] I used to buy a knotted bread-roll called "Japanese", or a cornet with honey and poppy seeds. The money I had left over was enough to buy several slices of *Parizer*[3] salami. *Parizer* used to be good back then. It had a friendly pinkish colour and smelt like fresh meat. Maybe the filling was not quite natural, but I didn't know it. You could eat it, it had no cartilage remnants, and it didn't smell of petrol[4]. There was also a cake shop, an *Aprozar*, and I don't know what else.

Then we moved over to *Pantelimon*[5] and I already had

1 In communist Romania the overwhelming majority of stores were owned by the state. Each neighbourhood had a so-called commercial area where the people could buy their groceries, household wares, electrical appliances, etc. Food stores (which incorporated the functions of bakeries, butcheries and dairy stores) were called *Alimentara*. Vegetables were sold in different shops, called *Aprozar* (short for *Aprovizionare zarzavaturi* – vegetable supplies), or *Gostat* (short for *Gospodărie de stat* – State-owned farm).
2 Leu – plural Lei, is the name of the Romanian currency. The name means lion, and it stems from the lion emblem of Dutch dollars in circulation from the 17th century in the Romanian principalities.
3 *Parizer* is a type of salami similar to the Italian mortadella. It was the basis for economic meals and was a staple of sandwiches.
4 In the 1980s, rumour had it that Romanian scientists had developed a meat-like protein from refined oil, and were experimenting with it in combination with soya and algae proteins.
5 Another neighbourhood of Bucharest; nearer to the village of the same name on the outskirts of the city.

my own room. We were no longer five people living in three connected rooms: now we were three living in four rooms. My recollections of that time are not too clear and are not very chronologically ordered either. Just images and pieces of conversation.

Then came the earthquake of '77, which caused serious damage to our new block of flats in *Pantelimon*, where the walls of the bedrooms collapsed, right where the beds were supposed to be; it was lucky we had not yet moved in. The earthquake saved me from an anti-rabies injection in my belly (Jack, the almost-blind dog living behind my block had bitten me; some two days later someone poisoned it), which would have been inflicted on me on March the 5th. On the 6th I saw the first collapsed building on *Ştefan cel Mare Boulevard*, after *Obor Passage*, as you go towards the hospital.

Then my grandmother Bebe got sick. An ill-fated cancer. My family kept me away from her, so that I could concentrate on my lessons. By that time, I was in School no. 51 in *Pantelimon*. I was no longer taking Russian classes. I was learning French instead. I even had a home tutor so that I could catch up. French was difficult, but I enjoyed clowning around, putting heavy stress on the Rs. My grandmother died one evening when I was preparing for the final exam paper of the term. It might have been Maths. They didn't tell me. I don't know what mark I got, I can't remember. But I remember the funeral, in the Catholic quarter of Belu Cemetery. That was the day I became less of a child, because the world is not fair. That was also the time when I started to understand this.

Then, I forgot again, or I pretended to forget, in order to hide deep inside my mind all that I had seen: crumpled walls, buildings destroyed by the earthquake, and – most of all – the sinister wooden coffin. That was the first coffin I gazed at from very, very near. And inside was a motionless being that vaguely resembled my grandmother. Like a doll. Then I understood that she was no more, and I felt alone for the first time in my life. Not alone in the sense that you are out to play and the other children are in, having dinner, or out at school. I was alone and abandoned. Left behind, an orphan. I cannot remember whether I cried or not, maybe I did. I was hollow on the inside, I was lost.

Memories become jumbled and disorderly. Just some images, words, and sometimes smells. How strange that I can recall smells. Like the smell of coffee that had overflowed on the hot cooker. The smell of natural coffee and, with the passing of time, the indefinite smell of horse-brew[6]. It smelled like rotting medicine. And again, from time to time, the smell of black market coffee – the golden 250 gramme packs of Wiener Kaffe[7]…

I finished the 8th grade[8] in School no. 51. It was near a church which was demolished. Or that's how I remember it, anyway. I remember a bulldozer and a crane with a dangling demolition ball. I remember revving engines and the smell of burnt diesel, and silent people carrying empty bags, passing by with small steps, casting furtive glances, so that no one would notice, and report their interest. I remember the militia with their exhausted Dacias[9] with blue protuberances,

---

6 Horse-brew – *Nechezol* (from a necheza – to neigh), mocking name given by the public to the (too little) coffee-based replacement generally sold in shops instead of coffee.
7 This coffee was normally brought in by truckers from Austria or Hungary, and was either sold or given as gifts/incentives. Wiener Kaffee was the most often encountered. There was also the superior Alvorada (gold or silver). The Austrian firm Alvorada producing these coffees is still in business. Another black market favourite was Eduscho (also still in business).
8 Romanian education has eight primary school grades, from age 6 to age 14. Then follow four high-school years, the grades 9 to 12.
9 Dacia – the national Romanian car. Based on Renault 12, Dacia models 1300 and 1310 were fabricated with some (minor) changes from 1969 to 2004.

which looked like bumps on the head, and functioned as warning lights. I also remember the big bellied *tablagii*[10] in their blue, badly cut and worn out uniforms.

Then came lyceum at *Mişu*'s[11], studying the mathematical-physics curriculum. Old building. New schoolmates. The first thrills. The first romance novels. At least we used to call them novels. Here the memories are very mixed, but I have a shoebox full of letters and black and white photographs from that time, and if I want to remember anything, I look at the albums, or into the envelopes filled with photos which were never mounted. I didn't have the time to do it. I didn't want to. Other priorities. I was nearly ready to fail my *Treapta I* exams[12]. The red line was exactly under my name.

Then came my target shooting period. It felt very good to hold a gun in my hands. Not because it empowered me – oh, no! I didn't think about stealing bullets, about attacking the regime or I don't know what. No way. I was testing the potential of my solitude. Just the gun and I, aiming at a target – a paper with circles – placed at 100, 200, or even more metres away. I forget... I was alone. It was just me and an object which acted on my behalf, like a slave, like a servant. I was testing my solitude rather too much at that time. At home I was alone doing my homework, if I felt like it. When I didn't feel like it, I used to read. I used to read like mad. I wouldn't remember very much about the

10 Militia men – so-called because of the epaulettes they wore; the term was derogatory, intended to imply corruption and incompetence; the term also denoted sergeants and under officers whose rank was signalled by metal strips on their epaulettes. Ranks are no longer signalled like this, but the term is still used as an insult to the lower ranks in the army and police force.

11 *Mişu* (pronounced Mishu) was *Mihai Viteazul* (Michael the Brave) Lyceum in Bucharest, now a National College. At the time it was the second most prestigious lyceum in the country, and the mathematics-physics curriculum was reserved for the top percentile.

12 *Treapta I, Treapta II* and the Bacalaureat were the examinations which defined the four years of lyceum education.

TV. Maybe just about Saturday night, watching Studio X on Bulgarian TV[13]. They had American films now and then, but they were dubbed in Bulgarian. Mannix in Bulgarian, Colombo in Bulgarian. Even John Wayne. In a way I found it funny.

In the second year at Mișu's, my school report looked really bad. They said I was going to fail the *Treapta II* exams[14] and that I would be better off heading to a vocational school. I can't remember who said this. Not my parents. Maybe our Class Tutor. After all she was the one who taught Maths. I gave up target shooting. I passed the *Treapta II* exams. Thirteenth on the list. I felt happy because I had taught them a lesson. But I forgot my great victory soon enough. Stupid...

I erased shooting from my life and my next year at school was spent in a perpetual party. The Saturday evening "teas". Rotated between every member of the group. Dancing, music on pirated tapes recorded at the cost of one Leu per minute, some sandwiches with salami and pickles, black market Pepsi[15] – brought from the factory in *Constanța*, the only one that still respected the original recipe – , home-made wines from the countryside (weren't we too young for wine? Maybe the alcohol comes from other memories). And, of course, the idylls, the kissing and groping, – the blues going on as the lights went off, or just a dim lamp, so no-one could see where your hands were busy. Then the friends' beds and the locked rooms.

Films on video towards the morning, when we all came out with our hair dishevelled and our clothes wrinkled, but smiling, and the boys, testing the manhood which had just

13 Southern Romania received signal from Bulgarian or Serbian TV.
14 Romanian high-schools required a first entry exam, for the first year of the Lyceum, and then another one, when students could theoretically change schools, two years later.
15 Pepsi was produced under licence in Romania from the early 1970s.

been aroused, employed Rambo's machine guns without understanding what the hell those guys were actually doing in Vietnam.

The *bac* was easy – or at least that's how I remember it. They all laughed at me – my colleagues, that is - when I announced that for my university course I had chosen the Civil Engineering School. They were aspiring doctors, or boys with dreams of aeronautics or electronics, girls dreaming of the School of Economics.

Civil Engineering was good for me. If it wasn't going to be History, then Civil Engineering was very good. But History and me is a different story. Not for now.

By comparison it ought to have been easier for me as an engineer. My parents had explained to me how one could be permanently seconded for employment[16] in closed cities[17] one could also earn good money on the building site for the People's House[18] if one had a *pilă*[19], a connection to fix it, then, afterwards, I only had to latch onto a trip to Yugoslavia in order to make my escape[20].

I passed the university entrance exams and then came the last summer holiday. And then came the letter[21]. The recruitment order. A wretched little document, badly printed

16   The communist state sent its graduate specialists wherever it seemed necessary to have them. The system could be avoided at a fair price, or with connections in the high places.
17   Cities like Bucharest which already had full employment. To be seconded to these areas implied the ability to exert unofficial or corrupt influence.
18   Nowadays the Palace of Parliament, the second largest building in the world after the Pentagon.
19   *Pilă* refers to the nepotism which pervaded the system. A *pilă* was a patron or 'godfather'.
20   Ceaușescu's Romania was in the 1980s a more or less closed country. Many Romanians tried to go on holiday to Yugoslavia and then try to filter through the border to Austria or Italy.
21   The Army was mandatory in Romania. Men over the age of 18 went for an 18-month stint in the armed forces. Those admitted to university were undergoing a reduced-term training of 9 months. Soldiers under this agreement were called TRs – *Teriști*, short for *Termen Redus*, reduced term.

and filled-in with blue ball-point, the blue of the Flaro factory (meaning the red *Flacără*[22] factory!?), which always looked faint and always leaked more ink than necessary. I had one last summer in front of me, so I forgot about the recruitment paper. I was drained by the examinations, and ecstatic over the promise of the coming seaside bacchanalia – I had some money and I was dreaming of girls, and of *Mamaia* beach[23] and *Mamaia Vermouth* –, there were also parties in the city itself, as people celebrated passing their university entrance exams, and there were even some birthday parties.

Later on, my parents brought me back to earth when we started talking about the wooden army chest[24] – you couldn't buy one of those anywhere. They were no longer making them, that is, if they were ever made by a business, and we had to find someone who had one available and would sell or lend it to us. I remember it was not easy to get hold of my chest, but in the end we did, after a long search. It was dark green and the paint was chipped at the corners and on the sides. You could see it was quite old and worn out.

My parents washed it and disinfected it; my father hammered some small nails in to tighten it up (it took him some seven or eight days, but in the end it was a work of art. If only I knew who got that trunk after me!). We lined it with white paper on the inside, so it would look cleaner and newer. One day I started to fill it up, which was not easy either. You needed socks of God-knows-what colour, white singlets, long johns, fleeces – things that seem strange nowadays when you only mention their names. All those things were, of course, impossible to find in the shops. I

22 The Red *Flacără* – the Red Flame.
23 *Mamaia* is one of the most popular Romanian resorts on the shore of the Black Sea.
24 The wooden travel trunk was a prerequisite for any conscript. It was invariably padlocked.

can't remember precisely, and I don't think I would like to, either.

It was September when I left. Alone? Yes, that's how I wanted it. But no, I had a friend recruited by the same unit. His father drove us in his matte white Dacia 1310 – at 70 kph, up to *Mărăcineni*, a poor region outside *Buzău* in the direction of *Râmnicu Sărat*, after crossing the bridge that was washed away by floods, then replaced and inaugurated by the president – and we were dropped off in front of the greenish metal clad gates of the unit. When I left Bucharest, my parents had been emotional. We embraced at the door and again at the lift. My mother was crying softly, but I was fine. I had the chance to be Rambo! It was an adventure. Or so it seemed.

I woke up in a yard full of wannabe men just like me who were sitting astride of their wooden trunks which all looked almost exactly the same – except that they had slightly different shades of green and brown. Everyone was looking around, completely disorientated. In that precise moment I felt myself to be part of a herd, and I've never managed to escape the sensation of being part of an idiot herd... neither in '89 nor after that! Sometimes, when I break out of the self-imposed sheep-fold of mythical Romanian space[25], I try to forget those years – all of them! And I try to keep in my mind only individuals, one by one, rather than everyone at the same time... Individuals who addressed me personally, and not the herd.

That was the time Simionescu appeared. He was going past on a narrow path by the side of the inspection field – the parade ground or assembly point, I don't remember the exact terms. I am not positive, but I think that was

25 The author uses the word *mioritic* which refers to the essential Romanian myth of *Miorița* which in Romanian eyes defines the identity of their nation – ergo mioritic space equals Romania.

the first time I saw him. He had an upright posture, not rigid, but distinctive. He was walking slowly, as if he was thinking of something and he looked at us with a bemused air. I knew the uniforms and the insignia of rank – four little stars on each epaulette, in a two-one-one formation. He was a captain. Maybe our eyes met, but I don't think so. Then a *tablagiu* came along and started shouting at us. Shouting things about getting into line, then threatening us with getting sent for a regulation haircut, or with being confined to barracks … The circus had started!

I keep asking myself whether I really glimpsed Simionescu that first day or whether it had been an illusion, a memory invented after the fact in order to give our story a more romantic flavour in my mind. I still can't answer that. I don't know. Maybe yes, maybe no. In my memories it was then that he appeared...

Chapter 3

Bucharest, December 2009

A GREY, FLAT SKY. Stupidly flat. Empty, without a bird, without defined clouds, like a backdrop of dirty, dusty canvas. I look into the abyss from the ninth floor. And I can't see a thing. Nothing. A deep, bottomless void is eating me from the inside. There's futility, much futility, disappointment and hopelessness. Crisis, desperation and a lot of resignation. I have learned this before. I've been learning this for many years. And what does it matter? History can repeat itself in a capitalist society too. Throw another coat on your backs, wait in yet another line, tighten the belt[26] another notch. Nothing new. Nowadays you can speak freely. In the marketplace, on the streets. So what? It's not only in the marketplace. The TV stations are throbbing with talk. So what?

I don't feel like going to work, or going out of the house, or even getting out of bed. I tuck the blanket under my legs, wrap myself like a mummy and lie there, eyes glued to the ceiling.

It's not exactly silent. Brakes and car horns are blaring – nothing new. The crisis has not killed the drivers.

Pfff... I'm terribly lonely.

The flat is empty. Nothing moves. Only one sound from a poorly fitted window frame – the whistling of the wind. Not loud. You can hear it only if you are attentive. It's like a muted whistle, which reminds me of Kaa from the *Jungle*

26 Unofficial motivational speeches used to encourage the citizens of communist Romania during the darkest days of penury in the 1980s.

Book. The wily snake.

Minutes go by and I don't feel them. I let them pass, as if I have too many. I let them expend themselves in the vacuum. For nothing, with no purpose.

I feel a cold shiver although the room is warm. I turn on the television with the sound off. On the news there is an agitated reporter. I should buy some insulation tape and secure everything properly, so as not to lose warmth, and to ensure silence. Outside, the horns and brakes of the latecomers can still be heard. It is still rush hour. Not 10 o'clock yet. A seagull dives in front of my living room windows. In silence. A seagull, lost or late himself. Where are the warm countries?

I feel like a bear in its den preparing for winter. A winter of solitude. I feel exhausted and disappointed, almost resigned. I stretch my arm out for the remote control, then stop. I lean towards the phone and look at the small red flickering LED light. Messages... Again work, problems. Or news.

I don't want bad news, or any kind of requests, demands, proposals. All I want is to be left alone.

Yet I check. There is a message from Sofia.

I love you!

That's all. I reply.

Me too.

Just that.

She is far away. On duty. In London.

Maybe she will come home for the holidays. Maybe I'll go there myself.

I don't know why I'm in this idiotic mood. It's as if I'm collapsing inside. I don't feel like going to work. Nobody will die if I don't go today. In any case we're at work for only a few more days, then everyone will start to disappear from the landscape.

Until after *Bobotează*[27] you won't find anybody in the office. I don't feel like doing anything: reading, eating, watching TV – nothing. I can't settle down. I can't find, either, a quiet space inside myself...

Sofia is far away. Little Lulu is far away too. I don't want to see anyone else.

Lulu left with her mother for Austria to learn how to ski. We talk every two, three or four days. She tells me how she learnt a new move. I talk to Sofia every day. We write to each other, we chat. I miss them and a simpler life. Do I? Isn't it just that I'm in a bad mood?

It has snowed. In fact, it's been snowing with a vengeance for about three days. They struggled with clearing the roads, and all they managed was to clean up the main thoroughfares. As usual. My car, in the parking lot, lies under a big pile of dirty frozen snow. The clouds are massing in the sky, preparing a new round of snowfalls. This winter is not going to forgive us.

I think about turning the computer on, to see what the world is doing. I don't have it in me.

Sofia haunts my thoughts.

The story started beautifully and, most of all, unexpectedly.

After divorcing Lulu's mother, I was completely exhausted. I remember I wanted to crash my car into a wall. Obviously that was extremely stupid. I was driving a Subaru Forester (Car Q came later on!) through Bucharest looking for a wall. I had filled the tank with petrol and left the office throwing the keys on Nati's desk – she was still with Trident back then. It was a Sunday afternoon, and it was dark. It was

---

27 Baptism of Christ. In the Romanian Orthodox calendar, on 6 January. It's the next to last traditional winter celebration, the last being St John the Baptist's day, on 7 January. As with many other important saints, St John's day is celebrated almost like a birthday by those bearing the name.

winter, too, maybe in February. Yes, it was the end of a dry and not too cold February. I think I drove around for two hours, on *Mihai Bravu*, on *Ştefan cel Mare*[28], then around the train station[29], up to the Military Academy, and on the quay of the river, and then, as usual, the phone rang suddenly. I was already bored because I had started to realise that I had no chance of killing myself. I had worked on the user's manual for the Subaru and I knew it was full of airbags and titanium bars. I would only have wrecked the car, without injuring myself at all. I was never a fan of meaningless gestures. If you want to kill yourself, at least look for the option that gives you a maximum prospect of success. A guaranteed solution. So, I was thinking of giving up but I had no formula to soothe my hurt ego. And the phone was ringing. Eventually I heard it and answered. It was a woman friend I had not heard from in a long while. She had called to see what I was doing. I told her the honest truth. She paused for several seconds, unable to tell whether I was joking or speaking seriously. She understood from my silence that I wasn't playing around. She told me to buy a bottle of white wine and come to her. This was an honourable exit from my suicide attempt. I said yes and hung up the phone.

From a non-stop booth I bought a bottle of dry *Recaş*, something ordinary and relatively cheap, plus a two-litre carton of Cappy orange juice. She lived in *Pantelimon*, near the Armenian cemetery, on the ninth floor of a block of studio flats. I didn't have to ring through the intercom, the door had been left open. I couldn't remember the flat number anyway. I only knew it was in front of the lift. She was waiting for me upstairs, smiling a little, with four glasses on the small table near the bed in the only room of the house.

28 Thoroughfares in Bucharest.
29 Following the route, this is *Gara de Nord* (North Station), Bucharest's main train station.

Two glasses for the juice, two for the wine. She wanted to kiss me on the cheek, but I started talking. She gave me a corkscrew and I opened the bottle while continuing to talk.

I don't know what happened afterwards, because I found myself towards morning, still standing, patrolling in the tiny studio flat. Three steps, turn, three steps, turn again. And I was still talking. By myself. She was sleeping in the bed. The glasses were empty, the wine uncorked and untouched. Same for the juice. I had the revelation it was morning so I shook a naked shoulder from under the blanket and told her I was going. She said farewell and pull the door after you. And this is how my first suicide attempt ended. I re-entered the struggle and then I forgot – for a while. Then… But this is another story and it's already too much.

Strange months of sadness and exultation followed, with mad passions consumed in two or three weeks. I was living a kind of rebellious adolescence that I hadn't experienced at such a depth during "the times of sad remembrance"[30], if you know what I mean. I lived through some wonderful experiences: Kirsten the German in Africa and Sandy the American in Germany, and I didn't think I'd ever say *I love you*, but I did and it seemed natural. There was also skinny Lori from an internet company and Lavinia, from the PR department, whom I think I actually loved deeply. I didn't understand afterwards, when I stood back trying to rearrange things chronologically, with a cool head, when exactly I had realised that enough was enough. I had consumed all the appetite for amorous adventures and felt very young. Finally, my divorce papers also made an appearance in an envelope. I didn't even open it. The definitive judicial decision. The chapter was over. We remained friends. And my Lulu had a Sunday father, a traveller to faraway places who came home

30 Times of sad remembrance – an expression used officially to denote Ceaușescu's time. It entered common usage but with a sarcastic overtone.

with memories – the red overcoat with black buttons from London, the yellow t-shirt with the Little Mermaid from Cape Town, the pink vest with Bibi Bloxenberg[31] from Frankfurt and so on.

It's no use making the story even longer. I had managed to reach a sort of balance. I passed over the Greek summer with Eleni, and also the two months of the lost manuscript, with my young colleague and her fluffy dog. Only the Greek woman kept haunting my memory from time to time. Her eyes and her hair were unforgettable. Whenever Misha Pushkin resurfaced, I always had a friendly smile for her in my thoughts.

At the same time I experienced some regrets. Not big ones, though. I was working on two fronts and in those days – it was in 2008 – things were heading in a good direction. Several months passed by like that. Sometimes I took a teacher out to an Indian restaurant, sometimes I invited one of my authors for a coffee, sometimes I went out with my friends for a nice dry red wine. Then came the end of 2008 and the newspapers started shouting that the crisis was coming. And it came. Everything started to fall and in the winter of 2009 I was feeling that things were slipping. I was losing my security again.

Then I met Sofia. It was in a restaurant in *Piaţa Amzei*, the *Pearl Harbour*. At a table where I wasn't supposed to be – say now that you don't believe in destiny. We talked all kinds of nonsense that evening. Some friends say that they realised then and there that something would happen between the two of us. I don't believe it. There was something, a spark, some kind of magic, call it what you want – but it wasn't that obvious. Or maybe I was too attentive to her. To cut a long story short, we met again, several times, in the same

---

31 German children's series about an apprentice witch.

restaurant. A kiss. Even more. Unchained passion.

Then came that stupid mission. I didn't feel like going to Africa. I had seen the southern part of the continent in 2006, and that was enough. Somalia was not at all my dream destination. And there was nothing I could bring my kid, Lulu, from there. God forgive me, the only things those people had were Kalashnikovs and a lot of poverty. And a terrible tribal system. What a crap mission.

Of course Misha was the primadonna in the cast of the show. As usual, he packaged me up and threw me into the pirates' clutches. But he knew what pedal to push. Sofia. She had disappeared. Those people were playing rough. The secret services went in, the four big players – what madness. If it hadn't been for her, of course I would not have accepted the mission. Misha blackmailed me and played his hand perfectly. It wasn't the first time he had done it. It won't be the last, I am sure.

I didn't do much in Somalia, and I even acted stupidly a couple of times, getting into punchups and firing some rusty shitty guns, but all was well in the end. We all escaped relatively easily. I was left with several new friends. Sofia suffered a lot. It was terrible, but it passed.

And now we are together. What a strange relationship we have, across Europe. I could not go after her to London. I had enough to work out in Bucharest as it was. I could not break away from everything. I think I was also afraid. Everyone says that after the first divorce, men run away from signed documents faster than devils running away from the smoke of incense.

Ha, I'm beginning to be amused remembering Caragiu[32]

---

32 Toma Caragiu (1925 - 1977) – well-loved Romanian stage, film and TV actor, and a fine humorist. He died in the 4 March 1977 earthquake. The sketch alluded to in the passage above is a critique on the bureaucratic communist system thinly disguised as a monologue of Mephistopheles'.

and his sketches from those dark years. I am not running away from any signed papers. We love each other. We love each other passionately. But we haven't found our place yet, nor our peace. My peace. It's my peace that's missing, and that's making her suffer. Uff...

I am still in the living room, absent-mindedly watching the news roll past on the silent screen. Accidents, strikes, parliamentary debates.

I look at the time. It's 11. In London it is already 9, she's at work. I call her.

"Morning, sweetheart!"

"Morning, my love. How are you?"

"I'm home. Doing nothing."

"You fine?"

"A bit dizzy. And sad."

"I really miss you, my love."

"I miss you too."

"I love you."

"Me too."

Silence.

"Are you very busy?" I ask.

"No, just regular busy. What's the news?"

"No news. The usual end-of-year madness."

"When should I expect you?"

"I haven't got around to buying the ticket. I don't even know when the last books need to be sent to the printers."

"OK, my love. You come here when you can. I'll be waiting for you."

"I kiss you."

"I kiss you too. I miss you. A lot."

"I kiss you."

The conversation stops here. I am sad again. I'd like to be there with her. But I can't leave. Promises I made and the crisis tie my hands. I feel stuck in a sticky spider's net.

It rings. Pushkin. The last man I felt like talking to.

"Yes, Misha."

"Are you happy to hear me?"

"As always, I am dying of pleasure. What do you want from me?"

"You are extremely impolite. I don't want anything. The New Year's coming and I was thinking…"

"Misha, there are three weeks left."

"Yes, of course. I was thinking that if pass through London, you could also pay me a visit. In the same place…"

"The pink house in Crystal Palace?"

"Yes, the same. I was thinking you might want some work."

"Not from you, Misha. Last time I was just about to leave my bones in Africa."

"Yes, my esteemed friend, but you saved Sofia. You found your balance, your other half."

"You are an insensitive bastard, Misha. Leave me in peace. I am in no mood for your stupid games. I have enough trouble on my plate as it is."

"Stelică, what you need is money. I know it. I wanted to offer you a job, but you know your own business best."

"You, give me a job?! Is this something to sort out, again, in some benighted corner of the world - like the devil's mother's house?"

"No…" He's silent. "It is something even more special." And he falls silent again. "Anyway, we'll talk, Stelian. Happy holidays – that is if we don't talk again in the meantime. Regards to Sofia. If you pass through London, do pay me a visit. Happy New Year."

And he hangs up.

He's ruined my entire day. I won't visit him in London.

And now I really have to wake up and start working. I still have to write a couple of stories for *Flacăra* Magazine. I am in no mood and I have no inspiration. But that's the way it is.

Chapter 4

Buzău, October 1985

I AM RATHER DISORIENTATED. The first days passed, and I didn't understand... Shouting and absurdity. Humiliation and useless verbal violence. And they claim that this is the school for reserve officers. More like a prison. And everybody says that this period of training would make men out of us. Bullshit! A bunch of impotent illiterates crushed under the slippers of fat, smelly wives. Idiots. They shout at us in complete desperation. This is how you instil discipline!

They cut my hair, but not too short. The barber was a civilian. Probably from the town. He didn't care much for the bellowing of the higher ranks. He was an old guy with a wrinkled face, short grey hair, and very quiet. In fact, the only thing I heard him say was "Finished", after he'd done each man. First, the sinister screeches of the scissors. Then, ten minutes later, another "Finished". He clipped several tens of big boys like me without a break. I was actually one of the bigger ones. Some looked as if they were only 14 years old. That's how small and underdeveloped they were. Not all of them were my future colleagues from Civil Engineering in Bucharest, some were from the School of Bridges and Roads in *Iaşi*. We didn't all get the same haircut. In his quiet way, the old fellow had his likes and dislikes. I never saw him again afterwards.

In the dorms we started to look each other in the eye. Hard to say whether it was curiosity, envy, or fear.

I don't recall the first night. Maybe the day had been too

full of events. I think I had a good sleep. I had tried on my uniform – it was still summer wear. The morning started at about 5.45 a.m. The shouting again. I was beginning to get used to this. The cold water in the sinister washroom area, with walls smeared with paint and several cracked tiles, set in crooked and incongruous patterns. The shouts: "Faster, faster" or "To the parade ground – assemble!" or "Soldier X, as you were! Rest of the squad assemble!"

X – I forget his name, although I saw him again after 1989 – was this beanstalk of a man, almost 2 metres tall, slightly amorphous and quiet. Many years later I suspected him of being from the Securitate[33]; his father was a big shot up in *Ardeal*[34]. Who knows? Does it matter?

On the second or maybe the third day, they gathered us all in the parade ground. We were the TR[35] company (reduced term!) consisting of four platoons. The first three were sent to do agricultural work[36]. They were sent somewhere in *Buzău County*, to pick potatoes, tomatoes and other vegetables. We, the boys of the fourth platoon, stayed in the unit, to do administrative work. The others laughed in our faces. They were going to have fun, drinking, little peasant women. They departed happily in their creased uniforms, in marching step, and singing a crazy song that we always mangled up – "Our pride's[37] under the *drapel*" or something like that. We turned that into "our pride's under the *rastel*[38]". The sub-officers used to get angry. "Start again!" then "March

33 Securitate – the feared Romanian secret police, with a very wide informant network (albeit smaller than the one of the East German STASI).
34 *Ardeal* – the Romanian version of the Hungarian word for Transylvania.
35 TR – termen redus; referring to students who had a shorter term of service.
36 During the last decade of Ceaușescu's rule, the army had become a very cheap force of labour, being sent to clear the fields or pick-up the crops, to buildings works, etc.
37 Pride – rural slang for penis.
38 *Drapel* – flag; *rastel* – gun rack.

forward in time with the music!" After several attempts and about ten circuits of the compound we would all calm down. After the three 'agricultural' platoons had left there were some thirty people remaining in the unit, plus the guards and the officers.

Two days later, while we were on parade, an officer turned up in front of our platoon. He was wearing a blue uniform, air force or paratroopers, I couldn't distinguish from a distance. He shouted out "Who knows how to do technical drawing?" Nobody reacted for ten seconds. Then I raised my hand timidly.

"Come here!"

I managed to say something like "TR soldier Munteanu N. Stelian, permission to report."

"Yes."

"I did technical drawing in school from 8th grade to 12th grade."

"Tomorrow morning, after breakfast, you're to present yourself at HQ to the duty officer. Understood?"

"Understood. *Să trăiți!*[39]"

I was not yet accustomed to saluting the way they did in the American movies. I think I was saluting with a bemused air. Luckily nobody noticed. Or they just pretended not to notice.

The guy in blue – he was a captain – received me the next day in his office and put in front of me a piece of paper, an ink well and two pens, one with a wide nib, the other with a fine nib. He was testing my knowledge. I wrote several words down.

I don't remember why I studied technical drawing to such a depth. It had started as something experimental

---

39 The words are part of a military salute to a superior. Literally, 'long life to you'. In common parlance, it has passed into every day speech as an equivalent to a phrase such as 'yes, boss'.

and optional in my grade VIII, as pre-preparation for the university. I was tempted because my parents, who were also technical, could help me. Then, during the lyceum years, I stuffed myself full with studying technical drawing, although I was still dreaming of the Faculty of History. A deeply buried dream. Rotring sets for technical drawing[40] appeared in that period. I don't know what those pens were actually called, because the Romanians changed any brand name associated with a special product into generic nouns. The same had happened to Xeroxes, which nobody called photocopiers.

So, I had received from my parents a beautiful Rotring set – six pieces, various widths. They were for the university, and I decided to keep my mouth shut and not use them for the benefit of the Romanian army.

I think I passed the test very quickly. I was taken to a room full of desks and officers who looked at me without too much sympathy. They gave me a desk, a chair, and brought in work. Following a pattern, I drew all kinds of weapons and vehicles. I made drawings of the enemy's weaponry. I wrote titles, filled in diagrams, and even drew the margins for baccalaureate dissertations. You know what I mean – there were two lines: a thin one and a thicker one at a distance of 2 centimetres from the left side (the strip in which you punch holes for filing), and 0.5 centimetres on the other three sides.

I spent a month in that office, while the others were doing agricultural work. I worked from morning till late at night, but I relaxed after 4 p.m, when the "cadres" left – this was the proper and slightly mysterious term for "military cadres". I was a smoker then and my parents sent me packs of Kent

---

40   Rotring – German manufacturers of specialised pens and implements for technical drawing. They are still in business.

cigarettes to help me open doors[41], but I just smoked them myself. From time to time I received tins of *nes* - Amigo instant coffee[42].

One evening, I had my first visit.

I had half climbed on the desk because I had to write a title using the 8mm-wide nib on a giant map. The window facing the square was open, and there was an eerie silence. Not even the dogs were barking. Maybe it was about 10 p.m. They had sounded lights out. In the hallway of HQ it was quiet, then I heard footsteps. Strange. I opened the door of the room where I was working, on the ground floor, and I saw somebody in the half light – we only had one light bulb burning, we were economising. This person was opening or locking a door which was never opened. It was a door like any other door, with a number, but nothing written on it. And I had never before seen anyone going in or out through that door. Now there was a man there. I mumbled a salute and went back to riding my big map. Everybody usually ran away from that office. It belonged to the CI officer, that is Counter-Information. In ordinary speech, the unit's Securitate man. Nobody knew his work hours, and nobody wanted to have anything to do with him.

I continued to write with my ears pricked up. I heard a key in a lock, the door opening and closing, then opening, then all of a sudden the man was in my office. He was wearing an army uniform with captain's insignia and the infantry arms on his lapels. Young, handsome, tall, blond with blue eyes – a combination of James Bond and an SS officer – I think I smiled a little seeing him. He smiled back at me. I tried to

---

41   Kent cigarettes were especially prized as small bribes, a system of barter which developed strongly during the harshest years of the communist regime, and whose remnants are still in place despite official efforts to get rid of them
42   Amigo instant coffee was made in Brazil, and it was also used for small bribes. *Nes*, short for Nescafe, was a generic term for any instant coffee.

climb off the desk and salute him.

"At ease, I don't want to interrupt you."

"But …"

"I have a request."

"Yes."

And then I noticed he had in his left hand a tin of *nes*. Amigo, naturally, which I think was the only instant coffee you could find, and only in Shop[43], not in regular stores. I'll tell you more about Shop some other time; not that I would know too much about it, but still...

"I wanted to drink a *nes*. I ran out of sugar. Do you happen to have one or two extra spoonfuls?"

"Yes. Sure."

It wasn't good to refuse him. And I actually had some sugar. I didn't use more than a level teaspoonful per cup of *nes*. I put my hand into the desk drawer and pulled a tin of Amigo, now filled with sugar, and stretched it out to him. He looked at it nonplussed, for a moment, then he understood.

"Would you like a cup as well? We drink together. You provide the sugar, I provide the *nes*."

"Yes, of course," I answered half heartedly.

"We could talk a little. Do you smoke?"

"Rarely," I replied prudently.

"I have Kent cigarettes. Would you like one?"

"No, thank you."

I took out two cups and two stainless steel spoons, scratched from so much rubbing[44], and a little bent. Each of

---

43 Shop, in English in the original, was the name for stores where only foreign tourist could make purchases using hard currency. Romanian citizens were generally forbidden to buy from there (they could not hold foreign currency legally), but rules could be bent in some cases.

44 The method of preparation for old-style instant coffee was to mix the coffee granules and the sugar with a little water until they were transformed into a frothy paste. This ritual was performed with a spoon in the drinking cup.

us poured the coffee granules and started the mixing ritual. Tradition had it that coffee tasted better if it was frothy. No joke.

"I haven't got any hot water. Cold water, if you…"

"Wait a little." He came back with a small enamel pan and a Soviet made instant water boiler, whose technical name was a "thermoplunger"[45], which he plugged into the wall socket.

"What are the boys saying these days?"

Although I was expecting questions, I think I was extremely startled. He had started too suddenly. He noticed. He looked at me for a long while and continued with the friendliest smile he could produce.

"I am curious about what they're saying at your age nowadays: music, films, chicks?"

I pulled myself together quickly and it was my turn to smile very, very thinly. Just enough for him to see my lips twitch.

"I return late to the dorm. They are all asleep. I have no way of knowing."

"Yes, you work hard. I heard. But what about in the mess hall? What about on Sundays? I have a boy myself, a little younger than you, he's 16."

He stopped because he saw my expression. I think it was opaque and blank. Maybe a little aggressive, too.

"You don't feel like making conversation."

"I am sorry. You know, I have work to do."

"Yes, I know that, but I was thinking you might want to…"

"I only want to work."

He looked me in the face again, with extremely cold and

---

45   A metal implement, usually a coil similar to those in washing machines, which was connected directly to the wall socket and plunged in a cup or pan of water, generating heat.

razor-sharp eyes. It hadn't been difficult for him to work out that I knew who he was and what he wanted. He had done his duty and asked me to talk. From my point of view, he'd done it badly. But it wasn't my job to pass judgment. I only wanted him to get out of the room, and escape.

"I understand. Pity."

I leaned towards the map and stretched my hand for the pen.

"In any case, if you hear anything that might be damaging to…" and he paused a little. "If anything comes up, you can report to your direct superior, to the platoon commander or even to me. Any time."

He knew it made no sense to say this, but he had said it the way they did in the movies when they read out the rights of someone being arrested. Following procedure, formally. He took a cigarette out of the pack and left it on the table. He then took the half drunk cup, got up and went out the door.

"Thank you for the sugar," I heard from the hallway.

And I never saw him again.

The second visit of that night was friendlier. One of the boys from the telephone exchange barged in with a steaming metal plate. On it were several pieces of fried meat and a quarter of a round, dark bread.

"We thought you might be hungry. We had a gift from the kitchens 'cos it's our boys' turn to work in there today. You're here all alone, working... Got a cigarette?"

I pointed at the cigarette on the table.

"Aaah, you're a prince! But it's your last one."

"I have others, take it."

"Merci. If you get bored, come and see us. We can chat a little. Bye."

Everybody was in a mood to chat a little.

I ate unhurriedly. Then I drank the *nes* and smoked a cigarette. A Kent. Then I started work again. I was beginning to get sleepy but I wanted to finish the job.

I think it was about 12 when I received my third visit of that agitated night.

It was Simionescu.

He was very tall and thin, with an incipient bald patch. He was smoking, holding the cigarette in his left hand. Further up on his arm, on the same side, there was a red band with white lettering. OSR. Regimental duty officer[46]. I gave yet another start when I saw his giant figure barging in.

"At ease, soldier. Carry on!" he ordered.

He put the cigarette in the corner of his lips and took a deep drag. He then collapsed into a chair. Full uniform, rank of captain (I knew that already), the badge on his lapels bearing a divider and a cogwheel. Engineer.

"Much to do?"

"I have to finish writing this map by tomorrow."

"You are Munteanu, aren't you?"

"Yes, *să trăiți*!" I replied in a feeble voice.

"Do you know who I am?"

"The regimental duty o…"

"No, fool. What is my name? What do I do here?"

"No, *să trăiți*!"

"Stop *să trăiți* -ing me, we're not on the parade ground."

He looked around, with tired eyes, for an ashtray. I gave him an empty food tin, half-filled with crushed cigarette ends.

"Yes, you've done quite a bit of work."

"Excuse me, but whenever I work… and the window is open."

He laughs.

---

46 Literally meaning *Ofițer de serviciu pe regiment* - OSR.

"That's your problem. I heard of you. They say you know what you're doing with technical drawing. Where are you from?"

"Bucharest."

"What faculty you are you enrolled in?"

"Civil Engineering, Bucharest."

"Good, good. I am Captain Simionescu. I might, probably, also need you. I'll see whether I can convince this lot to lend you for a while. I am responsible for the vehicle pool. There are technical sketches to be made now and again."

"I understand."

"If you have any problems and I am on duty, you come straight to me. Just to save too much debate afterwards. Better if I know about it."

"Yes, understood."

"Good, Munteanu. I am going back to my place." He got up, headed for the door and then turned and came back. "Did that fellow come to see you?"

"Yes."

"And?"

"He wanted some sugar."

"His mother's sugar! So?"

"I am here all the time, with my nose in the maps. That's all."

"Ahuh! Good."

And he went out of the room.

That's how my first encounter with Simionescu went. I worked for another hour and then I went to bed. In the dorm, my colleagues were breaking wind and firing it up with deodorant sprays. These were called flamethrowers. The winner was whoever produced the longest flame. The only problem was how to measure it. And this is where the debates of the night started. Great fun.

Chapter 5

Bucharest – Vienna, Feburary 2010

THE RINGTONE SCREAMS FROM ONE OF MY POCKETS. I drop the frying pan because I've just burnt myself on it. I was cooking an omelette,in the middle of putting it together, pouring the eggs over the hot olive oil. I answer the phone in an angry mood. I really didn't feel like a conversation, especially because the screen said "Unknown number."

"Yes!"

"Am I disturbing you?" I recognise his voice.

"Misha, you are always disturbing me."

"The hell I am – you're a spoiled brat."

"What do you want?"

"To see how you are."

"That's why you're calling from unknown numbers."

"I'm in Vienna, in a hotel."

"So?"

"So wouldn't you like to come by?"

"No."

"Why?"

"Misha, you haven't caught me on my best day."

"Pity."

This game of his annoys me... He's coming forward, he withdraws.

"Te hell with it, Misha! Just say for once what you want."

"I have a gift for you."

"What's the occasion?"

"Just like that… for New Year's Day."

"We are in February."

"It's only now that I could get it. If you didn't come to visit me when you were in London…"

"I didn't go to London for you. What's the gift?"

"You will have to come here and see it."

"I can't."

"Why?"

"No money."

"I'll send you the tickets, you'll take the train. It's more pleasant. I'll even take care of the accommodation."

"What if I don't feel like it?"

He is silent for a moment. Then he changes his tone.

"Listen, we've played enough. I have a job for you. And a present. I know things are not rosy for you at the moment. Quit the histrionics and pack your bags fast. There is a ticket in your name, in your post box. You are leaving tonight. Don't bother to comment. I know you have nothing better to do. Clear?"

Yes, he's right. I have nothing better to do. February is a dead month. No new titles, no magazine, no income, no money. Only nerves, calculations and hopes.

"Clear, Stelică?"

"*Să trăiți!*"

"And your mother too!"

He's funny when swearing. His Romanian is elegant, he doesn't say "your mama" he says "your mother." Such a very strange man. I don't have the arguments to contradict him.

"Fine, Misha. I'll climb into the train this evening," I said, calming down. "Wait for me."

He's calmed down as well. In fact, he never gets angry. When he seems angry, he's merely playing a role.

"I'll wait. You know very well that I'll wait." And bang, he hangs up.

I am alone in the sleeper compartment. I've bought two cans of beer and some crispy poppy-seed pretzels. A couple of newspapers too. I packed my bags to last me three days. He didn't say it, but I don't think I would be staying much longer. I didn't take any other accessories. Some time ago I had exchanged my Beretta for a Colt. A real jewel: Colt 1911 A1M1. Well, it was Misha again who brokered the deal. I've left it at home and I feel naked.

I am not sleepy. The noises of the train are soporific and it's warm in my compartment, but I am not sleepy. I go to the restaurant car and order chicken breast with French fries and a red *Fetească*. A coffee and a bottle of still water. There are only a few people around. I exchange smiles with a bearded guy who is also drinking red wine. He raises his glass to me in a toast. I do the same. That was all. For a moment I ask myself whether this might be one of Misha's men shadowing me. I am paranoid.

I eat and drink in peace. Sofia is in London, Lulu is on holiday. And I'm on the way to Vienna. Maybe I'll find some sales and get myself something nice. My BlackBerry blinks red: "Safe travel. Bon appétit. And good night. Misha." I look around me for a moment. I'm paranoid for sure. I continue to eat and drink.

Message from Sofia "I love you. Sleep well. Am thinking of you. S." I reply "Love you too. Have beautiful dreams. Will call tomorrow. S." The train goes through stations rattling noisily, chuffing and whistling. I feel as if I'm in a time tunnel. I open the newspapers and start reading the gossip columns. Maybe they'll send me to sleep…

It's morning. The watch says there's about a half an hour left. The conductor tells me we have a twenty-minute delay. No problem. Vienna is a special destination. I would come back here any time. The train will stop in Westbanhof. A couple of steps away from Mariahilferstrasse.

Sms: "From the station straight ahead. 400m on the right. Before the church. Hotel Haydn. You'll see it. Restaurant ground floor. I'm waiting there. Misha."

Not bad at all, because after a night of deep sleep I was starting to get hungry. Although it's not the best thing for your digestion to sit next to Mikhail Sergeyevich Pushkin while he tries to convince you to take part in some miracle of a mission in a forgotten corner of the world.

I realise that, strangely, I am in a good mood. I step inside. The place seems to have just opened its doors. There is no-one inside; no-one with the exception of Misha and a waiter who is changing an empty glass for a full one. Cognac, of course. Or schnapps!

"So good to see you!"

"Likewise!"

We embrace with a show of emotion and kiss each other's cheeks. Three times. A little theatrical.

"Would you like to eat?"

"Yes, I am hungry."

"A glass of something?"

"It is a bit early. Apple juice."

"These people say the Viennese Breakfast menu is good."

"Whatever you say."

He lights a Rothmans cigarette. You can still smoke indoors in Vienna. Misha then hails a waiter. As usual, I have a feeling that he's an habitué.

"I am listening, Misha."

"On an empty stomach? There is no hurry."

I am silent and I am waiting.

I look at the quiet street through the windows. It is too early for pedestrians looking for today's bargains, and, for tourists, February is not a good month to go walking around the town. The sales are over, and everybody is out skiing.

Then comes the food – cold meats, cheeses, butter and brown bread, comfitures, tea and coffee. I start eating without hurry, staring into space. Misha smokes methodically and takes a sip from his glass now and then. We study each other from the corners of our eyes. The eternal game of cat and mouse. I am absolutely convinced he wants something from me. He actually tried to convince me to visit him in London. I stayed there for a few days, and all the time I had I gave to Sofia. I don't even know if there were many occasions on which we went out walking.

"Finished."

"Was it good?"

"It was wonderful."

"Schnapps?"

"No, I would like my head clear when I hear what you have to say."

"It's about a gift, Stelian."

"What was that proverb about gifts?"

"That was about gifts from the Greeks[47]."

"Greeks, Russians, Romanians…"

He smiles while he blows a big circle of smoke. He looks at it proudly.

"The gift is upstairs, in room 128. That's where you're going to stay. Shall we go now? We can come back after you've seen it."

"Is it that big?"

"No, but it is cumbersome."

"Fine."

---

47 *Timeo Danaos et dona ferentes*, a phrase from Virgil's Aeneid, saying "I fear the Greeks bringing gifts".

The waiter doesn't look worried because we are getting up to leave. The entrance to the hotel is through a gangway from the street. We take a lift and go to the mezzanine. Misha nods a hello to the reception. A solid-looking man, with an Indian appearance. Then we continue through a corridor and straight through the door of room 128.

It is a strange room, on the corner of the building. The big bed looks out onto the street through a huge window. The room is also furnished with a sofa, two armchairs and a coffee table. On the sofa lies a big, long, rectangular package. It is wrapped in coloured paper and tied up with a big bow. A little funny. Weird, even.

"This is the present. You can unwrap it."

I tear the paper haunted by the blackest foreboding.

A long black leather case. On it, a note in English, like a label: it's a warranty certificate. I read it.

Steyr–Mannlicher SSG 08 sniper rifle with stock folded
Caliber(s) 7.62x51mm NATO (.308Win)
Operation Bolt Action, Rotating bolt
Barrel 600 mm (23.6")
Length 1182 mm (46.5") / 960 mm (36.8") folded
Weight, empty, w/o scope 5.7 kg (12.5 lbs)
Feed Mechanism box magazine, 10 (7.62 NATO)
Made in Austria by Steyr AG…

I don't open the case. I sit down in an armchair.

"What do you want from me, Misha?"

"Nothing. I know you did target shooting in the old days and I thought you might like to train once in a while."

"Misha, I am not an idiot! This gift is not just like that, for… training!"

"Oh yes it is. What if you lost your touch? Or your sharp eyes?"

"What do you want me to do now with a rifle with

telescopic sights?"

"Oh, nothing, Stelian. Not now! I would like you to play a little with it. Look here –" he says and takes a medium-sized blue envelope from his pocket, "here are the ownership papers for the weapon, plus a permit for target shooting at the Neustadt Sports Facility. You have the address in here, too, all in English. You will find the operating manual inside the case, as well as all the necessary pieces and, naturally, cartridges. I thought it might be useful. Do you know that film – with Jack Nicholson, was it? – called Anger Management? It's the same thing with you. So that nothing bursts – *Bozhe moy*[48], God forbid – in your head."

"You are the one whose head has something wrong with it, Misha! How could you give me a gun with a telescopic sight!? Who do you want me to kill?"

"Oh God, you're way off track. I didn't think of that. But now that you have mentioned it, I might be able to find a job for you."

"You must be mad, I am not an assassin!"

"Why talk so loud? People might think we are quarrelling."

"But we are quarrelling."

"Not at all. By no means. It's a gift, nothing more. Go on, play with it. Forget any troubles. And we'll talk…"

I keep quiet and look at the floor. The carpeting is beige and perfectly clean. Pushkin sits in the other armchair. He takes a deep breath. I am sure he's looking for another cigarette. He should be happy. I think I reacted a lot better than he expected. But he doesn't light his cigarette. The room is probably for non-smokers. He puts a hand on my shoulder.

"Stelian, don't jump to any conclusions. Don't think

---

48 Bozhe moy – My God, in Russian in the original.

about anything. It's a gift. Go and play with it. I paid your hotel room for three nights. Here's your return ticket and 500 Euros. I think it's enough. I'm off. We'll talk."

He gets up. From the door, he says:

"When you are free and in the mood, give me a sign. Sms, e-mail, carrier pigeon."

He laughs and goes out of the room before I manage to abuse him "Your mama's cunt, Pushkin!"

I left everything in the room as it was. The black leather case unopened, my travel bag, the blue envelope with the documents. I only took a one hundred Euro bill, locked the door and went back to the ground floor restaurant. The waiter seemed to be expecting me. He led me back to the same table and, without a word, he brought me a small glass of schnapps and a double espresso. I look at him curiously, so he says *"The other gentleman told me to bring you this... With the compliments of the house. Anything else?"*

I shook my head. I didn't feel like anything else. The room was beginning to fill up. There were customers appearing at the tables and only at that point did I begin to realise how hot it was there. Massive old wooden furniture, with a shiny dark brown finish, slightly used, chairs upholstered in burgundy red velvet, candles in candleholders... The atmosphere was fully Mitteleuropa[49] of the '30s. I looked at the waiter and he smiled at me, enquiringly.

"Yes, Sir?" and he approaches me.

"Nothing, thanks a lot."

I drank my schnapps in one gulp. It wasn't all that strong,

[49] Mitteleuropa - German for Central Europe. The word has political, geographic and cultural meaning, describing a geographical location and also the cultural identity of a German and Austrian-dominated Central Europe.

but very aromatic, sweet and sour. I then sipped my coffee. No sugar, no milk. Tasty.

In fact, what did Misha want from me? To kill? To change my trade? To return to the sport of my youth? All of a sudden I saw myself in the role of a *contract killer*. An image I couldn't superimpose on my own face. I have forgotten the crisis back home. Books, bookstores, prices and debts. Last time I handled a gun was in Somalia, less than a year before. That was madness, my brain muddled from the heat and the desperate fear that I might lose Sofia. At that time, I had stormed the court of a pirate king, yelling and firing two AKMs, without hitting anything. They were all under cover. After a minute, they downed me with a single bullet. A sniper. No, not even a sniper – it had been the Professor. I have no news of him. I have no news either of Sofia's parents, who remained there, or of Donovan the American, or of that pretentious Brit, or of the little old Italian tangled in the web of the Holy Alliance. Was I feeling any…?

I realised suddenly that my fingers were starting to itch. The longing to get away? The desire for action? The criminal instinct? The money? The debts?

Who was it that Misha Pushkin wanted me to kill?

Chapter 6

Buzău, January 1986

THESE MEMORIES ARE SLIGHTLY FADED. They are milder, due to the passing of time. A little embellished and less frightening. The instinct for self-preservation has probably modified them until they have become bearable.

Something woke us up... I don't remember what. Just an infernal noise. A siren or the shouts of a top sergeant or a patriotic song from the wheezing tannoy installed in the dorm. My first sensation was that I was about to shatter like a block of ice dropped on the floor. I couldn't feel my legs, and, on many occasions, I couldn't feel my arms either. The blanket was rigid, thrown over the heap of clothes – layers and layers which clothed me day and night. Always the same. Hidden somewhere near the armpits was the bottle of vodka I had received from home. One bottle lasted seven days. One hundred mils daily, before going to bed. I used to draw lines with a marker on each bottle, measuring the daily ration, so that I wouldn't drink more or less than I ought to.

It was dark outside and it was only the dim glow of four light bulbs, 60 watts each, which kept us from bumping into each other.

Near me, another blanket would be moving, and a guy, his face battered and hung-over, would be opening his eyes for the first time, and glancing around with a murderous air. Up above me, Paul was always quicker. He would be the first to come to himself – in about 40-50 seconds – and he would stick his nut out around the side of the bed, red hair flopping down, unwashed and spiky.

"Come on. Leave it alone, mama's boy. Wake up!"

I would grumble something. I don't know what. I think that even back then I didn't know what I was saying. It was surely not cursing – they weren't even words. My mouth would be gummed up after the alcohol, the gluey Cristal[50] toothpaste and the last meal of the evening, potato stew. It didn't matter anyway. Nobody would have understood what I was saying.

Already the first barrack-mates were sliding towards the hallway. They were sliding for real. The mosaic floor was covered in a fine layer of ice. Then started the search for our army boots. Sometimes the night sentry, more insomniac and more perverse than the rest of us, half-dead with the cold and starved of booze, re-arranged the order in which we left our shoes. Cursing would follow. Rich and loud. The hallway of the dorms was tiny, leaving barely enough room for the hundred and something pairs of boots.

The first thing I looked at in the morning was the half-filled glass of water on the metal bedside-table. By the thickness of the ice in the glass I tried to estimate the temperature of the room. Several millimetres of ice, several degrees below zero. Outside it was -25. I kept wishing that the glass would break one day. The laws of physics which I still had in my head told me that water increases in volume as it freezes. Therefore, my glass should have cracked. But it never happened.

The next thing was to try and sit upright on side of the bed. Then the bottle, the unscrewing of the cap, and a "good morning" swig as payment on account from the hundred

50 Cristal toothpaste was the most common oral hygiene product in Romania.

mils to come that evening. I would then hide the bottle quickly in the wooden crate which I locked carefully every time. That was the moment when the first shivers caught me. I would have to move. As far as the bathroom, to throw a little water – very cold – on my face and hands. That was it. I could not remember the last time I had been fully undressed. It was a real adventure to urinate; I can't even speak about the rest. I felt that the cold was conquering another little piece of me, night after night. The shivers came every two or three minutes.

Paul from the town of *Tecuci*[51] used to throw his legs over the side of the top bunk, chasing me away.

"Hai. Giddy up!"

I am trying to remember how many layers of clothes I was dressed in. A singlet, a T-shirt and a body shirt, a khaki shirt, two pullovers – one of them beige, from home, one of them regulation khaki, then the army jacket. I had already been wearing all this on me for ten days. I didn't know much about lice and bedbugs and fleas. I was hoping they could not survive the cold. It did not matter anyway.

The bathroom only had traces of tiling on its walls. The Turkish toilets had cracked windows. Constipation, therefore, looked like a strategy for survival. The jet of urine raised steam, expending even more of the body's heat. Then dry soap on the hands and face and a mouthful of glacial water with the eternal Cristal toothpaste (I can't remember any other brand from those times), followed by running on the double to assembly on the parade ground, and finally the drill.

When I looked at myself in the cracked bathroom mirror I could see that my face was creased with black lines of dirt. I only had the black-and-white image of the world from

---

51 *Tecuci* – small town in Moldavia, eastern Romania.

Tarkovsky's *Stalker*[52]. Actually, mine was a world in grey-and-beige. Pure white didn't exist any more. Anywhere. Everything was either ashen-white or beige-white. A dirty, bedraggled white, nuanced by beige or grey.

No one bothered us too much during the drill. The officers knew there was no heating in the barracks and that sleeping could be a risky operation from which you might not even wake up. But, as we all liked to say, nobody died from it. Our officers didn't look too happy either. The town of *Buzău* itself only had heating and electricity for a few hours daily[53].

Until one day when we found out we were going to be sent to unload coals in the train station. To me, it felt like hard labour for convicts, but the gossips in the unit were talking about it as a great achievement. Because the town hall had no labourers to unload the coal wagons for the heating of the townspeople, they had called in the armed forces[54], as usual, and it seemed that we were going to receive, as payment, a full wagonload.

It was a sinister night. The station was lit only by two dim lights. Near it, the coal train was illuminated by a neon spotlight hanging from a pylon, and by the lights of the trucks. At first, I tried to avoid both the light and the fine coal dust getting into my eyes. Then I started moving like a robot. No thinking involved. The shovel was stuck to my fingers, from which I had removed the gloves so as not to

52 *Stalker* (1979) is a seminal film by Russian director Andrei Tarkovsky (1932–1986), widely regarded as one of the best film directors in the world.
53 The time of the action, the 1980s, was the worst in contemporary Romania from an economic, political and social point of view, due to the way the Romanian state was led under the dictatorship of Ceaușescu. In the 1980s, in order to pay the external debt of the state, everything that could be exported was sent abroad and a major programme of "saving" and "economising" was started, which included power, water and gas cuts.
54 It was usual for the army to "lend a hand" to the state, so that soldiers were often used as cheap/unpaid labour in the fields and factories, for menial jobs, loading and unloading, and even as extras in historical films.

soil them. I couldn't feel my back any more, or my arms. And I think, at that point, that I couldn't see anything. Simionescu was there as well, directing the trucks and giving brief orders. I couldn't hear him, but I could see him. He was angry and waving his arms a lot.

I don't remember how long it all lasted. Six or seven hours perhaps. The sun was coming up on the horizon, yet everything around us was still black night. Darkness...

Back in the barracks, we only washed our hands and faces and took our vodka ration – some had slurped various dubious liquids in the corners of the train station – and went to bed exactly when the solar disc was detaching itself from the line of the horizon.

They didn't have the heart to wake us up that morning, so they let us sleep until late in the afternoon.

When I woke up, I looked at my glass. The water was liquid. No traces of ice. I looked around me in a daze. Several scores of grey ghosts looked at each other in bewilderment. Slowly, we started to feel the difference in temperature. I cannot imagine exactly how many degrees centigrade, probably not too many above zero... The usual shivers didn't kick in. Not immediately.

Then came an under-officer who announced, at the top of his voice, that we were going to take a warm bath.

A warm bath!

They took us on the run to a low building where we used to do our gas-mask training. It felt like being in Auschwitz. We stripped off our khaki clothes in a corner, and the last layer, the singlet, peeled off with some of my skin on it. I threw it in the dustbin. We took some left over slivers of soap in our hands and then we were lined up against a wall. They took a fire engine hose and turned on a jet of water. I can't remember now and I can't make an estimate of how hot the water was – probably tepid – but, in comparison, it was a miracle of heat. They fired the hot water hose at us for a minute or so, then we were ordered to use the soap. Then another stream of hot water for another minute, to rinse the soap off. And that was it.

We got dressed again in our dirty clothes. Some of us had kept a clean flannel or singlet in our luggage. Most of us didn't.

About two weeks later, we swore our oaths of allegiance and I returned to my desk and my maps, my *nes* and my Kent, BT or Apollonia[55].

Afterwards I remained in the office until it was my turn to be on guard duty. I don't know who wanted to do me a service, maybe even him – although I hated him for it – , because I got assigned to the guard tower at the vehicle pool. It was a tall sheet iron tower, with windows all around it. It vibrated badly in the wind, and even though all the windows were in place and intact, the glass was not insulated with mastic, so a draught came whistling through from all sides.

During the second watch, in the dead of night, I would stand and listen to the storms pounding through the valleys to the left of the base, through the buildings and the cars with empty petrol tanks, which it would be my duty to protect with my submachine gun and four live calibre 7.62 mm rounds in the clip. I would also have a sheepskin coat over my army greatcoat, and some type of monstrous overshoes covering my boots, along with three pairs of gloves on my hands, on top of each other. The wind kept on putting out my matches so I could barely light up my cheap cigarettes, which I had although it was forbidden to smoke on duty. In order not to take my gloves off I smoked the cigarette using two burnt matches as a holder. I had a revolving search light

55   BT and Apollonia – Bulgarian and Albanian cigarettes, very popular during the communist times.

on the watchtower, which I was supposed to use for checking on the cars. However, the electricity was always cut during the second watch, and our unit was left in darkness. I kept on asking myself what would have happened if the enemy had decided to attack in that very moment. It was an idiotic question. No enemy could have reached us in that blackness, through potholes and ravines.

One night, something happened which was very similar to the incident in that movie, I think it was called *The Blue Gates of the City*[56], when the guard is caught sleeping on duty. Pintilii (with two Is), taciturn and reserved, was from the town of *Pașcani*, and he always was allocated all sorts of idiotic duties. At that point, he was in the remotest corner of the base, near the football ground. There was no shelter around, with the exception of the wooden kiosk where the field telephone line was located. The wind was blowing. It wasn't a cold night, but the place was haunted by a morbid legend. It seems there was a mad former army major in the region, who had been expelled from the army, and who prowled around at night, killing isolated sentries. We were all paralysed with terror.

It was not clear whether he was human and had not yet been caught by the militia, or whether he was a ghost, because the major was already dead. We had no notion of what a zombie was in those times, it was too capitalist[57].

I think Pintilii had fallen asleep – either sitting on the ground or supporting his weight on the kiosk's wooden pillar. The electricity was off, and all I could see was darkness. And noises: rustles, cracks, maybe footsteps. I was afraid too, and

56   *Porțile albastre ale orașului,* in Romanian. 1974 film about WW2 events in which an officer shot by his own men returns to the unit to fight the retreating Germans.
57   A reference to the fact that Western films started to make fewer and fewer appearances on Romanian screens in the 1980s.

was holding my gun in firing position. The trigger guard was set on automatic and I was fixed motionless in position.

All of a sudden I heard a long bellowing:

"Haaaaaaaaalt! Halt – who goes there? Stand still or I shoot!"

In the second of silence after, followed the unmistakeable sound made by the safety catch releasing the first bullet into the chamber. I froze. The ghost major! Our officers had scared us saying the USLA-people[58] could come in secret to mine the base and steal the flag. It would have been some sort of test of our vigilance. We were terrified.

I recognised Pintilii's voice. Normally, the three warnings should have been uttered one at a time, not all in a go. It was clear he had been sleeping and woke up in fright.

"Hold it, *băi*[59], I caught you sleeping on duty!"

"Don't move or I shoot!"

"*Băi!* I'm Major Dragnea. I caught you, you unfortunate good for nothing."

"Down on your face, now! Don't move!"

And the lights came back on - surprise! I took the searchlight and turned it in that direction.

The scene was out of the movies. They were not very far away, and I could see well from above. Pintilii was looking down the barrel of the gun, and – I suppose – finger on the trigger. I would have needed binoculars to tell. Some ten metres in front of him, the major was lying on the ground, growling something in a subdued tone – probably curses. Pintilii kept on yelling.

"Don't move! Or I'll shoot. Keep down. Don't move!"

---

58   USLA – *Unitate specială de luptă anti-teroristă*, in Romanian: Special unit for anti-terrorist combat, Special Ops.
59   Informal and discourteous mode of address.

Dragnea was a dirty dog. He behaved viciously towards us whenever he got the chance. He was the unit's propaganda chief from the Communist Party[60]. One day, he had measured my hair with a ruler and noticed that it was one centimetre longer than regulation. He ordered me to get a haircut. Down to zero. The officers from HQ saved me. They didn't want a skinhead office colleague.

"*Băi*, call the guard. Fuck your mother and all her ancestors. You'll see. I'll rip your foreskin off. Fuck you..."

"Don't move! Keep down. I'll shoot," the soldier kept yelling.

It was like being in the audience for an absurd theatre play. And I am sure Pintilii would have really fired. The circus lasted for some five or ten minutes until the guard commander came.

"Halt, who goes there?"

"Guard commander!"

"Password."

"*Mihai Viteazul!*"

"*Ștefan cel Mare*[61]! Light on your face!"

I would have laughed, had it not been for my terror that the finger could pull the trigger, making me a witness to a murder "live on-air." The position of the gun remained unchanged. Pintilii, without wavering, was still aiming it at the major's head, now raised out of the mud pool in which he had thrown himself.

The flashlight was on the face of the guard commander.

"Pintilii, it's me, Vasiloiu. Lay down your damned weapon or you'll shoot us all."

"No, no... Halt! Halt or I shoot! Permission to report,

---

60 All military units – in fact all state institutions – had a propaganda chief.
61 *Mihai Viteazul* (Michael the Brave, 1558 - 1601) and *Ștefan cel Mare* (Stephen the Great, 1433 - 1504), two of the greatest and most esteemed Romanian princes.

comrade chief warrant officer, I don't lay down anything! Comrade major wanted to…"

"*Băi*, you unfortunate good for nothing, I caught you sleeping! I'll finish you! I trample you into the ground! The court-martial will eat you up!" the officer kept shouting from his prone position.

"Comrade Major, let's try to arrange this… please do not provoke him."

"What?! How dare you, Vasiloiu?"

"Halt! Face down! Don't move!"

The scene was now far too long. The weapon was in the same position. Pintilii's hands should have been numb by now, which could have led to a dramatic end. Then Simionescu came on the spot. He glanced in the direction of my searchlight. I suppose he knew I was there. He also turned on his flashlight and threw the beam on his face, sideways. He signalled to Vasiloiu and the replacement guard to step back. He approached the major in the mud pool using small steps. Simionescu was the RDO.

"Pintilii, this is Captain Simionescu, the duty officer. You recognise me?"

"Yes, comrade Captain."

"Pintilii, I am going to get closer to Major Dragnea, pick him up and then go with him to HQ. Did you hear?"

"Yes, *să trăiți*."

"So you understood what I will do now?"

"Yes, *să trăiți*."

"After we get farther from here you will lower your weapon and leave Vasiloiu to change you with the replacement sentry. Is that clear?"

"Yes, *să trăiți*."

"Did you understand?"

"I understood, *să trăiți!*"

Everything was sorted out in a matter of minutes. I finished my watch and, when I was back in the building, I looked for Pintilii. He was in a bunk in the guardroom. Sleeping. The next day, nothing happened. No complaint, no punishment. As if nothing had occurred. Nobody saw Dragnea for two days, but the story about the way he bit the dust while threatened with a gun by Pintilii made the rounds of the county. Everybody was pointing at him and laughing behind his back. Pintilii was a kind of local hero for a while, and then everybody forgot him.

Chapter 7

Bucharest, March 2010

IT'S EVENING AND I AM ALONE. The windows are open. End of winter chill. And the smell of gas burning, mingling with the scent of fresh grass. Slightly nauseating but manageable. I should be more optimistic. Spring is coming. And I talked to Sofia over the phone. It was a kind of dialogue of the deaf. Each of us talked about our own problems. Each of us absorbed in our own job. A little awkward.

I am now trying to decide between a tin of fish – something longish, in tomato sauce, with a colourful label – or a thick and juicy omelette with cheese, ham, and dried herbs mixed by myself following an original recipe, which had no logic to it. But before that, a stimulant would be good. I have a little whisky in the house somewhere.

Only two lamps are burning in the living room – a small table lamp and a tall standard lamp. The light is diffuse and the sound of the TV is turned down. As usual, I don't feel like the news. Accidents again, murders again, and our eternal and fatal crisis with no solutions.

I pour the aromatic liquid into a glass. The remnants from the bottom of a one litre bottle of Johnny W. I drain it to the last drop and throw the bottle in the rubbish bin under the kitchen sink. That was that. I look for ice and add two cubes in the glass. I abandon the food for the time being and slide into an armchair, my eyes fixed on the silent screen. Outside, car horns and brakes – as usual. Rhythmic music in the background. And a football match. Sounds which are coming from the pizza place on the little street nearby.

I calm down gradually as I sip the cold liquid little by little. I consider taking a long hot bath and maybe I'll choose the tinned fish after all. For the sake of convenience.

As usual in my life, calm moments – either sleeping or just relaxing with my eyes wide open – are interrupted by the ringing of the telephone.

I hear it but I don't know where it is. I look for it in the house. In the bathroom, on the small shelf under the mirror. A mobile number. Unknown.

I hesitate. A couple of seconds. Then I answer it.

"Yes?"

"Good evening. Sorry for disturbing you – I am trying to contact Mister Stelian Munteanu?"

"Yes, that's me."

"I am Diana Simionescu," says the feminine voice, and, puzzled, I start being more attentive.

"I am glad. How can I help you?"

"I would like to invite you to take part in a show. On the TV."

"What show? On what channel?" I make myself more comfortable in the armchair, ready for a discussion where I have no obligations.

"At Star TV."

"I do apologise, dear lady, but I've never heard of it in my life."

"It's newish and not all cable networks have signed up with us. But we are growing…"

I throw a wry smile at my TV screen, still mute, stuck on a news channel, and I switch to Discovery. No doubt they are growing. Yet another lot who are throwing money through the window on talk shows featuring beautiful, skimpily dressed girls.

"Of course, of course. And what can I do for you?"

"We have a cultural slot of one hour, live, evenings from 7 to 8. It's called Culture in the contraflow."

"Strange name for a show."

"It makes an impact, don't you think?" I feel her sending me the smile of a TV audience warmer.

I am bored and blasé. And this conversation has started to be too formal and slightly stupid.

"Of course. I agree. When and what are we talking about?"

"Thank you very much. It's about the book market and the volumes published by Trident. You have a special series of books, and they are surely of great interest to our…"

"Madam," I interrupt her rudely, "there is no point in continuing to laud me to the skies, I've already agreed to take part. When?"

"Er… Tomorrow evening?"

I have lived through the sensation of being the last minute replacement many times. When beautiful girls asked me to escort them to parties where I hadn't been invited in the first place, when I've been asked to talk at a book launch about a volume published in the previous ten minutes, or when I've been asked to stand in for a TV show's chief guest, celebrated and important, who developed indigestion, was indisposed or called out to a government meeting. I was always a second class VIP. And I always accepted it, out of convenience and laziness, but also, of course, because I was getting something out of it.

"Did you hear me? Tomorrow evening?"

I had to bite my tongue to stop my initial answer. Even a TV station of the fourteenth rank was using me as a reserve. I took a swig of whisky. It was just a Johnnie – the average, everyday walker. I put on a smiling face, reflected in the TV screen where Rommel was fighting fiercely in North Africa, and I said:

"Of course, Madam. I'll be there."

She giggled, briefly, predictably.

"I'm happy, Mister Munteanu. Shall I give you the address?"

"Could you e-mail it to me? It's a little difficult for me to write anything down at the moment," I replied, holding the glass in one hand and the remote in the other.

"Yes, I will e-mail it to you. I have your Yahoo address."

"Perfect."

"Thank you very much. We'll be waiting for you at a quarter to. Have a wonderful evening. Good bye."

"*Sărut mâna*.[62]"

Shit. A wonderful evening. I took another sip of whisky. Rommel had already been defeated.

Yet another day had passed. A day like the one in the song of the Pioneers and the Falcons of the Nation[63] – "A day in which you haven't done anything is a day you've lost." But, sometimes, even days during which you did too much can also be lost days, when nothing is good and nothing satisfies you.

I was wearing a faded blue jacket bought in Vienna last year, at the sales between Christmas and the New Year, with a striped shirt and jeans. Sofia used to say that was the way I dressed to dazzle easy lays. "You're going again to turn the heads of that TV lot?" I had no intention of turning

---

62 *I kiss your hand*, in Romanian. It is generally addressed to women of all ages, and, in the family, to one's elders of both genders.

63 Pioneers and Fatherland's Falcons – *Pionerii și Șoimii Patriei*, in Romanian, were the youth organisations of the Romanian Communist Party. The Pioneers were aged 8 to 14, while the Falcons were the regime's answer to Scout Cubs, covering ages 5 to 8.

anyone's head. I only wanted show off a bit about how many amazing things I know and how clever I am.

This TV station is in an old warehouse in the *Militari* district. I don't know what used to be there before. Some factory from the communist times. A bored porter watches something on a worn out television set. Obviously he is watching another company's channel, not Star TV. A vigilant bodyguard asks for my photo ID. I give it to him and he checks me against a list. He gives it back, without looking me in the eye, and mumbles:

"First floor, on the left. It's written on the door."

I changed my mind about saying *sictir*[64] to him. I hadn't actually caught what he was saying about the writing on the door. I go upstairs anyway.

On the first floor, on the left, are the toilets. That's what's written on the door. This makes me aware once again that we are a country of bodyguards and waiters. Either fools or brutes. The door on the right says "Newsroom" and I go in.

There are three people inside. The man doesn't look up from the computer when I slam the plastic and glass door. The two women fix their eyes on me. Young. Elegantly dressed. TV make-up. Striking. Same style, although they don't look the same.

"Good afternoon. I am Munteanu. I was looking for..."

One of the women gets up. She's tall.

"I am glad. I am Diana Simionescu. I was waiting for you," she says, using the polite *vous* form of address.

"I am afraid I got here a little too early."

"It doesn't matter. We can have a few words about the show, about your publishing house..."

---

64 *Sictir*, from the Turkish *sikdir*, translates literally as *fuck you*. It is used liberally in Romania and countries from the Balkans formerly under Ottoman influence.

She offers her hand. It's a little too low for her to be expecting me to kiss it. It's a small hand which I grasp and lift delicately to my lips. Bending slightly, I place the most chaste kiss on the pale skin. Tricks and illusions. Games. She's startled – she didn't expect this. Every time I make use of this stratagem I get the same results. Softening them up. She smiles. I look her in the eye. Dark blue...

"Would you like a coffee?"

"Of course."

"This way."

She walks ahead of me along a corridor. She is tall anyway, and she is also wearing high heels – 7 or 8 centimetres high. My eyes go down from the black, shiny hair – probably dyed – to the tight fitting dress of dark mauve, then further down her back. When she stops in front of the coffee dispenser, I had reached the ankle-high boots. She turns to me and smiles.

"What kind of coffee?"

"Espresso lungo, no sugar, no milk."

Her lips keep forming themselves into a smile. I'm in a funny mood today, ready for a bit of flirting. So is she. I have the impression that with her it's premeditated. She wants to ask me something. Or it's just the show. It's obvious this station does not pay fees to its guests. I didn't need the money anyway. I am ready to enter the game. Any game.

"Should we sit here?"

An ordinary square white table. Regular office equipment.

"Of course."

We sit down. We look at each other up close, from a distance of less than a metre. She sits with her legs crossed so that the hem of the dress only reaches a little bit above her knee. She keeps her hands around the coffee mug as if warming them up. We watch each other in silence. I am waiting.

"Why are you studying me, Mister Munteanu?"

"Can we be less formal and address each other on first name terms?"

"As you wish."

"Stelian."

"Diana. Dia."

"Stelian. Stelu."

She nods as she drinks her coffee.

"What are we doing here? Are we playing games?" she asks, eyes fixed on mine.

"I don't know. You tell me. What will we talk about?"

"Your publishing house. News. The book market. Culture in general."

"Do you have a plan?"

"Of course. I did some research. Have you brought any books?"

"Oh yes, I thought... for the audience. If anyone phones in, prizes."

"Excellent," and she laughs with all her face. "I am glad I managed to convince you to come in on such short notice."

"I suspect another guest disappeared suddenly."

"Got ill. But you did feature on the list. In less than two weeks it would have been your turn."

I sip the coffee which had started to get cold and seemed more tasty. I like my coffee cold. Heat only attacks your taste buds and...

"What are you thinking of, Stelian? You are not here."

"I was thinking of coffee and tastes."

"Are you a fan of coffee?"

"I like to experiment with various brands and types. If I have the chance."

"Maybe we'll have some better coffee one day. This is company refreshment. Apologies if it is not up to…"

"Hey, hey, I'm not fussy. It was just part of the conversation, waiting for the show to start."

"There are fifteen minutes left. Would you mind if I leave you here for a minute? I am going to have my make-up fixed and check all is ready."

"I'll be waiting."

She stands up and goes. I am convinced she feels I am looking at her from behind. She senses it because her body now seems catlike, as if my eyes were stroking her from the nape of her neck to the ankles and back.

The TV show went all right At least this is what she said. And the director. And the camera crew. The Bookfest[65] is getting closer, the local book fairs are already happening, and the crisis is reaching its climax. We had topics. I tried to be charming, vehement, wise. To keep the audience switched on. She made several good points with a lot of aplomb and charm, sometimes contradicting, and sometimes agreeing with mc when it was appropriate. I don't feel tired. I am in good shape.

She looks at me from the studio door.

"Should we get a good coffee?"

"Now?"

"Yes. Feel like it?"

"Where?"

"In the centre. *Piața Romană*[66]. At Costa Coffee. Do you know it?"

"Yes. Let's go."

---

65 One of the two annual major book fairs in Bucharest, the other being the Gaudeamus.
66 *Piața Romană* (Romană Square) is one of Bucharest's main places of meeting, fully central, with cafes, shops and restaurants very close.

"Perfect."

"My car is parked in front," I say.

"So is mine. I'll meet you there in half an hour. The first one to get there chooses the table."

She smiles and runs away. I pick up my bag and follow her. I exit the building in time to see a red, two-door 307 driving off fast through the gate of the former communist factory. From the metal gates, which are always open, grin several rusting letters. Car Q is where I left it. I throw my bag in the trunk. I hadn't even given her a business card. Useless.

I get there in 38 minutes. I park on *Căderea Bastiliei* Street[67] in a narrow space on the same side with the Academy of Economic Sciences. I walk quickly to Costa's – she is at a table. I can see her through the window. She is stirring a huge cup with a spoon. I come in, she sees me, and pulls out my chair. A normal, friendly gesture that surprises me.

"What would you like?"

The waitress is already near the table.

"Right now, a Schweppes Bitter Lemon."

"But you said…"

"I am trying to get my energy back; you are too fast for me."

"Fast or too fast?"

"Both."

"My father says that about me. But he is the same."

I don't know what her father is doing in this discussion. She looks calmer now, less of a burgeoning TV celebrity, and more of an intelligent woman.

"What are you doing working for that station?" I ask suddenly.

"There was no other job available, and I didn't want to

---

67 Fall of Bastille.

use my father's connections."

Again the father?

"Why television?"

"That's what I wanted. It has been my dream since forever."

"And… Do you think that, during these times, the television industry will survive? Everything seems to be falling apart."

"I studied journalism. That was where I got this one." Her left hand waves in front of my eyes. Fresh manicure, dark nail polish matching her dress, and a narrow wedding ring in yellow gold on her ring finger. I hadn't noticed – you're getting old, Stelian. You did look at her left hand…

"Marriage?"

"Yes." She is laughing. "You are probably asking yourself how come you haven't noticed it before."

"I admit it. My photographer's eye should have been quicker."

"I don't wear it on-air. Now that I am going home I like to keep up appearances. And so does he."

"Are you playing 'Mr and Mrs Smith'?"

"Yes. I don't know. It was madness, a demented passion in the last year. We got married after three months. Nobody believed it. We didn't invite anybody to the civil ceremony. We just bought the wedding rings and placed them on our fingers. We didn't go to the church. He didn't want it. Then our emotions cooled down after some years."

"Many years?"

"No. About three years and a half."

"And now?"

"He's in computers. He's absent, more and more. Up and down the country. I suspect he's out of line from time to time."

"And then?"

"We'll stop this one day. It can't go on *ad infinitum*. My best friend is a lawyer."

"Why have you told me all this?"

"I don't know, I just felt you would not hurt me."

"God forbid – why hurt you?"

"A woman, almost alone, young, in television, is vulnerable."

"Maybe yes, maybe no. You caught me watching you when you left."

"Yes, I felt your gaze. But it was different from other men's."

"Pfff… Well, Diana, believe me, I don't know. So what are we doing now?"

She smiles all over her face, like before. A knockout smile. She makes a sign and the waitress comes back.

"May I take your order?"

"The gentleman would like to order."

I watch her perplexed. Mute.

"You asked what we are doing. Answer: we are having a coffee." She turns to the waitress: "He'll have what I'm having."

I don't say a word. For a second. Two. Three. I take a long look at her. I read her face, her navy blue eyes – she has glasses on the table, so it's not from contact lenses –her thin but not too thin lips painted in a pastel shade of red, the slightly pointed nose, the tall forehead with a fine line, running parallel to her contoured eyebrows.

"What are you doing? Are you studying me?"

"Yes. And I have nothing to say."

"I ordered a large mocha for you, as well."

"A large mocha? A large *moacă*?"[68]

68 *Moacă* – slang for face. Can be translated as the English mug, meaning both face and a dupe.

75

"Strange. I feel good with you," Diana declares, fixing me with her eyes again, and touching with her fingers my left hand, which is holding the glass. As if by chance.

"Me too," I say.

"We should have a drink from time to time."

I nod my head to indicate my agreement. Somewhere deep inside a thought begins to take shape.

Chapter 8

Buzău, May 1986

I YAWN AS I LOOK THROUGH THE DIRTY WINDOW. The window was dirty but not because it hadn't been washed. It had been, but without much success. With cold water and no detergent. And with our own spit, when some crazy sub-officer ordered us to make it shine.

It is sunny and it is Sunday. All the go-getters had left. I couldn't manage to get leave to go, not even from a colonel in Bucharest. Too many hustlers. More than half got their passes due to their *pile* with HQ, with the military hospital and even with the Ministry of Defence. Generals and Securitate men. No problem. I'll have a quieter day here.

It is sunny and the unit is almost deserted. We have a month and a bit to go. AMR 55[69].

I am thinking of going to HQ and negotiating with the officer on duty about playing some old discs on the internal radio station. Some old-time rock, or some newer disco music. Some girls would be nice, too.

Two or three weeks ago I had been working late. Until early, that is. It was around 3 o'clock in the morning. I had smoked a lot and drunk a lot of *nes*. I had done a difficult job with a lot of text and different fonts. It had taken me nearly 14 hours with almost no breaks. Afterwards I couldn't sleep.

---

69 AMR 55 – acronym meaning "still 55 days left". AMR stands for *au mai rămas* – "still left". Soldiers and their relatives marked the time left on calendars with AMR followed by the number of days.

So, at three in the morning I was walking around the base, while those of my colleagues from the 1st platoon, who were on guard duty, kept yelling at me "Light on your face!" I swore at them and they swore back in a friendly manner. That was the game.

Suddenly, I had the idea of making a quick dash to the village. It must have been in the early hours of the Sunday, so I was sure to find a bit of a do going on in the village. I was not really on speaking terms with the local boys, but it was well worth joining in from time to time. Dancing with a girl, and maybe getting lucky in the dark. Some sweeties, a little present, a foreign cigarette, a *nes* at the break of dawn – all made an impression.

So I strolled lazily to the sentry hut at the main gate, the place where every Sunday there were tens of parents jostling each other, holding 1 Leu plastic bags, as they were called, full of all kinds of goodies and black-market or "shop" produce. Food, drinks, cigarettes…

When I was four or five metres away from the hut, I stopped all of a sudden. The windows were open and I could hear through them a continuous moan, as if somebody was having an endless orgasm. For a moment, I thought somebody had a video player and the boys were watching porn. I was wrong. It was live porn. I got closer and some boys came out. They were from the 1st and 2nd platoons, and even some of our men. They planted themselves in front of the entrance, guarding it.

"What? *Băi!* Draughtsman! You came too?"

I looked at them in disgust. They were eaten up with envy because I worked at HQ and had an easier schedule.

"What do you want, greenies[70]? I'm off to the village to

---

70 *Verzituri*, in Romanian. The term is derogatory, coming from the colour of the uniform, and it was applied freely to army conscripts. Another name was 'castraveți', cucumbers.

look for something. Fresh meat."

They started laughing, especially Sandu, who was a beanstalk from the 1st platoon.

"What? *Bǎ*! Are you stupid? Can't you hear the fresh meat moaning? Why would you want to go anywhere? Put 5 Lei in the collection plate and join the queue."

I didn't get it at first. It took me the time it would take to count to ten. Then I realized: it was a proper gang bang. There could have been some twenty or twenty-five boys. Each boy operated for five or seven minutes, according to his own strength. Then changed over. They wiped themselves quickly, pulled up their trousers, laughed stupidly, slapped the girl's buttocks and that was it – next!

I couldn't.

Out of fear. Out of embarrassment. I don't know why, but I just couldn't. I didn't even go to the village. I dropped in at the kitchens and made a transaction in illicit pork scratchings, exchanging four BT cigarettes for them. I then returned to HQ to brew up another *nes*.

I had given up on women. Just for that night, not for ever. But Sundays are too beautiful. I had to try for a grope in the village. I had several battle plans and I was preparing to apply them.

I knew Simionescu was again on duty, and he could cover for me if I disappeared to the village. I was about to go and tell him, when Gore from the telephone exchange barged in from the hallway, shouting:

"They've dropped the bomb, they've dropped the bomb, comrade Captain!" and he flew past me into the duty officer's room. I got there, my steps shorter and less hurried, and knocked on the door.

"Yes!"

I went in. Gore was speaking incoherently, repeating

"bomb" after every five words. Simionescu was looking at him without understanding.

"Shut it in your mother's cunt, Gore, and don't keep on shouting!"

"But it's the bomb, comrade Captain, it's the atomic bomb. We're all going to die. They've just announced it. We should do something. The bomb!" And he didn't stop repeating himself.

"Connect me with Army HQ, now." The tone was more than imperative. "Now, you hear? And call me when you're connected. On the double!" Gore shut up and ran off. "And what do you want, Munteanu?"

"Now? I don't think I want anything more. I'll come back later."

"No. Wait." He changed his tone and I noticed a shadow of a smile. "Let's see what this madman wants first and we'll talk afterwards."

"I understand."

"You're coming with me."

The room with the telephone exchange was small, grimy, full of apparatus and wires. It was like visiting the Technical Museum. Stale air. Small windows covered with blue paper for wrapping notebooks. The paper had been blue once. Now it was the colour of a turd. An enormous control panel, with holes and jacks from which cables extended. Telephones with dials and machines with cranks. Black, made of Bakelite. A metal filing cabinet. Wooden chairs. And two under-officers on secondment from Transmissions.

"I am connecting you with HQ, comrade Captain."

Simionescu was waiting in the hallway, looking on through the open door. I was also in the hallway, one step behind.

"Here you are. Connection to Army HQ. Comrade Major Popa." He was handed the receiver.

"Reporting! Captain Simionescu here, duty officer. Allow me to ask for details." Then he listens. I see him nodding. He grows increasingly red faced, his teeth grind, and he nods his head affirmatively, exposing his bald head, shining with perspiration.

"I understand. Of course. We shall take all measures. I understand… Of course. We are waiting for further orders. I understand."

He returns the receiver to Corporal Gore, who is now silent. He then turns and signals me to follow him down the corridor. He does not say a word until we are back in the duty office. He throws himself on the chair, which creaks menacingly, and looks for a cigarette.

"We are fucked! There will be radiation. A nuclear power station in Ukraine blew up."

For a second or two I don't manage to grasp what this means.

"A nuclear power station?"

"Yes, Munteanu, a nuclear electric power station. In Chernobyl. Somewhere above Moldavia."

"Well, but all the way to here?"

"Radioactive particles are scattered in the atmosphere. Radioactive clouds are travelling to the south and west."

"What must be done? I mean, what can be done?"

"HQ asked for the Geiger-Muller[71] counters to be activated so we can take measurements of radiation in the air and at ground-level. Also in the waters of *River Buzău*."

"When? Now?"

He inhales deeply from his cigarette and looks at the table. I am sure he would like to drink a *nes*.

"Munteanu, this is really bad. We don't know what it can

---

71 Geiger-Muller counter, also called a Geiger counter, is a type of particle detector measuring ionizing radiation. Used especially to detect nuclear radiation.

lead to. The medical units are making evaluations. We never had anything like this in Romania. Mother cunt. What should be done? The orders are not to panic."

"It's like there's a kind of atomic war."

He gives me an ugly look and makes a circle with his index finger on his temple:

"Are you an idiot? This is no game. Devil knows what will come from it."

I shut up, although I still have the impression we are in a movie.

Simionescu takes the phone and dials. He holds the receiver in his left hand and smokes nervously with his right. In the end somebody answers.

"Achim, where the fuck were you?"

Growling from the receiver.

"Eating. Good for you, bon appétit. We have an explosion at an atomic power station in Ukraine. I need Geiger-Muller counters."

Growling again. "Good. After you finish eating, it would be good if you came in as well." And he slams the receiver down.

"Munteanu, you're coming with me to the chemical and nuclear protection storage. They keep all this crap in there. Devil knows how they work."

There is almost nobody in the sun-filled alleys of our unit. It is nearly lunchtime. Those who had stayed in *Buzău* had received permission to go out to town. Everything is deserted.

I would also have liked to go out to the town, to the *Crâng Park* and look for girls. I would have had a furtive beer – regulations say alcohol and the uniform don't mix – and I would have eaten an indigestible *mic*[72]. On my way

---

72 Short for *mititel*, the typical Romanian skinless sausage.

back, I would have also have had a string of crisp pretzels. But nothing like this is going to happen.

The *Anti-chemical and Anti-nuclear* storage was a long, low shed. It looked like a former stable. They had threatened us several times with the chemical protection suits, contraptions made of greenish-yellow plastic sheet under which you heated up in three minutes, and we had used the gas masks during our exercises in the gas-chamber. I had escaped it because I had important stuff to do at HQ, but two colleagues had choked on that abominable gas. They had not suffered any harm apart from the fright. The gas had not been toxic, it was merely a deception. Hisses, whitish fumes and pungent smells.

Simionescu unlocks the rusty padlock and we go in. We switch the lights on, and look at the shelves and dismembered racks, stacked with equipment of all sorts, and stretching into the distance.

"What does a counter look like?"

The captain starts laughing.

"It's a black plastic box. Happy?"

I make no comment. It was an idiotic reply typical of an *APVist*. End of story. He appears to know what he is looking for, and after I follow him like a puppy for five minutes, he stops in front of a shelf and points to the devices.

"Here they are. Take three of them, I hope they'll be enough."

Then we go back to HQ.

Here my memories are again a little misty. The counters were indeed some black boxes, but I don't exactly recall if they had a cable with a stick on top, like a sensor. I tend to believe they did.

Back in the office, we place the Geiger counters on a

table. Simionescu lights up another cigarette. People gather around us – the guards' commander, the DRDO, meaning the Deputy Regimental Duty Officer, and the boys from the telephone exchange. We all look at the black boxes as if they are foreign cars[73].

"Does anyone know how to use them?"

Silence.

"Right. You're all a bunch of shitheads."

He takes one of the boxes – black and made of Bakelite, with that international symbol for radiation which people know from the films. It has a label in Russian, printed in minuscule letters.

"Does anyone know Russian properly?"

"I know how to read the letters, comrade Captain," Gore blurts out.

"We all know the letters, smarty pants. I meant what it says on this label."

We all knew the letters because watching Bulgarian TV[74] had become a national sport by then. Well... in fact, a sport for people in the south who filled their balconies and the terraces of their apartment blocks with metal plates, manufactured in dark corners. This was where private initiative started.

While Simionescu is fiddling with the apparatus, the box opens suddenly. The top part slides backwards and reveals a dial with lines and numbers, and a pointer flickering left and right. But that is nothing: in a moment the thing soon starts emitting a terrifying ticking.

We all turn to stone. And the noise doesn't stop, while the pointer keeps flickering round the screen.

---

73 Foreign cars, especially western-made, were rarely seen on Romanian roads, and they were known only from magazines and films. People used to gather around and stare at them.
74 Also using the Cyrillic alphabet.

Everyone present has a stupid reaction: we look around as if we could see the radiation and dodge it.

"Mother cunt, this is not good."

"Listen, Comrade Captain, there's one of the boys in the kitchens who's from the *River Siret*[75] area and has a funny name like Mateiciuc. He could be Russian or Ukrainian or something, and he might know the language."

"Is that so, Gore? Bring him in here, on the double!"

The corporal, happy to be of service, leaves on the run. The counter is still ticking. We sit and look at it enthralled. And yet again we looked around to check whether the radiation is in the room.

Iurie Mateiciuc is still wearing the fat-stained kitchen apron round his middle, and his sleeves are rolled up.

"Have a look, soldier, what does it say on this label?"

The man – in his twenties, to go by the breadth of his shoulders – takes the box in both hands, with no fear, and starts spelling out the words.

"On opening... will be used... for... stabilising... the mark out... or sample, or the piece – don't know how to call it – which is found in the lid of the counter... Stabilising will be made... with pointer on position 100."

I can't remember how long it took, maybe half an hour. Mateiciuc was spelling things out without knowing what it was about. As if he was reading a piece of school work.

In the end, they managed to stop the ticking after they calibrated the apparatus and took the sample out of the lid. Everybody was wondering how come the batteries were still working after all this time – it was rumoured they were from the '50s. Mateiciuc said he had seen somewhere on them the

---

75 Near the border with Ukraine.

inscription "1953г." with a Cyrillic letter г, which makes it short for год in Russian (pronounced *god*), meaning *year* (not God as in English).

I was standing with Simionescu on the bank of the stream, near the bridge, and we were watching the lazy flow of the muddy water. I seem to remember I was playing with the end of the probe not knowing whether I should plunge it in the river. He was smoking, looking at the horizon, dreaming or preoccupied. The two of us were alone. I think he wanted to escape from the walls of the unit for a while.

"Leave that bloody thing, or you'll manage to break it in the end."

"But, comrade Captain, are we doing this sampling or not?"

He blows the smoke in my face, trying to make me want one myself, and says:

"What's the use of this mother cunt, though? They asked us to take measurements in order to give us something to do. Whatever happens this is bad news. Lucky I've got no children..."

"Will it have an effect?"

"It certainly won't do any good. They'll feed us iodine and they'll keep washing the streets, but we can't say where the rain from those clouds will fall."

"So far there's isn't a single cloud in the sky."

"Come on, Munteanu, this is no joke. I am dead serious."

I sigh, looking towards the other side of the river, where some ragged children are playing in an eddy near the bank. He sighs as well. Deeply.

"Shouldn't they announce it to everybody? I mean the people out there, the population."

"An official announcement will be made around 16.00,

so that they don't ruin the people's Sunday completely. As if anyone cares about our Sundays anymore..." Then he stops, thinking that he had said too much. But he can't help himself:

"Do you know that joke with *Bulă*?"[76]

"Which one, there are loads of them."

"The one which ends with – 'that was all that was missing'."

"Yes, I know it."

I tell it to myself and laugh out loud. It is sunny and the skies are blue, and, somewhere, radioactive clouds are floating over Europe. The joke says that *Bulă* was in a career guidance class at school. The teacher asks the children if they feel that there is anything missing about life at home. Ionel says that they are missing a new radio, but his father would buy it and pretend it was a present from Father Frost[77], Costel says that they are missing a window curtain, but his mother would buy one next week. Only *Bulă* says "Comrade Teacher, there's nothing missing in our house." "How come, *Bulă*?" she asks. "Simple. My elder sister came home last night and told mama she was pregnant, and when father heard this he screamed - that was all that was missing – so nothing is missing now."

"What do you lot care, Munteanu? You are all young. You have plenty of years ahead of you. But us..."

I turn to him, trying to understand what he wants. I understand, but I want to provoke him.

"Plenty of years for what?"

---

76 *Bulă* is a character found in the majority of Romanian jokes, sometimes as a child, sometimes as a grown-up, but always not very bright and much put-upon.

77 In communist Romania atheism was state religion. The use of names of religious celebrations was discouraged. Officially, there were Winter Celebrations (*Sărbătorile de iarnă*) instead of Christmas (*Crăciun*), and a Father Frost (*Moș Gerilă*) instead of Father Christmas (*Moș Crăciun*).

"To find a place, somewhere."

He stands up, sighing. I am convinced that he wants to say more, but doesn't trust me enough. Even if he does speak, what would be the point? Gossiping around the corner, telling jokes while queuing for food?

"You know, I was born in a small town. It's called *Nehoiu*, in the mountains, near the curve of the Carpathians. My father worked at a stud farm. There were many pedigree horses back then. After that period they introduced tractors on the collectivised farms and the peasants had nothing with which to feed their horses. They began to raise horses again in the '70s, when I was in high-school, taking extra-mural classes because I had to work. They were raising horses then, for the militia. I wanted to stay in *Nehoiu*, but one evening, at twilight time, I sat down for a chat with the old man, my father's father. He had come to visit us from a village near *Tecuci*, in Moldavia. He had fought on the frontline during the war, and he told me stories about army life, about fighting alongside the Germans, then alongside the Russians on campaign to Budapest and to the Tatra Mountains. And I liked the army, I would have liked to be in the cavalry, but they abolished it."

Then he seems to return to the riverside, as if coming back from far away. He realises that he had said too much, as if he had forgotten about me.

"I was carried away by my memories. I am boring you, Munteanu. I liked the idea of being an officer. The uniform, the insignia… I believed… I haven't seen the old man since then. He died in his own village. I couldn't attend the funeral, I was in officer training. Then life took me onward. I forgot about him. I didn't even lay a flower on his grave. Never. But that's life…"

He stops suddenly and looks at me intently with his light

brown eyes, sweat on his temples and the military cap sitting back a little on his head. He is thinking he had spoken too freely. Or maybe it just seems that way. Why does he trust me?

"Let's go to the unit. I am hungry."

Chapter 9

Bucharest, March 2010

THE GADGET ON MY HIP RINGS. It's the TV fairy. That is, Star TV – a kind of TV station. I answer.

"*Sărut mâna*, what a surprise!"

"Good morning, I am glad to get hold of you."

"Was it hard?"

She sounds puzzled. She doesn't know what tone of voice to use. Irony, a little joke? She lets it go.

"I would have liked us to see each other."

"You would have liked?"

"I would like. When do you have time?"

"I have nothing much to do. One afternoon? Or around lunchtime?"

Her voice sounds very professional, and that makes me think she doesn't want to see me just for the sake of it. Business again? Or payback? Like "I put you on my show, now I want something..."

"Lunchtime is OK too. Where?"

I don't answer her question. "Is there any special reason you want to see me?"

"I'd just like to... but yes, there is a reason. I have a proposition to make. A book."

"A book? With great pleasure."

It's only the second meeting and she's making demands. I remember that I had sensed something premeditated about her style. Had everything been planned? The show, the coffee, our chat, the smiles, the hands touching? Could it be so devious?

"It's not my book. Don't assume that."

"I wasn't."

"You're lying!"

"OK, we meet and talk. Is it urgent?"

"Don't you want to see me?"

Before this we have talked a couple of times over the phone. Banalities, a guilt-free flirtation with nothing at stake. And now, a book?

"Of course I do. But..."

I leave her in suspense for a moment. I'm going to try a little game of my own.

"But?"

"I was thinking of something a little more tasty. Not just coffee."

"What are you thinking about?"

"Dinner."

"Where?"

She doesn't refuse. I jump to the next step. Now we'll find out.

"My place."

"Where?"

"My place. I cook something, we drink a glass of wine. I'll even brew coffee."

It's her turn to be silent. I am thinking about the odds: 50-50. I am also thinking about Sofia.

"No."

"No?"

"It's not wise for us to meet at your place. I am not comfortable... Please understand me. It's... it's not the right time. Or maybe it's not the case."

"That's fine. What now?"

"You find a place and call me."

And she hangs up. I'm left holding the phone to my ear. What interest do I have in this lady? For a moment I decide not to call her again. Inviting her to my place had been a trap. None too subtle. Although I would have liked to have a pretext to cook for somebody. Sofia is far away and my friends don't barge in on me. But it wasn't such an elegant move. It could have been interpreted as…

No restaurant comes to mind. I give up and return to the laptop and my economic situation. Stock and sales. Pfff, these things are insufferable.

Two days go by. It's evening, chilly, pleasant, springtime. I have window open towards the street, like always. I am seated in my armchair and I turn on the television. I start zapping with the sound muted, like always. I stumble on Star TV. I start laughing, all by myself. This means cable operators have finally syndicated it. I remember the phone call I owed. I look for the number and dial it.

"*Sărut mâna*, Munteanu here."

"Good evening."

"I wanted to apologise, I was a little…"

"Nonsense, you forgot!" Her voice sounds contented and amused.

"No, but…"

"It doesn't matter. Have you decided? I need to reach a conclusion on the manuscript. My father keeps pestering me."

"You know, these things take time, I can't just sling it together."

"Stelian, I don't want you to sling anything. Let's meet. I'll tell you about it. You read and then decide. OK?"

I released the storm.

"OK. Do you know *La Birlic* on *Pache Boulevard*, near ProTV?"

"So that the competitors see me?"

"I don't think…"

"I am joking, we're no match for ProTV. I know the place. We can talk in peace there. When?"

I up the ante:

"Why lengthen this? Now."

"OK, I'll be there in an hour's time."

"In the non-smoking lounge."

"Perfect. See you. Bye."

"Bye."

Wow, she was fast. I jump in the shower. A book? Maybe it's something interesting. Who could her father be?

The restaurant is not full. In the non-smoking lounge there's no-one. Of course, I had leave home in a hurry. I didn't want her to get there first, like the last time. I greet the *boss* – I've known him since that time I was running with that damned manuscript across the length and breadth of Europe – and I order a cheap beer, a Holsten, and an espresso lungo. The light is diffuse, there's a continuous hum, the table cloths are cherry-coloured, just like the walls, and the atmosphere has a slight undertone of decadence.

"May I sit at your table, monsieur?" she says and laughs at her own joke.

"Of course, madame." I kiss her hand. I also hold the chair for her. A waiter gives me a long look from behind a curtain and makes a sudden appearance.

"What would you like?"

"I am hungry," she says. "I'd like a Bulgarian salad. Are you not eating?"

"No, *merci.*"

She puts her hand in her purse and takes out a memory stick sheathed in a sort of red plastic holster.

"Here is the book."

"Don't you think you should tell me what it is about?"

"Well yes. You will laugh at this, but I told dad that I'm seeing you to offer his book, and, at first he was shocked. Then he started laughing and said 'how strange it is that life puts everything together'."

"I don't understand."

"It's simple. You have my father's memoirs on this memory stick. I did the typing and corrections."

"And?"

"My father is General Gheorghe Simionescu."

A coup de theatre! Not for one second had I made the connection between the family names. There are plenty of Simionescus. I hadn't seen the General in a while. I think the last time was immediately after the revolution. He had appeared on television from time to time in the aftermath. There had been all kinds of TV shows and scandals... but we had not met face to face for a long time. There were all sort of conspiracy theories woven around him: that he had worked for the Securitate, that he had access to the Ceaușescu family accounts, that he had been involved in Milea's "suicide" and, especially, that he'd had a hand in capturing the fleeing Ceaușescus[78]. I don't know who was the source, but these stories kept springing up in the press from time to time.

"He told me he knew you and that he would be honoured

---

78   The story of the Ceaușescu family's accounts is an enduring Romanian mystery. The rumour had it Ceaușescu had millions of dollars in foreign accounts. These were never recovered. Vasile Milea was the Minister of Defence who committed suicide (or was "suicided") for allegedly opposing Ceaușescu's reprisals against the revolution in December 1989. The Ceaușescu couple fled the communist party HQ in Bucharest at 12.08 on 22 December 1989. They were captured after several days, imprisoned in a military unit in the town of *Târgoviște*, some 80 km NW of Bucharest, tried summarily, sentenced to death and shot on 25 December 1989.

if his memoirs were to be published by Trident."

"Yes, of course." I am a little at a loss and don't know what to say. "I know him, of course, and I am honoured. I did not expect this."

"Do you have any reservations?"

"None, I am convinced it will be a fabulous book."

"We should sign a contract, shouldn't we?"

"With him or with you?"

"With him. It would be nice if we could pay him a visit. He lives most of the time in *Telega*, near *Câmpina*[79]."

"I know *Telega*."

"We could go together. He told me he would like to see you again."

"Of course, with great pleasure. You two decide and I will come. I am certain the book is a very serious affair."

"I enjoyed it. You should read it. There are some things you will understand better than I do."

"I am certain."

She smiles, and I ask myself if there is anything behind it. A provocation? An offer?

"I think I'll have some wine. Red. We should toast the collaboration."

I nod to the waiter and order a bottle of *Fetească neagră*[80].

"Diana, in all honesty, I would never have thought you were Simionescu's daughter. You don't look much like him."

"I resemble him too little. Meaning not at all. That's how fate had it."

I don't insist. The wine fills two glasses.

"*Noroc!*"

---

79 Some 60 km NW of Bucharest, towards the mountainside.
80 *Fetească neagră* – an old Romanian local vine producing a dark, aromatic, semidry red wine.

"*Noroc*, and best of luck in everything you do" she replies and smiles enticingly, sipping from the tall glass. Somewhere, as if by chance, our hands meet again, just for a fraction of second. And for a moment I look at her with different eyes. An appetising woman, elegantly dressed in red and black, with navy blue eyes which fix me with a curious stare, dark shiny hair and fingernails painted red, bright red. In the yellowish glow of the restaurant I watch her closely, my thoughts starting to scatter, once again reaching far back, and far away.

Chapter 10

Buzău, June 1986

IT WAS A WONDERFUL DAY. Not only because it was sunny and not very hot. Because we were going home. That was it! It was all done. Enough! We were waiting for the travel permits. We had packed our bags. We had handed in our military uniforms and equipment. We had paid the market value of items which were lost, stolen or which we were keeping as souvenirs. A beret, a belt – silly trinkets.

I am sitting on the edge of the bed looking down. I am a civilian again, dressed in old jeans and a blue short-sleeved shirt made of a fabric imitating denim. I had a nice green shirt I liked better, but I had seen enough green during the past months so, for the moment, that was enough.

In the long bedroom there are no discoloured and patched socks hanging on drying ropes. It doesn't stink anymore of soya salami, combined with the effluvia of unwashed feet, and smelly farts from cabbage salad with beans cooked in garlic and onions.

It is quiet. It is deserted. Just the wooden trunks standing on end near each metal cot. Somewhere far off a door creaks and slams shut. My noisy colleagues are in the yard smoking the first cigarette of civilian life, making their goodbyes and making promises, which they themselves don't believe in, that they would write or call.

I have a moment to myself. I am alone in this space in a way that I hadn't been for a long while. I can draw a line and close this chapter in my life. I am no more of a man. I am no

97

better prepared for life. And I am no more skilled.

"Am I disturbing you?"

I give a start and raise my eyes. Simionescu was looking at me from his full height, shiny bald pate inclined towards me.

"No. Did something happen?"

He reassured me with a gesture of the hand.

"Nothing. I wanted to say goodbye."

"Oh... yes, I wanted to drop in myself, but I thought you'd be busy."

Lamentable lie. In fact I didn't think there was any point in looking for him. He had been humane and rational. One of the few, but, in any case, he was *APV*, and over the last nine months and I had seen enough and lived through too much, if not because of him, because of others like him. I needed a break. A longer break.

About two weeks previously there had been a wakeup call in the middle of the night. They had got us up around 3.30 in the morning. But not with noises and sirens. Quietly. "Get dressed and kitted up." We were taken to the yard. The engines of the trucks were running. The ammunition depot was open and the crates were being carried to the trucks. Then they also loaded us up. We had remained in place for 40 minutes or so. Then we had been sent back to bed. No explanation. It hadn't been just an exercise. Or maybe it had. I cannot know. I had looked around for him in that mad hubbub, and when I saw him I had enquired with my eyes. He had only said "take it easy, it'll be fine." Back in the dorm, we had all fallen asleep, with no worries.

"You didn't expect this, did you?"

"Frankly, no."

"I'm just a bastard *APVist*, no?"

"Mmm..."

"You're a civilian. Now I have no power over you."

"These months have not been the happiest of my life."

"I am certain of it. But there is no guarantee about the next few months."

"No, but I will be free."

"Free – nonsense! You have only changed the boundaries. You have widened the area a bit. And you think you're free?"

"I am on holiday. I am a student. I want to go to the seaside."

"Yes, I know. Well, you have gained space. I wanted you to know you have been one of the few I felt to be different. I can't say exactly how. More normal. Less deformed. Keep your spirit free. If you can. And, most of all, look for a place of your own. A place where you can feel safe and happy."

"Happiness is a notion which is too vague, too general."

"No, happiness is simply the capacity to enjoy any thing, big or small. I think you have this capacity. Try not to lose it."

And he offers me his hand.

"Have a safe journey."

I feel his warm, sweaty palm. The grip is strong and complicit. His eyes are sad. Only for a moment. He takes four small steps and, from the door, he turns back to me, just like Colombo the TV policeman, and adds:

"You remember that night with the Counter Information fellow? I came to see you after he'd gone. It was very strange, but I trusted you had told me the truth."

"About what?"

"You told me then that you refused him."

"I didn't refuse him. I only told him I didn't know what was happening in the dorm. I could not have afforded to refuse him, I was scared, comrade Captain."

"Same thing. But I believed you. I was convinced you were not an informer."

"Nowadays, people are what they can be."

"That's a little too philosophical. We might meet again. I am here for the moment. Over the years, who knows? If you want to come back after you graduate. Or if you simply want to talk... Anyway. Look for me. Good bye, Munteanu."

"Good bye, comrade Captain."

He goes out, leaving the door open.

In a moment's time, from somewhere close-by, Paul, my colleague from the top bunk, gave a shout:

"Come on, they're giving us the documents. Let's get away from here as fast as we can!"

Chapter 11

Bucharest-Iași, April 2010

I HAD PLAYED WITH MY WEAPON for two whole days at the firing range. I had been almost always there by myself, and I had practised taking 200 and 400 metre shots. It had been harder at first. I could not get the breathing right. In the old days when I was doing target shooting at the Dinamo club[81], we started every training session with a run. Not more than 15-20 minutes. Then we stopped and reduced the rhythm of our breathing, trying to control it.

After two days, I had managed to hit a circle as big as a tangerine – some 7 or 8 centimetres – at 400 metres with all the ten bullets in the clip. It wasn't perfect, but it was satisfying.

When I was about to leave, in the last day there, I had looked in puzzlement at the weapon in its case, lying on my bed, and I didn't know what to do with it. It was clear I couldn't take it to Bucharest. Misha hadn't shown up in person, but he had left me a note on the coffee table in the room. And a key. The firing range also had private lockers, well locked and well guarded. I left the rifle there. Totally secure.

I then took my travel bag and left on foot for the train station. I drank a last coffee and a final beer. Then, the train. I called Sofia – she was busy, going into a meeting and she

---

81   Dinamo was the name of a network of sport clubs supported by the Ministry of the Interior. The best known was, and still is, the football club Dinamo Bucharest, but the clubs covered every sport, from judo to weightlifting and track running.

still had papers to complete. I laid myself on the lower bunk and started nibbling bread sticks, while leafing through a magazine. At some point I fell asleep.

I wasn't pleased to be returning to the swarm of problems in Bucharest.

It's been a month since then.

April is an important time for publishers. People buy books at Easter[82], either for their children or for their girlfriends, and regional book fairs were all grouped together in this period.

I am now in *Iași*[83] and, trying to forget about everything, I'm drinking a Merlot de *Purcari* from 2006 in the *Bolta Rece*[84]. I have three friends here, and I see them rarely. When we do see each other, we seem very happy. In fact, we really are.

I had forgotten to switch off my phone. Maybe I was waiting for a sign from Sofia. Or Lulu. The moment the phone buzzed and the LED light went red, I grabbed it hopefully.

"I am glad you are in *Iași*. We will meet tomorrow morning. For a coffee in the hotel lobby. Misha."

Always theatrical, he prefaced his appearances with messages of this kind. A sort of fanfare. James Bond style. For some time now I had been asking myself whether he had always been like this, or whether it was a development which came with old age. I had only known him for about four years, and he was already knocking on sixty then. I

---

82   Easter is the most important religious celebration in Romania, bigger even than Christmas, although the more important gifts are received in December rather than spring.
83   The former capital city of Moldavia and still the most important in north-eastern Romania. Very close to the border with the former USSR and nowadays Republic of Moldova.
84   *Bolta Rece*, literally "the cool wine cave", is a celebrated restaurant in *Iași* which has played host to come of the literary giants of 19th and 20th century Romanian cultural life.

would have liked to meet him when he was younger, or very young, in the '60s – a young KGB officer during the times of de-Stalinisation, the missile crisis, Kennedy's assassination. He told me once that he had spent many years in Romania. A slip of the tongue (or maybe he had said it intentionally) by which he confessed to a fling in a village in *Bacău County*[85]. I think she was a Romanian-language teacher, and he had learnt the language perfectly at that time.

We never had the chance to talk like intimate friends. There were moments, in fact, when it might have been likely, but Misha knew how much to say and especially when to be silent. He usually lit up a cigarette, sipped a cognac or a coffee and entered a dream-like state. Or he counter-attacked with a new subject which felt completely incongruous[86], but was surely premeditated. I have never felt that Misha was completely human. Perhaps only after the explosion in Rouen, when he saved us from the tentacles of the Greek connection, or after the assassination attempt on the Greek, his mysterious daughter, Eleni[87]. That was only for a couple of seconds, though, before he immediately re-assumed a mask of detachment, calm and calculation.

I walk out of the restaurant into the pleasant chill of springtime and phone Sofia. She answers immediately.

"Yes, my love. How are you?"

"Having a glass of wine."

"Did you get to *Iași* all right?"

"Yes, I had a clear road. Many police speed checks, as usual, but all fine."

"I'm glad. I miss you."

"And I too, my love. Was your meeting OK?"

85   County in Moldavia of about 700,000 inhabitants.
86   The Romanian expression is *'ca nuca în perete'* — "like a walnut against the wall".
87   Stelian is referring to previous cases described in Hrib's novels, which feature recurring characters, e.g. Misha, Eleni, and Sofia.

"Well… Hm. There is still work to be done. I'll stay a little longer. Have some rest."

"I will. You too. Love you."

"Love you too. Good night."

"Good night, my love."

After Somalia, Sofia had a difficult time recovering. Hospitalised in Hargeisa, convalescence in Bucharest. A short holiday in Montreux, and then Toni – who called to say that he needed me back home urgently. A body had appeared in a place where it couldn't have been; and a person had turned up who didn't exist. This was another story which turned out to be a soap bubble in the end. Sofia started lecturing again at the School of Political Sciences. The course was hers. It was her speciality. Then, all of a sudden, the opportunity to go to London came up. It seemed, on the surface, to be a reward for the hostage rescue mission, but I think it was more to do with some people's desire to tear us apart. Out of sight, out of mind… they didn't succeed. Maybe we grew a little distant, but that was it. Trident business doesn't allow me to be with her, full time, in London. I would have loved to take care of the books from there. Whatever people might say, London is the world capital of *publishing* – when the Frankfurt Book Fair is not happening. I would have loved to quit Bucharest as soon as possible, to run away.

I descend the stairs to the wine cellar. I'm going to drink some more wine. Maybe I'll have some juicy *papanași*[88] as well.

I didn't set the alarm clock.

I woke up without it between 7.30 – 8. The previous night

---

88 *Papanași* is a Romanian dessert of the doughnut variety, but the dough is prepared with cheese curds and cream. They are served hot out of the deep-fryer with more cream and jam.

I had overdone it. Now it's 8.45 a.m. It's sunny in *Iași* so I open the curtains to let the light in. I turn on the shower and lay out my clothes on the bed. Misha is bound to be downstairs already. I am not hurrying. The idea of making him wait is my revenge for all the moments when I felt he had manipulated me. But not quite all of them.

I go down to the lobby. I see Misha at a small round table surrounded by three armchairs shaped like shells. One of them is occupied by him. The others are empty. I reach the table at the same time as a waiter. Perfect synchronicity.

"Morning, Misha. I'll have a regular espresso and an espresso lungo with milk. And a still water."

He smiles ironically.

"Aren't you eating something first? You're pouring coffee inside yourself without eating?"

"You're so caring."

We shake hands.

"What business brings you to *Iași*?"

"I was coming from *Bălți*[89]. I heard you were around so I thought we could talk a little."

"You heard?"

"Well, you know, things get heard."

The waiter brings my order.

"You know what I'd like. Bring me a cognac and a coffee. And for the gentleman, two ham and cheese sandwiches. On toast and butter, please. The slices should not be cut too thick, and make it brown bread, if possible – you know, for the waistline," the Russian adds.

I burst out laughing.

"You are one of a kind, Misha! A demanding fusspot."

He's laughing too. The atmosphere becomes more relaxed. Not for long, though.

89 *Bălți* is on the other side of *River Prut*, the natural border between Romania and the Republic of Moldova.

"So what's going on nowadays, Stelică? How are things?"

"The same."

I gulp the short espresso down and then take a mouthful of water. I pour a sugar sachet in the long one and stir it methodically.

"Are you here to ask how I've been, or…?"

"Don't you miss a holiday to Vienna?"

"For training?"

"Yes, a month has passed. So you don't want lose your sharpness."

"Don't worry."

"I'm not. Did you think about it?"

I act dumb.

"Come, come, Stelian. You know what I want, but you're avoiding the issue. You know you are in a bad situation and there's no other solution. It would be a pity not to use your skills. I have a target for you. An easy one. An exercise."

A shiver goes through me. This means killing.

"I don't think I can, Misha. You understand? It's beyond my power to accept. I can't… Not for money."

"Can't you say the word? Nobody's listening. You can't kill for money? I don't think you've got any other solution. What I propose is very honourable."

"Honourable my arse. I am not a killer!"

"It's a contract."

"This is like being in a film."

"We're all in a film, a film made by someone else."

"Good. You're a philosopher now!"

"I'm a realist. And I offer you solutions, that's all."

"To the devil with your solutions. I can't."

"But you will, Stelian, because you will have no choice."

"Are you blackmailing me?"

"No, I am warning you. I am letting you know... I'm off now. You pay."

He stands up and crushes his cigarette nervously in the ashtray. Not too nervously. Just a bit. Calculated.

"Do you have the money to pay or should I leave some?"

"Are you insulting me?"

"No, I am waking you up to reality. I bet that you don't have more than one or two hundred in your wallet. Isn't that so?"

"So what?"

"So nothing. You do what you want. You'll receive a message. Think hard. Really hard. We'll speak."

He leaves.

Chapter 12

Bucharest, December 1989

I WAS IN A *MAXI-TAXI*[90] ON THE 21ST. People called it a *sexy-taxi* because, from the outside, all you could see through the windows were bottoms. The bottoms of the people standing inside the bus, bent double. A ride was worth 5 Lei in those times and the passengers left their tickets behind when they got off, which made the drivers rich. I had even calculated it. If for every full circuit, which lasted about one hour, a driver resold twenty tickets, it meant that in eight hours he was pocketing about 800 Lei – and that was big money back then. In twenty working days during the month, he could assemble 16,000 Lei. Ohoo, I can't even imagine the potential of all that money in those times.

There was a *maxi-taxi* going through the centre of Bucharest, which terminated at the Opera, right near the restaurant. From there, I would then climb aboard a trolleybus to *Drumul Taberei*[91]. It was 10 or 11 in the morning, and, through the crowd of bodies in the minibus I had managed to secure a narrow avenue of vision by which I could see through the window. In practice, all I could see was a strip of the street. At the University, the minibus stopped and stayed put. The passengers started mumbling quietly. Everybody knew something was happening. They had all learned of the developments in *Timișoara* from Radio Free Europe or from friends in *Timiș County*. Those who'd had the courage to telephone. There were all sorts of rumours

90 A mini-bus used as public transportation on some routes.
91 One of the most populous neighbourhoods of Bucharest.

which said that the *Banat*[92] had risen, and, together with the army, the people were marching on Bucharest. On the other hand, rumours also said that the army was ready to erase Timișoara from the face of the earth. These were the kind of reports being bandied around by idiots or professional rumourmongers. It was certainly one of these two parties.

Through my tunnel of vision, I saw columns of demonstrators. They came from *Piața Unirii* and were marching down *Magheru Boulevard* (I wonder what the name of the boulevard was at that time?) towards *Piața Romană*. In fact, I think there was something about to happen in the square in front of the Central Committee building. This was the site of Ceaușescu's favourite balcony from where he delivered his lectures on the topic of "dear comrades and friends" or "lay another coat on your shoulders".

I started to be terrified. There were thousands and thousands. Placards, slogans, portraits of "The Comrade", shuffling steps and expressionless faces. The texts on the placards condemned the meddling of foreign powers in the affairs of the Romanian state. The inevitable, soporific phraseology but, this time, it seemed, much more venomous. I suspected that *Timișoara* was lost. I had good friends there. I remained staring into space, while the minibus stood motionless and the mass of people, scattered over the entire width of the boulevard, flowed past slowly. My hands were busy with a long blue tube full of sheets of tracing paper, and a big cloth bag staffed full of my papers and manuals.

I was standing jammed up against my fellow passengers

---

92 *Banat* is a historical province occupying the greater part of western Romania. It was conquered by the Turks in the 1552 and then by the Habsburgs in 1716. It has been part of Romania since 1918. It is very ethnically diverse, with Romanians, Serbians, Hungarians, Swabian Germans, and Slovaks living side by side. Part of the historical *Banat* province is in Serbia. The county capital, *Timișoara* (Temeschwar) was the starting point of the 1989 Romanian revolution, on 16 December.

and I could not move. I would have liked to get off. I had no revolutionary thoughts, I simply wanted to contemplate the powerlessness and sadness of the marchers. I would have smoked a cigarette, and been resigned to the foolishness of my fate in an insignificant corner of Europe. I was about to graduate so that I could end up on a building site from where one could sign up for a trip to a country which was a bit freer – meaning Yugoslavia – from where one could try to escape. Far away, as far away as possible.

My memories from that time now seem very foolish. Running away was my only dream. Not because I felt oppressed or because my freedom was curtailed, but because I was fed up of cold and queues, of tasteless Chinese chocolate, of cooking oil pumped out of a tank, of sugar straight from a sack, of the *Petreuş Brothers* chickens, and of "tacamuri" and all the shit[93] which made made me feel as if we were at war.

After a while, the minibus started off. The column of demonstrators had passed us by. Half dazed, I got off in Opera Square and crossed the street to the trolleybus stop. I reached my colleague Ioana's place after 12, and, from the radio, the voice of "The Comrade" could be heard. He had started his speech.

Ioana and I were working on a housing project. A block of flats with a restaurant on the ground floor. Even when we were drawing floor plans we were dreaming of food. (Nowadays the apologists say that we weren't dying of hunger and that there was no one rummaging through the rubbish bins in those days! True enough, nobody died of

---

93   The Petreuş Brothers are two very popular traditional musicians; in the slang of late 1980s Romania, the name was given to a bag containing two emaciated chickens sold instead of one regular chicken. *Tacâmuri* was chicken feet. The "shit" referred to were soya-protein salamis and sausages, which Romanians looked back on after the revolution as symptomatic of their deprived condition under the dictatorship.

hunger – or, at least, I didn't hear of anyone dying of hunger. And the militia didn't allow anyone to rummage through the rubbish bins. Not that you would have found anything! But was that one of the ideals that we fought for: not to die of hunger? I'll say no more!)

We spread our blueprints out on the table, as well as the Rotring pens and a heap of papers with many calculations, then we started working. She dealt with the numbers, I dealt with the lines. In the background, the radio with its commentary. A background sound to which we paid no attention, until we heard people clamouring and a voice – Ceauşescu's or his wife's – saying hesitantly "calm down, please calm down". I can't recall the exact words. We rushed to turn the television on. Something was happening. Then the broadcast was interrupted for a little while.

It's not clear to me what happened next. Something was happening. The demonstration was over. I tried to talk on the phone with my father, whose office was in the centre of the city. He said "Stay calm and get on with your work". Clearly something was happening.

Later on Ioana's parents came home. There was a rumour that a barricade had gone up at the University. Nobody knew for sure. Everybody was trying to tune in to Radio Free Europe. The reception was poor. But the word was circulating mouth to mouth: a neighbour would whisper something in the hallway, another one at the corner of the building. A group was still resisting at the University.

Dusk was falling and, through the windows of the first floor, we were looking straight into the courtyard of what was then the home of the Ministry of Defence. Although the *Drumul Taberei* district is higher up than central Bucharest, I could not see anything.

We worked, or pretended that was what we were doing.

We were waiting for a sign. I ate with Ioana and her parents, one fried egg and a chicken wing each. I had decided to stay there overnight.

Late in the evening we heard gunshots and saw tracer bullets shooting across the night sky. We felt shivers of horror then. Had they also fired down on the ground? Towards the people?

I slept fitfully, with one eye half-open and my ears trained on the Russian-made radio that was the best at catching the signal from Free Europe. There were rumours, suppositions, estimates...

In the morning I telephoned my father again. He had walked to his office. He only said "At the University everything is washed down and clean". I didn't comment. I didn't know what to say.

Suddenly, someone found out about General Milea. I think it was Free Europe again, which had announced something. He killed himself. He had been killed. The legends took flight.

Around nine thirty, we started to hear the columns of demonstrators. They were marching down to the Centre, flooding out of the *Drumul Taberei* district, and they covered the entire width of the street.

It was sunny, warm, and the skies were almost clear. I don't know how I managed to get dressed as fast as I did.

We went out ourselves. The column of people was packed tight. That was the first time I saw flags with a hole where the crest of the Socialist Republic of Romania used to be. There were many of them, taken from the workplaces. Then I noticed that people were also grouped according to the place where they worked. The day before I had seen another column, with messages which said exactly the opposite. I wondered whether these were the same people, and obviously they were.

At the Military Academy we were joined by officers in uniform, who placed themselves at the head of the demonstration. "The Army is with us!" the crowd chanted. I can't remember where we stopped. In any case, I missed the flashes of action when the helicopter left the roof of the Central Committee[94]. All day long I took pictures of happy people, who were making the V sign with their fingers and chanting "*Ole, ole, ole, ole, Ceaușescu nu mai e!*"[95] along with other highly ambitious messages.

I think I believed sincerely in the revolution. Just like many of the others. I also remember seeing a black man yelling "Down with the dictator" and making the V sign. Probably some foreign student. Fervent freedom was contagious, irrespective of nation.

When our feet started to hurt, we started back towards *Drumul Taberei*. Around *Cotroceni Bridge* I saw the first TABs passing by at full speed, flying their flags with the hole, helmeted soldiers behind the machine guns. Stray groups of confused people had started to whisper "There is shooting. There is shooting at the Central Committee! There's shooting at the University!" The shooting was beginning, and so were the first doubts...

I got home as night was falling. I ate something and sat with my eyes glued to TVRL, that is TVR with the L for *liberă* added on, after its recent liberation. It was broadcasting non-stop sloganising, appeals, and orders. At that time I didn't notice the chaos. I was still enthusiastic. Various rumours continued to spread.

When I heard the first volley of shots right outside my windows I think I froze. We threw ourselves face down on the floor. After five or ten minutes, we realised what was

94 When Ceaușescu and his wife fled Bucharest.
95 "Ole, ole, ole, ole, Ceaușescu is no more!"

happening and we turned off the lights. After about half an hour the first bullet penetrated the house. It went through the glass panels of the balcony, through the double-glazing, and stopped in the wardrobe among the overcoats. I noticed later on that it had gone right through a winter scarf and two pairs of woollen gloves. A completely mad night followed. The people occupying the television station were appealing to the army for help, terrified of the columns of armoured vehicles which were on the attack. I talked to my parents – they were home, in the east of the city – and they said that they could see tanks passing along the boulevard. "Ours?" I asked. "They seem to be," they replied.

I stayed lying on my belly, with the television on and the sound turned down. A good idea – I can't recall who came up with it – was to take refuge on the stairwell of our building: there were no windows so we had more protection. All the neighbours were there, armed with knives and ladles. They said we had to defend our block of flats, so as to prevent terrorists coming in. After a while, one neighbour remembered that there was a deaf old man living on the ground floor. Hopefully nothing bad had happened to him. A leadership group went to ring at his door. He didn't open. They tried the door. Unlocked. About seven of us went in. The apartment looked like the aftermath of a battle. The lights were on, the television was screaming, and, here and there, bullets had bitten off chunks from the plaster and the furniture. The old man was upright, walking around happily with a small pan in his hand. A more robust neighbour tackled him to the floor, as if he was playing rugby, and dragged him out of the flat; another one turned off the lights. The television remained – screaming.

We spent the entire night like this, weapons in hand, accompanied by the music of volleys of gunshots outside and television commentaries inside. We had a small interval when the television announced that our water supplies had been poisoned, and a neighbour came out of her flat, foaming at the mouth, holding her toothbrush in her right hand, screaming "They've poisoned me, I'm going to die". She was calmed with a brutal slap.

When morning came, we were all dizzy. They had not found Ceaușescu yet, although they were chasing him, I think. We ventured outside again. A bit more carefully. The camera was still hanging around my neck. Check points had appeared, boys with tricolour arm bands and sub-machine guns hanging from their shoulders. Fingers on triggers and no trigger guard. I asked myself then how many innocent people had died, out of stupidity or incompetence, in this hubbub. Collateral damage – I think this was the label they used some years later, in another war. Obviously the collateral damage was not important, as long as the Revolution succeeded! Revolution must always succeed, no matter what the cost may be. And if the forces who matter are supporting the right side, then of course, the Revolution will always succeed.

Those boys with AKMs and eyesight already clouded by tiredness – and maybe drink – made me take apart again and again the zoom lens of my Soviet-made Zenit camera (Zenit type E, old and a little damaged, bought by my parents in the '80s) in order to check I didn't have a home-made pistol or bomb hidden inside it. Useless to tell them it was impossible and that what they had seen in films was all a fantasy a la James Bond.

Then, at one of the checkpoints, further on down the road, surrounded by other officers and lower grades, I saw him. He already had a bigger star, he was a major. And the inevitable tricolour arm band. He was giving orders. I was sure he would not notice me. But the checking of my papers and my Zenit was taking a long time, so he got closer. He gave me a swift look and suppressed a smile. He snatched the ID card from the hands of the blond boy with crossed eyes and finger on the trigger and said, pointing at the camera:

"The comrade is a journalist." He then changed the tone and continued in a conspiratorial voice "He is with us!"

The young soldier nodded affirmatively, I screwed the lens back on the camera and followed Simionescu several steps further away.

It was only then that he offered me his hand.

"I am glad to see you. I was convinced you would be out on the streets, but I was not hoping to meet you…

"I am also glad… *the army is with us!*"

"Yes, *with us*. I believe it's not yet very clear who is this 'us'…"

"Are you well? In these mad days..."

"Yes, I am fine. I'm stationed at the Central Committee from tomorrow. Maybe you'll come by to see me. There will be a need for people like you. Now is a good moment…"

"I don't know, I wouldn't want to get involved..."

"Munteanu, there won't be too many chances. It's now or never. Think seriously!"

"I promise to think."

He shook my hand very firmly.

"I am not joking. Many things will change. At least on the surface. Fishermen in murky waters will appear soon. In addition, the structures will be rebuilt. This confusion will not last too long. Make a decision fast."

"I have the school..."

"You'll also have time for school. Join the structures. In politics. We need people like you. I know some others too."

"Fine," I replied dryly.

We parted. He looked at me with sadness. He knew I wasn't going to look for him, and I never did. During the following days, he appeared on the television. I saw him just as I did Iliescu, Caramitru, Dinescu[96], along with many others who have completely disappeared from public view since that time.

On the 25th, they shot Ceaușescu, it snowed, and people were already experiencing the delights of Christmas. Then came the crazy year that was 1990. During the Mineriad[97] I heard nothing of him. It was only later on, in '96 or '97, that I found out he had continued to climb up through the ranks.

---

96 Ion Iliescu (b. 1930), first president of post-1989 Romania, for three mandates; also an important member of the communist regime until he was "marginalised" in the 1980s. Ion Caramitru (b. 1942), one of the leading Romanian stage and film actors, former Minister of Culture (1996-2000). Mircea Dinescu (b. 1950) dissident and poet. All three are major figures of the Romanian revolution, members of the FSN (*Frontul Salvării Naționale* – the Front for National Salvation), which took control of Romania after the fall of the communist government. Caramitru and Dinescu quit the first post-revolutionary government during Spring 1990.
97 Mineriad – in Romanian, *Mineriadă* – is the name given to the brutal interventions of the miners in three rallies against the neo-communist government established in 1990. The miners were given free rein from the government to discipline the "layabouts" protesting against the new regime. The biggest and gravest display of force was during 14-16 June. Two anti-government mineriads, protesting against subsidy cuts, followed in September 1991 (resulting in a change of prime minister) and January-February 1999 (resulting in the crushing of the miners and the arrest and imprisonment of the ringleaders).

Chapter 13

Telega, Prahova County, April 2010

IT'S FRIDAY, AND IT'S ALREADY 14.45. I would have liked to leave earlier on my trip to the mountains but – as usual – all sort of problems cropped up. Administrative crap, papers to sign, nauseating phone calls, e-mails that needed immediate attention, hysteria of the "It must happen right now" variety. Especially on Mondays and Fridays. I stayed there, trying to solve as many things I could, until I told myself that Monday would be another day...

Car Q is rather dusty and dirty. The colour has become a matted greyish brown, its original metallic aquamarine of which I was so proud two or three years ago has been hidden under mud and dirt. I haven't washed the car in a long time. In fact, sometimes, I even forget to put diesel in it. The yellow light signalling a minimum reserve in the tank is always lit. I have learnt to ignore it. One day I'll manage to get the idiot's breakdown[98].

The road is busy but I am not in a hurry. I don't have a fixed time of arrival. The Simionescus are expecting me after 5 p.m. I'll probably get there around 6. I feel a little emotional, I haven't seen the General since he was still a major, and then only for a few moments. I had skimmed through his manuscript, on the computer screen, squinting, and skipping from word to word. It looks interesting – memoirs. Cool. Fresh material, short essays about the society of today and yesterday, memories of youth, political games from '89 – well,

98 Expression meaning to be left stuck in the middle of nowhere with no fuel at all.

a kind of hotchpotch written by a confident and especially coherent hand, given that we are talking about a first time author. A good start. With a little editing it could become a very saleable item. I don't understand as yet what he is aiming to achieve with the book – promote his daughter's career, scare someone, payback, or, pure and simple, to close the door on a chapter of his life. Simionescu is well known, even if he had stayed in the shadows recently. All sorts of stories about him were being thrown around by the *bad boys* of talk-show journalism, who circulated stories, ranging from the one that he shot Milea to the one that he was, in fact, the liaison between our Securitate and the American CIA. Fairytales. Of course, in the manuscript there were no such confessions. It would have been impossible. On the other hand, I might convince him...

Almost on auto-pilot, I'm driving through the settlements of *Prahova County* – rolling past village after village, each as unremarkable as the other, houses, fences, people in the courtyards with home-made wine in plastic bottles and over-ripe vegetables for sale, apathetic, resigned, expressionless faces. Blasts of car horns and curses from people in a hurry driving brand new jeeps accompany me. I am thinking that, if the General would let me fiddle with it a little, I could make the text more engaging. I'd give up some of the ballast of rhetorical questions and multiple adjectives.

Diana had called me about three days before. Late in the evening. Around a quarter to midnight. I was half awake, squinting at a programme on the AXN Crime channel.

"Aren't you coming to *Telega*?"

"When?"

"Friday evening. My father is there. We'll have a barbecue. Drink a glass of wine. We'll stay in the fresh air. You talk

about the book, sign the contract. Shake hands on it. What
do you say?"

"Yes, I could use some fresh air."

"Do you have the address? Write it down."

"One second."

"It's *Telega Vale* number 1854."

"Is that all?"

"Yes. Can you manage it?"

"Of course. I'll give you a call when I reach you and you
come out."

"Good. We'll be waiting for you around 5 p.m. I'll already
be there. See you."

A short discussion. I wondered why it wasn't him calling
me. I thought that, perhaps, she had not told him about me.
Or that she had not told him that I would come. No, that
would have been too strange. The General knows everything.
What, then? In fact, who really wants the book published?
Could it be that Diana wants it more than her father?

It was getting dark slowly – with a combination of rain
and nightfall. I push buttons on the radio and the sound
of the music gives me a shock. James Blunt's guitar and
hoarse voice in "Tears and rain" lead my thoughts to Sofia
and the huge distance between us. I feel like turning the car
round and starting out for London. I am unsettled. Could
it be that I have agreed to this madness with Simionescu's
memoirs because his daughter smiled sweetly at me and
touched my hand, as if by chance, on two occasions? Or
could it be because she caught me admiring the line of her
back all the way to her bottom? A short break, and then
down to the ankles. I feel the need to step on the brakes. To
turn back home.

Simionescu deserves a chance, however. I never trusted
him completely. I always withdrew when he made a step

towards me. I don't know why I didn't trust him, I can't explain it. That's how I felt. So why am I surprised that he didn't call me now?

At *Câmpina*, I turn off the National Route 1 and enter the town. It is a small town besieged by people from Bucharest at the weekends. I cross it via the high street – filled with cars parked higgledy-piggledy – and then I turn towards *Telega*, after the Grigorescu Lyceum. The road is winding, descending to the exit, and I cross a partly ruined bridge over *Doftana*, I think. I didn't bring the GPS with me, but I, more or less, know the roads in the region. Tibi, the photo reporter from *Flacăra* Magazine, explained every detail to me – his parents have a house here.

The road is empty and unlighted. I proceed up to *Telega* and the asphalt-clad, narrow road invites me to keep on driving. I feel like driving on for a long while, without a target.

My eyes are closing. I feel sleepy. I yawn, cracking my jaws, and I don't bother to cover my mouth with my hand. On the radio I can't find good music anywhere. All the stations seem to feature people talking, and when I hear sad music it doesn't do me any good. I'd like to call Sofia. I had told her where I was going and she didn't seem too happy about it. She didn't comment, but the tone of her voice suddenly changed.

I have reached the centre. The town hall, a monument, little shops, several people eating sunflower seeds by the side of the road, then a left towards *Telega Vale*, over another bridge near which a rusty plaque announces that it had been reconstructed with funds from the European Union. I pick up my mobile phone and beep Diana.

It's not yet dark, but the looming clouds cover the landscape with gloom. I slow down and switch the lights to full beam. I see her in the middle of the road, one hand raised and waving.

I park on the right-hand side of the road. I am such a lout. I didn't buy anything. Neither flowers, nor wine. I am entering their house with a finger up my arse[99].

"Welcome to *Telega*, wandering stranger!"

"Glad to find you, princess. I have just realised that I didn't bring you anything. It's not polite to come empty-handed."

"Don't worry. My father is already cooking on the terrace at the back of the house. We're very hungry."

She's in a very good mood, and behaving naturally. More naturally than I had ever seen her behaving. The street is so badly lit that I can only just see her. She is wearing discoloured jeans, an open brown jacket under which a white blouse conceals her breasts.

"Are you well?"

"Yes, of course. Why?"

"You are quiet. Different than usual."

"A little tired. It was a long week."

"Right… You know, I think my father is a little bit emotional. You, becoming his editor, after so many years."

"I feel emotional too. I think."

"You'll get over it," she says, and presses her mouth down on my cheek, kissing me with a loud smack. "Papa, Stelian is here!"

I enter hesitantly through a metal gate. The house is small and old, whitish – a timber-frame plastered in traditional style. The roof is lined with sheets of galvanised tin. There is a ground floor and a converted loft. The whole house consists of only a few rooms, four entrance steps and a sort of veranda. From above the General is looking at me. He is

---

99 Expression meaning to go empty-handed on a visit, a faux pas.

as tall as I remember, his back a little bent now. His baldness is more accentuated, and what hair he has left is all white. He has a superior smile and I see a face with the same lines that I had noticed on TV. Too deep to be covered by make-up.

"Good evening, Mister General!"

"Fuck your mother, Munteanu, I call you here for a barbecue and you start out with the official language."

"I see you haven't changed your style of address. Still direct and military."

"After a lifetime of giving orders, it's hard to change."

We both laugh. Heartily, but a little uncomfortable. He's wearing a coloured apron with an advert for chicken soup, and a thin navy blue sweater. He offers me his hand – I feel it is as strong as it used to be years ago. He grips my hand tightly, then hugs me unexpectedly and whispers in my ear:

"I don't have many people, who I recall with any pleasure, from other times. You are one of them."

He surprises me by the way he spits out this line.

"Why do you say this, Sir?"

"Stelian, let's give up this official style of address, we've known each other for far too long. Call me Gigi, Jorj – whatever you want. I'd prefer to call you just Stelică."

Just because we have known each other for a long time, doesn't mean that we comprehend each other. I keep this retort to myself and instead I just say "OK".

"Let's drink a *ţuică* [100]. Diana, would you like some?"

"No. You go ahead."

He asks me inside and we go through a hallway and exit on the terrace at the back of the house. It's no bigger than 3 metres square, bordered by two apple trees, three plum trees, and several rows of seedlings, onions and other vegetables.

100   *Ţuică* or *palinka*: plum brandy of varying alcohol content (from ca. 30% to ca. 60%), very common in Romania and Hungary, generally home made.

It's all covered by a huge red umbrella on which raindrops have already started their mad dance. There is a wooden table with a yellow oilcloth and three stools – that's all.

"You'd prefer to sit inside, so that we won't get rained on."

"No, it's perfect here. Clean air."

"This is my little empire. Since I retired from that grand hotpot, I took refuge here."

"And you wrote."

"Yes, I did. At first, I did it because Diana kept flapping her mouth. I was not convinced it was the best thing to do. Then I started to get bored with sitting around and cleaning, so I started writing."

We sit down and he pours a yellowish liquid into two glass thimbles.

"Take care. This is not weak *Prahova ţuică*. It's a stiff one. *Palinka* from *Zalău*[101], a gift from a former colleague."

I smell it – he's right. It's strong. I taste a little, I gulp it down. He refills the glasses.

"I propose we take a break. We still have to talk, don't we?" and he laughs. "When you feel sleepy, you can go to sleep. Tomorrow is another day."

"True. Are we talking in famous quotes?"

"No, it was just a way of speaking."

"Already arguing?" Diana asks, placing a dish of cold meats on the table.

"No, my dear. Men just have a way of talking between themselves. More brutal, more ejaculatory."

"I don't believe you. But it's your business. If I'm in the way…"

I feel as if I'm in the theatre. A theatre of amateurs. Like

---

101   *Zalău County* is in Transylvania. The *palinka* made there is deemed to be of the strongest variety, sometimes triple distilled and going to 60% or slightly more in alcohol content.

TV dramas in the old days, with a Party secretary speaking in parables to young apprentices. In fact, I don't know what I was expecting from this meeting. A meeting with a difficult author. A possible future author.

"Should we talk about the book?"

"Won't we eat first?" he proposes.

"I admit to being hungry."

"I cooked skewers of chicken and pork. A few trout, too – a gift from a neighbour."

"I'll bring pickles and French fries in a moment," Diana shouts from the minuscule kitchen.

I eat in silence and chew slowly, looking into a void. Only the chicken. I don't touch the fish, afraid that the bones might stick in my throat. I am experiencing a slight regret that I came. I would have stayed at home and I would have fallen asleep like an idiot in front of the television, watching a crap film, full of shootings. But I would have been in my house, sitting in my underpants, and probably holding a bottle of beer.

"Still silent?"

I look at her and I don't say anything. Neither does the General.

"You seem ill at ease," she adds.

"A little. The gherkins are wonderful," I say, changing the subject.

"Yes, they are," Simionescu intervenes diplomatically. "They are left over from last winter. We don't have many left. I pickled them myself."

"You have become domesticated... Jorj?"

"Are you picking on me, Stelian? Even now you can't get it out of your head that I am a bloody *APVist* who fucked up nine months of your life. Isn't that so?"

"It was not your fault, General, the system was at fault!"

"We all have been at fault."

"After twenty years, these philosophies don't matter any more. They're all worn out."

"True, too many years have passed. Everything gets forgotten."

He puts down the skewer from the kebab and looks at me fixedly.

"Will you publish my book?"

"That's what I was waiting for, to talk serious business."

"You know, Stelică, I tried to get on with you. As much as I could. I don't think I succeeded."

"It's not your fault. I couldn't… It's not the best period of my life."

"The crisis?"

"That too. I am at a crossroads. I need to make some decisions. Hard ones. Important ones. But these are my problems. I brought a contract. Read it and, if it is OK, you sign it and send it back through Diana."

I give a sigh from the depths of my being and breathe in the cold, clean air. The rain eased off a little. I yawn and hide it by putting both hands to my face.

"What about the book, the text? How did you find it?"

"Hm… To be frank, it needs more work. It's a little too…"

"Boring?"

"Yes. There are things that have been said thousands of times before. People are waiting for the big disclosures. And you don't have too many of those in there. It will be hard to market it."

"I still have enough connections with various TV stations."

"I wouldn't say so."

"Why?"

"Because Diana is wearing out the soles of her shoes at

Star TV. What the hell kind of TV is that?"

It was only after I finished saying this phrase, that I realised how crude I was being and I expected a slap on the face. But she doesn't say anything. She gets up from the table, picks up the dishes quickly and goes back inside the house.

"Was that behaviour necessary?"

"General, you have a beautiful daughter. You have a mysterious past. And a weak manuscript. What should we do next?"

He gives me a long look and says nothing.

"I think it would be best if I leave. It was not a good idea to come all the way here. Here," I say, and I put the little object, the memory stick, on the table. "I didn't copy the file. Have a nice evening."

I take a few steps in the dark, as far as the gate, then I hear his voice.

"I have some dry red wine. Would you like a glass?"

I turn back and look at him. There isn't much light, but I can make out the lines on his face, marks of sadness and past grief.

"Please…"

I sit back down at the table. He pours wine in two thick, tall water glasses.

"I don't have glasses with stems here – we're in the countryside."

"These will do fine."

"What's eating you, Stelian Munteanu?"

"Noroc!"

"Noroc! To health."

The fruity, dry taste of the drink soothes me. I can't recognise the grape variety. Probably some sort of merlot. Home-made.

"I would have liked you to write some stronger stuff. Conspiracies. You know what the masses want. We could market that properly."

"You mean lies?"

"Not lies, fiction!"

"You know well there are things I cannot say."

"Of course. But there is a middle way. Could you spice it up? I would need it ready by the middle of May."

"You would like to launch it at the Bookfest?"

I am surprised he knows about the book fairs.

"No, in November, at the Gaudeamus fair. It needs a longer marketing campaign, and it would be closer to December – we're still celebrating the *Revoluția*."

"*Loviluția?*[102] "

"The events of December '89. That's *politically correct...* So?"

"Fine. I'll do my best. I promise. You'll have the book by 15 May." And I see him smile again. "I am glad we met again, Munteanu, very glad. I am glad for the book, but also for my own sake. Search for your peace, my boy. Life passes us by too fast."

"We're starting again on this?"

"Stop. Whoa. I wasn't going to turn the subject round to cheap philosophy. Let's stop the business talk here. Let's drink wine and gossip. Maybe you feel like a game of backgammon?"

I try to remember the last time I played this. I can't.

"Yes, General. Red wine and backgammon... that's a wonderful programme for a Friday evening," and I mean it.

It's late. The rain has stopped a long time ago and the General has gone up to bed. We had drunk a full bottle of

102   Word play between *lovitură de stat* (coup d'etat) and *revoluție* (revolution).

wine, and half of another one. He beat me mercilessly at backgammon.

He laughed: "You must be lucky in love, my dear!"

It is past midnight and I look at the sky from the wet terrace. It's a long time since I've watched the night sky. Here, in *Telega*, the air is a lot cleaner than ours, in Bucharest, and I see a lot of stars, like a curtain painted in random patterns. I would have liked to know their names. As it is, I only recognise the Little Dipper and the Big Dipper and the North Star. Lulu asked me once about the stars and I didn't know what to tell her. I didn't want to invent a story either. I said I'd buy her a telescope and a book on astronomy. And she said "Nooo, I don't need those. I wanted to be a little romantic, you know, like in the movies" and she burst out laughing.

"Are you smiling, stranger?"

Furtive steps and the rasp of a lighter. A short flame and a manicured hand with red-painted nails offers me a lit cigarette. I sigh and rub my hands over my face, my eyes and my forehead. My head hurts. I smoke rarely and when I do, I only puff the smoke in and out. Fooling around. I have already given up smoking. I take the cigarette from her left hand and put it to my lips while still looking up at the stars. I feel her brushing her body against mine. Lightly, barely touching me.

"I was thinking of my daughter."

"Is she far away?"

"No, she's in Bucharest. I don't have the time to see her as often as I would like."

"I believe we set too many targets for ourselves."

"No, Diana, it's about options. About choice."

"And you have not made your choice yet."

"No."

She takes the cigarette from my hand, touching me briefly with her fingers, and takes two quick drags.

"I don't want anything from you, Stelian. I would have liked… I mean… You know what I want to say. I know it's not the right time. That place is taken. I'd be…" She takes a step to one side and sits on a stool. "But my father deserves this book. Please help him."

I feel I'm crumbling with fatigue, with powerlessness and insecurity. I don't know what to say, what to do. I gaze at the stars. I have an attractive woman at my side… I turn towards her and see her red lips, freshly made up. I see desire, and I also see, deep in her eyes, hopelessness and desperation, and I don't know why…

"I am going to bed. Good night."

She turns to me with a studied movement which I recognise: Kim Basinger in *L.A. Confidential*. "Just so you know: I filed for divorce."

The cigarette continues to burn in the ashtray. Somewhere far away a dog howls in sorrow at long intervals. The moon sheds her light on a numbed, silent and sad village. I climb to the bed in the attic room. The memory stick and the empty glasses are lying on the table.

Chapter 14

Bucharest-London, May 2010

THE BOOK FAIR IS APPROACHING and everyone bombards me with e-mails. I have had enough. I am home and I don't feel like doing anything. It's not a new mood. It's the same feeling that has been stuck to my forehead, for the past year, like a yellow Post-It note that refuses to fall off.

There – I have become a poet. I turn the laptop off and get dressed to do some shopping. The ordinary kind: vegetables and still water, maybe a can of beer. Maybe, who knows, a newspaper or magazine.

I open the door and an envelope falls on my old and dusty doormat, on which all my neighbours wipe their feet since theirs had been stolen. It is a bulging white A5 envelope.

I don't much like retracing my steps. But I do it now. I am curious. There is no writing on the envelope. It's clear that someone brought it and stuck it in the doorframe. I am surprised the neighbours haven't stolen it. I lock the door again and take a seat in the armchair in front of the TV. I have a hunch about what could be inside the envelope and it makes me uneasy. I hold it with the tips of my fingers, as if not wanting to leave fingerprints. So foolish. I tear the end of the envelope open, and several folded sheets of A4 paper, printed on one side, fall out. Photocopies of stories from the newspapers. After reading the first headline I freeze. Literally. The shiver of horror and fear is so powerful that I drop everything to the floor, stand up and run to the kitchen. I look in the fridge for an uncorked bottle of white wine and pour myself half a glass. I drink it in two gulps and return, breathing heavily, to the papers scattered on my carpet, face upwards.

General Simionescu accuses: "The failure of the Romanian political class is a consequence of the mistakes of January 1990!" and a long interview published in March of this year follows. *"I withdrew because I could no longer accept compromises, says General Gheorghe Simionescu"*, a cover story from the house in *Telega*, photos of him on the back terrace writing on his computer, from April. I search through the papers chronologically. The last sheet has a smaller article, a column from a paper printed a few days ago: *"General Simionescu, a figure who was rather reserved in the days of December '89 will publish his complete memoirs later on this autumn. It appears that the volume will contain…"*

He is absolutely mad. He has started the marketing campaign without discussing it with the editor. He hasn't even sent me back the signed contract. Once again it strikes me that this is Diana's signature. She is intent on hurrying things up in order to consolidate her own position in the media.

It's not this which terrifies me. I am actually worried by the anonymous envelope. It's clear what they want, that is, what Misha, or other people behind him, want. The KGB, FSB or God knows who else. They want to stop him. To stop the publication of the book and to liquidate the General. They are afraid he will write or say too much. I try to remember the pages of the electronic manuscript. I am now regretting that I only skimmed it without making a copy. What the mother cunt could be so compromising in it? Several stories with Iliescu and the CPUN[103], with

103 CPUN – *Consiliul Provizoriu de Uniune Națională*, in Romanian – the Provisory Council for National Unity, the body that took over Romania after Ceaușescu was killed in December 1989.

Verdeț[104], Dinescu, Caramitru and everybody else from back then. Nothing serious. Nothing incriminating or secret. Maybe I didn't know how to read it. Or maybe they do not know the contents of the manuscript.

And they want me to kill him!

I am certain they know I am going to sign with him. This is terrible: a book editor killing his own author. These idiots have either seen too many films, or are trying to get inspiration from the Stieg Larsson model. An author who dies just before the book is published will sell better than a living author. But we know, or believe, that Larsson died of a weak heart, while, I, on the other hand, possess a Steyr-Manlicher sniper rifle which is waiting for me in Vienna.

The red LED blinks. An e-mail. Address unknown.

"You have received the envelope. I believe you read it. August is a good month. He'll be in Vienna. To help you understand what's going on, 1,000 Euros are already in your account. It's not payment in advance, it's just proof that we know everything. Payment for opening the envelope, that's all. You should start getting used to the idea."

Unsigned. A strange address. I won't check my bank account. It's clear the 1,000 Euros are there. These boys are not fooling around. I know Misha too well not to be convinced: things are clear and precise.

I am afraid. I am very afraid. And I feel ill. My head hurts as if it's going to burst.

I look in my telephone agenda for Misha's number. I don't know what else I can do.

"Yes, Stelică. How can I help you?"

"You know too well!"

"You've received a letter?"

---

104   Ilie Verdeț (1925-2001), an important man in Ceaușescu's cabinet, also his brother in law, the first to establish a new government when the revolution started, only to be pushed aside by Ion Iliescu.

"Stop playing the fool. I can't do this."

"I don't think you have much choice. The crisis is getting deeper," he says, and he laughs into the receiver.

"I am scared."

"It's normal. It will pass. Think of the benefits."

"I can't think of anything."

"Calm down, Stelică. You'll get accustomed... And now, please excuse me; I have a little problem to solve."

He hangs up. He's putting me off. What to do? I have forgotten about shopping and I don't remember my schedule of work for the day. I have forgotten where I was going and who I was meeting.

A new e-mail. Another unknown address.

"Next payment on 1 August. 10,000. Then, there in Vienna, another 10,000. The remaining 30,000 afterwards. That's for starters. To get your hand in."

Cold shivers go through my body. I go into the bathroom and turn on the hot water. I'll take a bath.

I burn the envelope and the papers in the sink. I delete the two e-mails from everywhere. I prepare a foam bath and relax into it. 50,000? I could cover some debts. Some – not too many. It would be a start. I breathe out vigorously. My conscience does not seem to be a hindrance. Years of crisis. The misery in the country. The lack of opportunity. Despair...

Heathrow is a huge airport. I don't know how the struggle over relative sizes was resolved by the European officials: Frankfurt, Amsterdam, London... It doesn't matter to me. Terminal 5 is a monster, it looks like a pavilion for exhibitions. The trick is to follow the signs. There are many of them, all clearly written. Sofia couldn't come to pick me up. She still had work to do, too early for her to leave the office.

So, the Underground to Victoria Station and then seven stops on a suburban train. "You get off at West Croydon. Go up the North End for some two or three hundred metres, turn right on George Street until you see a Starbucks. It's the entrance right opposite. I'll leave a little red heart stuck on the window of the ground floor, near the door. When you see it you'll know that I am waiting for you with many kisses."

She's sent me all the directions by e-mail, and I received her message as soon as I switched on the phone, while I was still on the plane. Once I pick up my bag from "Baggage claim", I look around for the Underground.

I laughed a little when I read that the point of reference was a Starbucks. I am inclined to believe that she wanted to have a house near one of these places. She's hooked on their coffee. She also used to drag me to Starbucks in Bucharest, whenever she had the opportunity, in order to buy herself a drink whose complicated name was impossible to remember. It's strange that she is now living in the same district where Misha has that odious pink house which used to belong to I don't know what Indian nobleman, and is located across the road from the hotel where I stay when visiting London. Is anything a coincidence? I wasn't a great believer in conspiracy theories. However, I once had the occasion to ask myself what Sofia actually did for a living, and whether she hadn't met Misha before meeting me. But after Somalia, team work between us didn't quite work, because our superiors didn't want it that way.

The trip takes a long time. The Underground, then the train from a busy Victoria Station. My bag is not enormous, as I'm only going to stay four days.

She had taken me by surprise. I had received an envelope from her at the Trident office, a big envelope with my name on the front and hers on the back, containing photos from her newly-rented flat and a printed return ticket to London. She hadn't sent it by e-mail, so it was already printed. Both she and I regretted the days when communication was only on paper. In fact I can't remember the last time I wrote a letter on notepaper. In my own handwriting. The photos were nice, but it had been hard for me to imagine the house as a whole.

I found the place easily. There is a wooden door, painted dark brown, against a grey-plastered front wall. Near the door is a window, not very big, with no curtains. A red velvet heart embroidered with small white beads, like pearls, is stuck to the glass with Scotch tape.

A row of narrow English houses, squashed together as if they'd only had the space to build ten houses, but, instead, had been obliged to squeeze in twelve or fourteen. They seemed like toy houses.

She is always romantic. At least for a while now.

I check my watch. It's early. Not even 4 p.m. I sit on one of the steps. I always sit on the second step, sunk in meditation. She had sensed that I was not OK and that's why she had made the effort to invite me to London. We don't have a lot of money and we certainly couldn't afford to throw away almost 200 Euros. I don't know what she had given up – food, or some household item that she would have liked. I don't know what to say, what to tell her. She should know as little as possible. Or nothing. But I don't think I'm a good liar.

She does not need to know the way I will try to solve all my...

Suddenly there is a long high-pitched creak behind me, which gives me a start and "Boo! What are you doing, my love? Why aren't you coming in?"

Two steps above, Sofia is looking at me, all smiles. She's very *office,* navy blue trousers and white blouse. *Office* and sexy! I stand up and she jumps into my arms. I give her a long, long kiss, and embrace her a little too strongly, as I always do.

"Uff, I missed you so much!"

"Are you sure? What were you doing sitting on the steps?"

"Waiting. I thought it's too early."

"You should have rung the bell. Come inside."

She tugs at my clothes pulling me into the small hallway on the ground floor. I kiss her again while pushing the door with my foot. All smiles.

"Let me show you the house. Or are you hungry?"

I am a little confused and I don't know what to reply.

"I'd like to take a shower."

"Good. The bathroom is only one flight up. To the left, as you go up. The master bedroom is on the right. Leave your suitcase and clothes in there."

I have only just arrived in London and she is directing me. I smile.

"What? What's the matter?" she asks. "What's wrong?"

"You're jumpy."

"Yes, I've just managed to escape from the office. The boss kept asking for some reports and I didn't feel like working on them. Usually it's you who are jumpy."

I stick my tongue out at her and climb the narrow, creaking wooden steps. The bedroom is big. Sofia has placed a small pot of climbing ivy on the window ledge, from where it climbs on strings. There are also a few stones polished by sea, and a small red ceramic lighthouse. Her little marine corner. Again I experience that heavy sensation of drunkenness, through which I would like to pass beyond real time, and enjoy all these small details and pleasures endlessly. I drop my travel bag in a corner and start to undress. I hear her coming up after me and entering the bathroom.

"I am turning the water on so it gets warm; it doesn't run hot from the start."

"Thank you, my love."

She kisses me quickly and goes down the stairs.

"I still have an e-mail to send and I'm coming. You have toiletries on the side of the tub."

She has put the plug into the plughole and the hot water starts getting deeper. I splash a little in the water and come out wrapped in a huge towel she had brought from Bucharest. I go inside the bedroom, and I find her sitting in the middle of the bed, sheets pulled up to her chin and smiling cheekily. I know what this means.

"Mmm… My little pussy cat feels like playing?"

I slide near her and scents mix: her DKNY perfume, a cream that smells like chocolate, the freshness of the sheets, the shower gel. She watches me, following my movements only with her eyes; she doesn't even breathe until I touch her and my lips land on the left side of her neck and start descending very, very slowly until my tongue touches the aureole of one breast, coiling round, and caressing it. I can't see her eyes now, but I hear her panting and moaning faintly. My left hand touches the other breast, caressing it with the tips of the fingers, and then tracks along the line of the sternum, passes beyond her navel and stops down below, where pleasure starts. She grabs my hair and pulls it while I caress her relentlessly, and she pants louder and louder and moans rhythmically, and I feel her nails digging deep into the skin on my back, and she screams "I want to feel you, now!"

I throw the sheets off and climb on top of her. Our bodies

merge in an apparently chaotic and noisy dance. We forget to think about the neighbours, about troubles and debts and distances, and everything disappears in a vortex of unleashed senses, as if the world was about to come to an end.

Later, when we are lying spread out diagonally on the huge bed, trying to regain our normal heartbeats, I realise how much I have missed her and how hard life is without her.

"Is madam content?"

"Will you stop asking me this question? I told you it annoys me!"

"I keep forgetting."

"Ehh, you are indulging yourself. Yes, madam is very content. But I still have an appetite."

"Ohoo… Do you think we could take a break?"

"Don't tell me you are hungry."

"But I am."

"I didn't cook anything. What would you like?"

"You don't cook. Do you have any spaghetti?"

"I have everything. I thought you might want to cook."

"Of course."

Wearing a t-shirt from the bag and a pair of shorts, I go down to the kitchen. The flat is small. The ground floor has a living room, an entrance hall, and a kitchen no larger than two metres square. A table, a cooker and a sink. A kitchen cabinet and a fridge.

"I'll be right down," she shouts from upstairs. "I'll just throw some clothes on."

I rummage through the fridge to find the ingredients. A bunch of spring onions, bacon, parmesan. On the kitchen shelf there's a plastic box of fettuccini, long, flat noodles. I put on a middle-sized pot, half-filled with water, to boil. I add a spoonful of olive oil and a little salt. I cover it so that the water boils faster. The huge frying pan is ready on another flame. Again, olive oil. If only I had some wine or vinegar I would add it. I find a half drunk bottle of Romanian white wine, a Riesling, and I pour a dash into the pan. After it gets hot, I throw finely chopped bacon rubbed with a little basil and herbs of Provence (Sofia always has plenty of spices in the cupboards!). I stir continuously until the bacon becomes shiny and a little crisp. The aroma of the wine penetrates it, and I now throw over it the finely chopped spring onions and a little oregano. And I stir again. The water is boiling and I dump the pasta in. I break an egg into a mug, add two spoonfuls of cream and four spoonfuls of tomato juice and stir rapidly. The whole art of cooking is contained in the ability to do everything at once, so I can't know or see whether Sofia is in the kitchen. Because this minuscule space is not uncomfortable, I imagine she is still upstairs. The meat and onion are now done, and I pour the sauce on top, stirring continuously, allowing it to boil a little. The pasta needs to be stirred through as well, so that it won't stick together. I try to use both my hands without causing too much damage in the kitchen: lids fallen to the floor, broken glasses, upturned pots. This is the same as when you make love and use both hands – the effect is devastating. I drain the pasta of water, and I get the hot steam in my eyes. I put it back in the pan and pour two raw eggs on top, adding a dash of pepper with some paprika and curry powder. I stir again and throw in the contents of the frying pan, stirring gently so that the long strands remain intact. The only thing missing now is the parmesan, which I had contrived to grate during the whole process, and put in a bowl. Of course, this resulted in a few small, inevitable accidents, like two or three scratches on the sides of my fingers, which sting a little when they get near the hot pan... Done!

I turn towards the stairs to call her. A round of applause. She is looking at me from the second step, dressed in one of my shirts, pale blue, buttons undone – it looks like a cliché from a film – and she claps her hands.

"I also missed this; not just the lovemaking. I missed seeing you cook."

She stands up, comes to my side, raises herself on her toes and kisses me forcefully, holding my head in her hands. Long, agitated, deep, and perverted, her kiss takes my breath away. I forget my hands are dirty and I embrace her and turn her round, so that she is facing away from the small, fragile table. Subconsciously, I am thinking about the table back home with its sturdy stainless steel legs, and about the first scenes of love between us, right there, in my Bucharest kitchen. I uncover her breasts and take refuge with my face between them, while my hands wander further down. The wooden table creaks and I clutch her tightly, and my last thought before losing myself completely in her is whether I have turned the cooker off.

Later on, we are calm again. We put the pasta on the plates and she brings out a surprise – a bottle of Bordeaux Mouton Cadet 2005 which I uncork with great pleasure. I pour the wine in two huge glasses which look like a pair of breasts sculpted in silicon, and we drink and eat.

Among all the sensations and feelings and dreams mingled with reality, a thought bobs up to the surface: I won't say a word about the job to Sofia! I lack the courage to ruin this little corner of paradise. My only paradise.

Chapter 15

Râșnov[105]-Vienna, August 2010

THE MORNING IS COOL. Pleasant. And the air seems very clean. I like urban mornings. They remind me of mornings having coffee in London or New York or Paris. It doesn't have to be a big town. All it takes is cool weather, fresh morning air, and good, aromatic coffee. Or, at least, coffee which is acceptable and affordable. In New York or London it's not easy to find good coffee. But I have drunk it in Parma or *Brașov*, and even in dusty and unwelcoming Bucharest.

The restaurant in the centre is called, pompously, *Pub Cetate*[106], using the *Romglish* language which has invaded us, together with market economy. At the back, near the stairs leading to the fortress, it has a terrace with large wooden tables and benches. In front, on the pavement, they have only four metal tables with chairs made of the same material, like a café in a big, wealthy metropolis. The chairs are cold and reinforce my feeling that the air is fresh and chilly. I don't mind. At lunchtime the temperature will be around thirty-something Centigrade – again.

"Good morning, what would you like?"

"Espresso lungo and a fresh fruit juice."

"Orange or grapefruit?"

"Grapefruit, it's got a sharper taste."

"Right away."

---

105   *Râșnov* - Old town in southern Transylvania, some 200 km north of Bucharest. The town grew up around a former Teutonic fortress, and had a sizeable Saxon population.
106   Literally, the Citadel Pub.

I didn't even see the waiter's face. I breathe deeply, trying to store up the chilly air for later. There will be crowds of people and it will be very hot. Smells and noises. Sweat and screams. It's Saturday and I came here to attend the Festival of Historical Films. We also have a small book fair attached to it and we are trying to get some cash. Small change. And, for my part, this is the last chance to spend a weekend outside of my usual working routine. I should leave here and go directly to Vienna. Driving car Q, which is parked – still dirty and with no diesel – in front of me, at the end of the pavement. I'm feeling good about being alone.

I received the direct order three days ago. The 10,000 Euros reached my account on August 1. I will receive the next 10,000 next Thursday, after I check in at Vienna. The Anna Pension, a building on Ziglergasse, near the corner with Lindengasse. Less than a kilometre away from Haydn Hotel. These are the instructions I received. The rifle case will be waiting, in a big box delivered to me at the Pension. I'll have my complete programme next Thursday, together with the money.

Brrr… this is sinister. And it's cold. I get the shivers again. A light breeze is blowing, and, on the street, the first noisy tourists begin to appear. The coffee and the juice are waiting on the table, although I didn't hear the waiter bringing them. I take a sip from the coffee and drink half a glass of juice.

Diana had called me as soon as I got back from London to say the old man had rewritten the text, and that in August he would be going to take about ten days rest in Vienna. She proposed meeting to give me the memory stick, and to ask my advice about a good hotel in Vienna. I didn't feel like a meeting with either of them.

Using the pretext that I was very busy, I asked Diana

to send the stick over to my office. I recommended the Haydn Hotel, as my instructions specified, and especially the wonderful room 128 – the one with the panoramic view of the boulevard. She listened to me and seemed convinced. Very easily convinced. And disappointed that we wouldn't be seeing each oher.

"You know, I would have loved to have a coffee with you again. Just that."

"I am sorry. I can't quite manage to tear myself away from work."

"I understand. We'll see each other at the beginning of the autumn, then. Around September. When you start the advertising campaign for the book."

She's pouting and a little offended. Uff… It's not courteous to refuse a woman who wants to have coffee with you. But I don't have the guts to look her in the eye.

"Yes, of course. We'll see each other after the 1st of September," I replied.

"You know, I changed my car…"

"Right," I replied absentmindedly.

"I moved into my father's place. The paperwork was completed quickly. I'm free of all that now."

"I don't know whether I should congratulate you."

"No need. Goodbye, Stelian. Have a wonderful holiday."

"I don't think I'll have a holiday. I don't have the time."

"Good. Then at least enjoy this month as far as you are able, and in the way that suits you. With whoever you like… Bye."

I didn't get the chance to answer – she'd already put the phone down.

The memory stick came by courier. I didn't open the file. I just left the thing on my desk. I didn't want to touch it. Not yet. I could not bring myself to do it. I didn't know whether

I would be able to do it... even afterwards. But the contract was signed, and the next step was to fulfil its conditions.

I take another sip from the coffee and finish the juice. I am not convinced that I will manage to end all this well. End it well? How sinister that sounds.

I go and pay my bill and then drive up to the fortress. The best thing is not to think, to let time pass me by without noticing it, and I'll cross that bridge when the time comes.

There's almost nobody up on top. The four book stands, set up in military tents, are just opening. I try to evaluate the possible damage after last night's rain. It was only a quick shower, but heavy. My colleague Sorin installs the weapons for the *airsoft* shooting gallery[107]. An M14 rifle and a Thomson machine gun from the time of WW2. This is the theme of the Festival.

"Morning, Sorin."

"Good morning, how are you? Would you like to train a little? There's no one here now."

It seems that everyone is going to take care of my training. I load the rifle and assume the standing position. *Airsoft* is a game with plastic calibre 4.5 mm pellets propelled by compressed air. I keep thinking of the Steyr-Manlicher in Vienna. The M14 is not too light either, a well-made replica. I select single shot mode and pull the trigger. The noise is pretty pathetic, and it doesn't sound anything like that made by a real weapon. There is no recoil, and the pellet, as it perforates the paper target at 50 metres, scatters little threads of paper all around. I fire shot after shot and then suddenly I'm in a state of terror, and I drop the weapon, as if I had been poleaxeed.

---

107   Airsoft is a sport akin to paintballing which uses replica firearms to shoot small diameter plastic pellets. Airsoft is used for competitions, military simulations or training, or target shooting.

"Is anything wrong? You're not feeling well?"

"No… Yes, I am a little tired and my eyes are wandering. I'll go get another coffee."

"As you wish. Can I play until the tourists arrive?"

"Yes, of course."

I turn my back on him a little rudely, and drift over to the car which is parked near the Bathory Tower. I should pack my bags and leave for Vienna, it's a long way to go, and I think I'll stop over near *Arad*[108].

I don't know what to do with myself. I would like to call Sofia, but in London it's two hours earlier – and this being Saturday, I suspect she's sleeping. I give up and climb into car Q.

I didn't leave straight away. I spent the evening drinking beer with my friends and postponed my departure to the next day. A lot of beer. I still had time.

In *Arad* I slept at a transit hotel that my friends in *Râşnov* had recommended. The Apollo Hotel, where I had a good dinner and a good sleep. Good and cheap. I woke up dizzy, with a nagging pain somewhere deep inside. I had been asleep, but I suspected that my inner turmoil had kept my brain functioning.

I passed through the frontier with no difficulty. I had shown my passport and then "have a good trip". Somewhere in my luggage I had my Colt, in its box, arms permit attached to it. I had given up the Beretta several months previously, when the "good guys" made me a gift of a wonderful Colt 1911 A1M1. It was a jewel that I had never used, although I always kept it near me.

Vienna is already two steps away after circumnavigating Budapest through the south, on the M0. On the motorway,

108 *Arad* – town in western Romania near the border with Hungary.

I fought with a curtain of rain like a tsunami, from kilometre 38 to kilometre 90. There is still a little way to go and I'll be there. My heart pounds louder and louder. I turn the radio on and I drive at precisely 120 km/h keeping my eyes fixed straight ahead. On the loudspeaker, a CD is playing old tunes. I haven't changed it in a long time and it is too difficult to do it now. I'd like to hear James Blunt playing "Tears and rain", because it brings Sofia to mind, along with thoughts about my past and my future, and especially our future. A future which is rather hazy for the time being.

My eyes close of their own volition, and a long yawn brings back the glutinous aftertaste of the cheese I had in the morning. I concentrate as hard as I can to cover the last few kilometres without incident. I am on a kind of one way street. Cheap pathos. Lucky this is only a thought and I'm not saying it out loud. I would look like an idiot. A fool and a sucker!

I am in my room at the Pension. Room 1 on the top floor. An attic conversion with white walls, and red flowers in the jardinière hanging outside the window. The bed linen is fresh and smells of lavender. An enormous cardboard box lies on the hand-woven carpet in the middle of the room. It has my name on it, and the landlady told me that it arrived precisely two hours before me.

It still seems chilly, even though it is August and the temperature outside is over thirty degrees.

I break the adhesive tape and open the box. The long black case containing the rifle looks exactly as I left it. There is also a travel bag with summer clothing. T-shirts, trousers, sandals, a thin jacket, sunshades. What for, I wonder? A thin envelope, a map, a piece of paper, and a paper bag with a hotel key in it. The key for room 106 of the Haydn

Hotel. I open the envelope. A copy of a bank statement for an account. My account, in which, today, another 10,000 Euros has been deposited. After I unfold the map I see that the important places have been marked: the Haydn Hotel, the Anna Pension, the train station, the Hofburg. The map was there to mock me. I didn't need it. I had been in Vienna many, many times before. The wannabe English irony was probably the mark of Pushkin. On the piece of paper there were only a few lines: "Friday 04.15 a.m. Rifle, map, and travel bag. Leave the rest where it is. Saturn Building, 5th floor. Restaurant door will be unlocked. Windows open and close. Approx. 200 metres. Good luck. Afterwards, go to 106 HH. You are a tourist."

I exhale deeply, rubbing my hands on my temples. It's only Tuesday. They knew I would not arrive on Thursday, but earlier. They followed me. They transferred the second instalment earlier because they knew I was going to get here today. I have the feeling they are constantly following me. The poor General will be killed and I won't know why. I think about the memory stick left on my desk. Someone should make a copy. I don't know how to warn my colleagues, the phone is certainly under surveillance. I have no chance. I am playing along as they direct. God help me! And forgive me for what I am going to do.

I call Sofia. Then I hang up. I can't talk to her, she would realise that all is not well. She would be worried. She would sense something is going on. I will write to her. I will talk to her later on, in the evening. I call Lulu.

"Yes, daddy."

"Hi, Lulu. What are you up to?"

"Homework for tomorrow. English. What are you up to?"

"I am in Vienna."

"Aha. You are always going from here to there and never

staying in Bucharest enough. With me."

"Yes, Lulu, I know. Work keeps me on the road."

"Aha, I want a job like yours with plenty of travelling."

"We'll talk about it when you grow up."

"OK, daddy. Bye, daddy."

"Bye. I kiss you, my little wonder."

"Bye-bye."

Smack. Smack. She kisses me through the receiver. I do the same. Then she hangs up. She would like a job with a lot of travel, like mine… Uff, it was hard enough to explain to her what I was looking for in Somalia; what will I say now? Lies, lies…

I tidy up everything in the room carefully, and I dash out in search of a beer parlour. I want to forget.

Chapter 16

Vienna, August 2010

THE DARKNESS IS DISSIPATING RAPIDLY. Somewhere, hidden behind the sombre buildings, the sun shoots out its first rays. They feel hot. It will be scorching hot today. I take another look through the telescopic sight. I regulate my breathing. Calmly. Quietly. I breathe…

I should shoot. Now.

I am breathing deeply. I grip the butt of the rifle. I inhale again. Deeply. Trying to calm down my disorderly heartbeat. Chaotic. I feel my heartbeat vibrating in the butt of the rifle. My eyes are watering, my fingers are clenched on the trigger guard. I release it.

Now.

I am looking through the telescopic sight. The crosshairs are fixed on the heart of the man.

And the General breathes deeply, rhythmically, quietly.

I move my index finger and curl it carefully around the trigger. I take a quick look at the rifle, just to make sure everything is fine. It is fine, obviously. Everything is perfect. I take aim again and fix the crosshairs on the General's chest, on the left, where his heart is.

Suddenly, all our common memories explode in my mind. They are jumbled and on *fast-forward*. Coffees, red wine, guard duty, cold, fear, Chernobyl, squalor, hopes, dreams, the revolution, the book… His daughter, my daughter…

My pulse rate speeds up again.

I'm struggling to recover my equilibrium. My eyes are

watering and a drop slides down beside the sight and falls onto the metal of the rifle. It will rust. "Take care of your weapon as if it were your woman," they used to say in the army. One guy asked "You mean as if it were my wife?" Everyone laughed. Then they slapped him on the back, and someone said "No. Not your wife. We mean as if it were your lover, you dumb ox!"

Where are you Sofia?

I regulate my breathing. Index finger on the trigger. Crosshairs. Chest.

And, all of a sudden, I see him smiling. It can't be! He's smiling in his sleep. I have never watched a sleeping person so intently. Not even Lulu when she was little. I didn't have the time, and I regret those beautiful moments that I lost. Somebody once said children are beautiful only when they are little. No, they are beautiful all the time, but when they are little their sleeping faces display an enormous happiness. Just as the General sleeps now – like a happy child. He's dreaming of something beautiful.

My finger is rigid round the trigger.

He's dreaming of the book, or of Diana…

Or who knows what other memories. From his youth, from the army.

I inhale deeply. I exhale. I adjust the butt of the rifle against my shoulder. I aim along the line of sight…

The finger pushes…

And I give up!

I can't! I can't shoot.

My body is covered with cold sweat. My eyes are dripping. Drops of sweat and tears mingle and fall onto the weapon and down to the floor.

I give up. I can't kill the General.

I will lose all the money and Misha will be livid.

I reset the trigger guard, put the rifle down and lean back on the wall. My heart is fluttering inside my chest. I wish I had a pill. I can't shoot. I am panting and my eyes are still watering. I look through my pockets for a paper tissue. I wipe my eyes and pat down my temples. I put the tissue back in my pocket. I am not thinking of anything.

I start to dismantle the weapon. Methodically, and very calmly. I take the bullet out of the chamber and put it back in the clip. I unscrew the telescopic sight. Then the chamber. I arrange them all carefully in the oblong case. I look around to check that I have left no traces. I can't see a thing. And I leave. I take the case and the travel bag which contains the clothes.

I go down by the same route. On the stairs, I meet the employees coming to work. I am still wearing gloves, but nobody notices. I was out in time. I reach the street, and, with the case on my shoulder, I cross it diagonally towards the hotel. I always wait for the green light. I am in no hurry. I look around – nobody has any interest in me.

I am in front of the entrance. I take the lift to the mezzanine, pass by the reception desk and go to my room, which is around the corner, room 106. I don't know why they'd had to bring me here. To be closer? I enter the room, throw the bag on the bed, put the case down and turn the water on. Hot water. Steam. The noise of the water falling in the metal tub calms me, soothes me. I am still breathing with difficulty. Panting.

I take off all my clothes and get under the shower.

I wonder how long it will take before they realise I didn't do anything? That I have failed in my mission.

I spend a long time under the shower. I pour water on my head and neck and shoulders and back. I don't know for how long. Half an hour. Or maybe an hour.

When I emerge from the bathroom I listen at the door of the room – all quiet in the hotel. All the noise is outside.

The red light on the BlackBerry flashes.

They've got it.

A text message: "Bravo!"

Number unknown. Bravo for what?

I don't understand. Who is writing to me? What is going on here?

I get dressed rapidly, changing my clothes for those in the bag. I put all my belongings in the travel bag. I take the Colt out of its holster, check it and replace it on the belt. I dress *sport,* putting on the light jacket to conceal the gun. A peaked cap on my head. Sun glasses. A perfect tourist. I leave the bags in the room. I go out and lock the door. All quiet on the hallway. Again the reception desk. The stairs. I am outside.

It's already warm. I walk with a spring in my step towards the centre, in the direction of Hofburg. Nobody says anything to me. Nobody calls me. Nobody follows me.

I'd like a good cup of coffee.

Part Two

The truth is useful to those who hear it, but disadvantageous to those who tell it because it makes them unpopular.

Blaise Pascal

Chapter 17

Vienna, August 2010

I LEAVE THE CATHEDRAL PIAZZA BEHIND and wander the streets. Tourists carrying shopping bags and cameras start to appear. I touch my gun from time to time, and it makes me feel secure. I walk slowly towards the Albertina Museum. Behind the Opera there is a coffee house. The Mozart. Famous, expensive, and good coffee.

It's early; the coffee house has just opened and there are not many people. I used to know a Romanian waitress here. The first time I came to Vienna was about seven years ago. I was with the love of my previous life, and Lulu had stayed at home with her grandmother. We went in to order a coffee. We didn't know the prices. A plump blonde waitress, about forty in my estimate, offered us the menus. While we were arguing whether we should buy what we wanted or just stick to the budget, the waitress returned to our table and, without preamble, asked:

"Didn't you know this place was so expensive?"

I think we almost dropped the menus in surprise. I didn't expect someone to speak to us in Romanian, much less someone who, by her appearance, was every inch a pureblooded Austrian.

"I... I don't understand," I replied.

She probably felt that her approach, phrased in a Romanian accent that I found difficult to place in the *Banat* or in Transylvania, must have been brutal and inappropriate. She continued:

"I wanted to say this place is too expensive. The coffee is good but it's not worth that much money. But since you're here, take a mélange, we make the best in the whole of Vienna."

We both smiled and nodded our consent. I don't remember if was expensive or not, probably so-so. We didn't understand whether the initial brutal approach had been a marketing technique, but we left her 10% because that coffee, and I still have no idea why they call it that, was very good. We said goodbye and left. Since then I came back many times over the years, although I am not sure that she remembered me every time. I was either alone or with other women. I always ordered the mélange and we exchanged smiles. I had always wished that I had an aunt, and that woman had the precise air of an affectionate aunt, a little feisty but motherly, neither young, nor old, well groomed but not excessively so. Sometimes she asked me what was going on in our country. She wasn't interested in a particular town, but in the country, in general. She would tell me about a good apple juice or a dessert. Or she would bring a newspaper or magazine in English. We would never talk more than two minutes. I would leave 10% at the end and exit with *"Sărut mâna"* while she always answered with *"Tschuss!"*.

I search the room with my eyes because this is exactly the moment when I need to talk for a few minutes with somebody familiar. But I don't see her. The menu is on the table. I don't read it. I know exactly what I want. A stiff drink, a schnapps. I look for a waiter and a newspaper. I see nobody and nothing worth my interest. I look through the big windows. Nothing interesting.

"Good day, Mister."

I am startled. She's smiling all over her face – my aunty.

"I didn't see you. I thought you weren't in today."

"I started work a bit late. Little problems at home, with the little ones. What can I bring you? The usual?"

"Yes, the usual. Is everything all right?"

"Yes, I sent them to a summer camp… I haven't seen you in a long time. What's going on in the country?"

"I've been running around most of the time. What do you think? Crisis and hysteria. Nothing too good."

She smiles broadly. I don't know her name and I can't tell how big the little ones might be.

"As long as we're healthy[109]… I'll bring your order right now."

She turns her blonde curls to me and goes to the bar. I gaze vacantly through the windows. People are out on the promenade, looking around.

The door opens and a tall man comes in. Grey suit, white shirt and no tie. He sits at the table next to the entrance. Strange, he threw a quick glance at me. Maybe he didn't realise that I was observing him. Across the road, near a lamppost, I see another two men talking to each other. No suits. Instead, they are dressed in sport jackets. Strange, it's a bit warm for so many clothes.

Aunty approaches, puts the mélange on my table and, as she has never done before, she leans towards me and whispers:

"I don't know who you are or what you have done, but there are three gentlemen from the police in the kitchen who are about to come in. They have weapons."

I look at her shocked and questioning.

"I suggest you get up slowly and go towards the toilets. Instead of going into the *Gents*, turn left in the hallway and

---

109 *Noi să fim sănătoşi*, in Romanian. A very Romanian expression summing up a life philosophy: bad things can go on and happen, but as long as you are healthy it's still fine.

exit through the first door, still on the left, where there is an inner yard. They are not there. We use it as a loading yard. Don't run. Some of them are also in the room. Good luck."

She smiles again and leaves. I don't have the time to say thank you. I get up in a dignified manner and go towards the toilets. In the corner of my eye I observe the man in the grey suit. He's also watching me while pretending to check the menu. I move slowly, relaxed. I reach the toilets in six steps, the hallway, then the door on the left. I am not followed. Now I am outside. The courtyard is filled with big cardboard boxes and rubbish bins. I see an alley going off onto a side street. I walk with rapid steps, but I don't run. My mind starts to work – they've located me. What can I do now? Who should I call? Misha!

While I walk, I take the BlackBerry out and look for his number. I push the button. His phone is off. How did I guess? My mind searches for another solution. Who can I call? Where can I go? Out in the open like this I am vulnerable. I take the direction of the Opera. There's a big taxi rank there, in front of the hotel. I'll just get a taxi to… to where? I have money on my card. I should get out and go to Budapest. I look around circumspectly, while I walk along in a swift and decided manner. No-one yet. I clamber into the first taxi. I change my mind. The Prater seems a better solution. There are plenty of people there, and I can hide more easily until I find a contact who can offer me a solution.

"To the Prater, please. Thank you," I tell the driver in English.

The driver doesn't say anything. He drives off in the direction of the Ring. I think of the little town of Pressbaum. The small pension where a confrontation with the lawyer of the Popescu family had taken place. I never stayed in that place. I know where it is, but things ended up badly there, with the intervention of Special Operations and Misha's fatal gun shot. Where is Misha hiding? Why doesn't he help me? I call him again. The phone is still off. What the mother cunt actually happened? Who sent me the "Bravo" message? Why?

The taxi moves into the middle lane. Then everything happens incredibly fast. A dark blue Opel with a police light on top pulls in front of us and brakes brutally, blinding us with the red brake lights. Two more cars in the white-green colours of the police flank us. They turn on their sirens. Another car approaches from behind. They are all filled with armed men looking at me through the half open windows and down the barrels of their guns. The taxi stops in the middle of the road and the driver puts his hands up.

I was in the back of the taxi. The car doors open rapidly, and the cops, who are wearing helmets with lowered visors, point their Steyr AUG A1 submachine guns at me. A huge display of force. What the mother cunt is going on? I stay where I am. Motionless. My Colt is pushing against my ribs. A smiling face appears in the gap to the right. A blond gentleman with a thin black tie.

"Good day, Stelian Munteanu," says the man in Romanian, but with a very strong accent. He's not Romanian. "I am Inspector Klein of the Austrian Federal Police, Vienna section. Please step out of the car. With your hands on the back of your neck."

"But..."

"Mister Munteanu, you are under arrest. Please step out of the car. No sudden movements. Hands on the back of your neck. We know you are armed and we don't want any nasty incidents."

I slide across the car seat and get out. I put my hands up.

161

A policeman in riot gear, with a bulletproof vest and helmet, searches me thoroughly. On his left shoulder I see a black badge with a yellow border, a red sword and golden wings on a black background: the *Einsatzkommando Cobra*. EKO Cobra, the anti-terror unit of the Federal Police. So I finally got to meet the Cobras! People have always told me to be careful what I wished for, because wishes can come true. They confiscate my gun and handcuff me. Inspector Klein is standing in front of me. I have at least a dozen soldiers and policemen surrounding me.

"Can you tell me what is going on?"

"Yes, Mister Munteanu. You are under arrest for the murder of Romanian citizen Gheorghe Simionescu. This morning, in the Haydn Hotel."

I stand there with my mouth open.

"Didn't you understand me? I apologise, I have mastered the Romanian language only recently."

"No... I mean... how...? Why me?"

"I invite you to talk about this at the station. We have all the evidence. I propose we stop blocking the street. Please step into the car."

And he indicates the dark blue Opel. I climb inside, flanked by two regular uniformed policemen. Klein is on the front seat. The car drives off, siren blaring. Behind us, the taxi moves off slowly, looking for a new customer. A less dangerous one. The traffic is unblocked.

Chapter 18

Vienna, August 2010

THEY DRIVE ME ALONG ALL SORTS OF BOULEVARDS and side streets. I am too angry and scared to remember anything. Everyone was silent during the trip. No words; just the terrifying wailing of the siren. High speed. Aggressive driving. Then, a quick turn through an arcade over an alleyway, ending in the inner courtyard of a sober official building. A building like many others in Vienna: massive, imposing, grey, old.

The car stops and I am invited to get out. An entrance with six steps, a long hallway and a simple room. A table and two wooden chairs. A mirrored wall which, probably, conceals a video camera and anyone else who might be watching me. The walls are painted light grey, and there is a window with opaque glass panels behind which I suspect the presence of iron bars. Very sombre and classic.

I sit on one of the chairs and wait. Someone locks the door.

I don't wait too long.

The man who had introduced himself as Inspector Klein comes in and seats himself on the other chair. He has a file in his right hand.

"Can we start?"

"Of course."

"Stelian Munteanu?"

"Yes."

"Romanian citizen, residing in Bucharest?"

"Yes."

"45 years of age, born in Bucharest."

"Exact."

He looks me in the eye.

"Where were you this morning around 4.30?"

I am silent. In my turn I look him directly in the eye. For a moment, we are duelling with our eyes.

"I repeat: where were you this morning around 4.30?"

I offer no reply. A suspicion starts to take shape somewhere deep in my brain. This is a set-up. Somebody wants me to go down. Misha? Why?

"Mister Inspector, can you please explain to me once again what happened?"

He smiles drily, metallic, and apparently irritated. He is a thin, lean man, and not very tall. Because of his blond hair, blue eyes and pale complexion he seems to be a local, but I would sooner have assumed that he was Spanish or Italian. He opens the file and reads from a sheet of paper.

"Yes. This morning around 4.30 the Romanian citizen Gheorghe Simionescu, aged 63, was killed with a single gunshot, fired by a Steyr-Manlicher SSG 008, from the fifth floor of the Saturn Building, while sleeping in his bed in room 128 of the Haydn Hotel. Is this clear?"

I am left open-mouthed. How did they kill him? Who?

"But it is impossible, Mister Inspector!"

"What is impossible, Mister Munteanu?"

"For Simionescu to have been killed by a bullet from a Steyr-Manlicher at 4.30 this morning!"

"And how would you know that, Mister Munteanu? I repeat the question: where were you this morning around 4.30?"

I don't know what to say. I sense a trap, a set-up. He was killed? How? Why? By whom? There is only one hypothesis I can offer off the top of my head: there was another shooter. They didn't trust me to do the job and hired someone else. Maybe I was only the bait and I fell for it a like a sucker. Misha sold me out. But why had I deserved this? Impossible. Nobody does such a thing. You don't betray your own collaborators… Or… maybe it was an order. But whose? And why? Why did the General have to be killed? What did he know? What did he do in '89 or afterwards?

"Where were you this morning around 4.30?"

The inspector is calm and repeats the same question again and again. He is not in a hurry, and he's not running ahead of himself. He looks calm and confident.

When they put me in the room, they had searched me for a second time. They took my BlackBerry, my watch, a few papers which happened to be in my pockets – receipts, business cards I'd been given, the wallet, the passport, everything.

There is no other solution. I have to go with the true version of events. My truth.

"I was on the fifth floor of the Saturn Building."

He doesn't look surprised by my answer.

"This will be recorded. And what were you doing there at such an early hour?"

I try to formulate a phrase which would sound as neutral as possible.

"I was keeping watch on General Simionescu."

He beams all over his face.

"You see, this was easy. Let's move on. Motive?"

"You did not understand me, Mister Police Inspector. I DID NOT shoot Simionescu!"

"No? How strange. We found several traces of you in room 106 of the Haydn Hotel, and room 1 of the Anna Pension. The rifle, the cartridges, the clothes."

165

"I don't know what you're talking about. They are not mine."

"You are joking, Mister Munteanu. I don't think you intend to mock me, but the rifle is registered in your name. The rooms were booked in your name. Payments were made with a card which is yours. Do I need to add many other details?"

"But I did not shoot him."

"Mister Munteanu, we have all the evidence, including sweat stains left on the fifth floor of the Saturn Building. We can analyse them. We have statements from some workers who were coming in this morning, and saw a man of your description, who, on top of everything else, was wearing gloves. We even have the spent cartridge of the bullet fired by the Steyr-Manlicher."

"Do I look so stupid as to leave a spent cartridge on the floor?"

"Mister Munteanu, it's not my job to judge whether you are stupid or smart."

"Can I ask you something? I'm just curious."

"Go ahead."

"How is it that you learned Romanian? You don't seem to have any connection to Romania."

"I don't. I was born in Linz. But the number of crimes committed by Romanians has increased recently, and we needed people who can speak Romanian. I was sent to learn and I learnt it. Satisfied?"

"Yes, of course."

"Let's continue. What was the motive?"

"We are going in circles. It wasn't me who killed Simionescu. I was there but I didn't do anything."

"So what were you doing there?"

I don't know how to answer this question.

"What were you doing there with a sniper gun at that early hour?"

I am silent.

"I am listening, Mister Munteanu. Did you, or did you not want to kill Simionescu?"

"No. I mean…"

"Mister Munteanu, we can play this game for as long as you want. I will bring evidence and present it to the prosecutors. What happens next will be the business of the justice department. You will have to sign a statement, naturally. You are free to write whatever you want."

"But can't you hear what I'm saying? It was not me who killed Simionescu."

He doesn't get annoyed, even now. He smiles drily and cynically.

"You know, Mister Munteanu, this is like that joke about Shakespeare. *Romeo and Juliet* was not written by William Shakespeare, but by another man with the same name. British humour. Now you are taking me for a fool, Mister Munteanu."

"I don't, but…"

"We have too much evidence."

"It was not me who killed Simionescu. It is my weapon. I did stay in Anna and Haydn. But it wasn't me who fired the shot."

"But what did you do?"

"Nothing."

"You mean to say that, at 4 in the morning you went to the Saturn Building, assembled the rifle, aimed at the Romanian for some ten or fifteen minutes, then you took it apart, went downstairs, went to room 106 at the Haydn, washed, changed, and went out for a walk?"

"Exact."

"Ahaa. And just so you could drink your coffee in peace, you put a Colt 1911 in your pocket."

"No. It was… It made me feel safer."

"Does our town not look safe to you, Mister Munteanu? Is it necessary to walk through Vienna in broad daylight with a loaded gun?"

"That is not what I meant."

"So? Don't you think there are just too many coincidences?"

Again, I am silent. They've caught me in the net. I don't know who and why, and what they want, but they've caught me. I don't know what to do or say. They will also check the phone calls and text messages.

"We are going to contact your Embassy in Vienna, Mister Munteanu, if you believe this to be necessary. I think you should contact a lawyer. If you don't have one, we'll give you one, *ab officio*. I leave you to reflect on your situation. I will probably be back. If you need to make a phonecall, just call out. You will be heard. My colleagues will bring you something to eat and drink. Water. Good day."

And he goes out, leaving me without another word. The room is silent. No sound. Except from the outside: a low hum of voices, doors slamming and footsteps on the stairs. It is a very muffled hum. The door is thick. I don't want to escape. I cannot, and, moreover, I don't have a reason to do so.

I try to rearrange in my memory the events of the last few days, then of the last few weeks. Misha is the key to the problems. But Simionescu? I wonder what's happened to the manuscript? Once again I regret not having read it properly. Especially the second version. With the corrections. Somebody is very scared of what might emerge. And of what he might be revealing. Possibly. Could Misha have set me up? Does his FSB – which he says he left while it was still called the KGB – have something to hide? There were rumours about columns of armoured vehicles with Romanian insignia parked beside the roads near *Focşani* or *Vaslui*, filled with soldiers who spoke broken "Moldovan"[110]... From across the *River Prut*[111]. Soviet soldiers dressed in Romanian uniforms in December '89 – is this what they want to hide?

I wonder how the General would have come to know so much. He was a poor major back then, a major from a sapper unit in *Buzău*. What the *mother of the mother* is hidden here? Maybe there was an incident in *Buzău* which has remained secret. But, *good people,* more than 20 years have gone by: who cares anymore what happened back then? His Diana has no idea whatsoever! She can't even remember the revolution, she was too young. Or my colleagues? What's the point of this set-up?

I hear the lock. I jump to my feet. Is he back? Already?

The door opens and a policeman brings in a tray with schnitzel and mashed potatoes, plastic cutlery and plate, a half-litre plastic bottle of still water, and a telephone with an antenna. He places everything on the table and leaves without a word.

I whisper a "danke" and take a seat. The food is hot. I will be able to think better on a full stomach. Then I'll make some calls. I don't know yet where and to whom...

---

110   The official language of the Republic of Moldova is Romanian (albeit spoken with a distinctive accent and with archaisms and Russian loan words). During the Soviet years and under the ex-Soviet leaders it was called Moldovan. This led to the publication of a Moldovan-Romanian dictionary, in 2003, which, for the greater part, listed synonyms and even the same Romanian words on both sides.
111   i.e. from Soviet Socialist Republic of Moldova. *River Prut* is the natural border between Romania and the Republic of Moldova.

Chapter 19

Vienna, August 2010

I THINK ABOUT TWO HOURS WENT BY. I ate with gusto. The food was hot and tasty. I found myself thinking I would have liked some pickled gherkins. I licked the plate clean. Not literally. The policeman took away the tray. He wanted to take the phone as well. I told him in English that I hadn't used it yet. He mumbled something and left it on the table. I wonder when the battery is going to die. But I really don't know who to call. I am at a dead end and I have no solution.

The sun is very high in the sky. Although the window is small, the light from outside is very strong. I get up and start pacing the room. From one end to the other, back and forth. I am convinced that they are watching me from behind the mirror. For a moment, I feel the urge to pull a face at them, just for the fun of it. But it's not the moment to convince them that I am also a nutcase.

Time seems to weigh heavily. And I can't concentrate.

After a while I hear the lock again. The door opens and a man with the air of a top dog steps in. When I see him, I feel I know him, but I don't know exactly from where or when.

He looks at me, amused. He can probably see on my face the conflict caused by images which are reluctant to come to the surface.

"You've forgotten me, Mister Munteanu? Years have passed."

It is only after I hear his voice, speaking English which is calm, relaxed, measured and fluent, that I realise how I know him. And I smile, because this is a face I am glad to see. He smiles broadly when he realises that I have recognised him.

"Years have passed, Mister Munteanu. I am glad to see you again, even if the circumstances are not the happiest."

"I'm glad as well, Mister Commissar, I guess..." I continue under my breath.

"Yes. Chief Commissar. I am the chief of the judiciary police of Vienna, Mister Munteanu."

Steiner sits on the chair on which Klein had been sitting, his back to the mirror. I sit down myself.

"Do we continue together?"

He shakes his head.

"Not really. It looks as if there some very important issues involved. Matters of state security. General Simionescu is... *was* an important person in Romania. Since the announcement of his... expiry, many wheels have been set in motion."

Steiner has got a bit older. At close quarters, face to face with him at the table, I can see the lines on his forehead, and at the corners of his eyes. His cheeks have started to sag. But his eyes are still lively and clear. He had always seemed to me a very open character. I met him in Pressbaum, during the incident with the Popescu family lawyer. He was wounded there and Misha Pushkin's intervention seems to have saved his life. The Russian's huge 10 mm Glock fires single shots. On each occasion he's right on time, precise and deadly. The lawyer was killed. Steiner wasn't very fond of Pushkin because of that. He reproached Misha for aiming at the heart instead of just wounding the man. The Russian replied that he'd do better to say "thank you" rather than complaining. The debate between them remained unresolved.

171

"What is going to happen now?"

"I don't know for sure. We are going to find out soon. My colleagues are still gathering all the available evidence. It's possible the Romanians will want to repatriate you. I also cast an eye over the file. I didn't understand much."

"It wasn't me who killed the General."

"I don't know what to say. The evidence incriminating you is too clear."

"It's been stitched with white thread!"

"I don't know this expression."

"I apologise, I just translated a Romanian expression. I meant that it's a set-up."

"Possibly, Mister Munteanu. In any case, you were there and you had that weapon. But what you wanted to do with it is not at all clear to me. Not at all."

"Do you remember Mikhail Sergeyevich Pushkin? The man who put down the lawyer, that time in Pressbaum?"

"Yes, the Russian with protection from the very top. I wanted to confiscate his weapon, but the boys in Intelligence told me he was one of ours."

"I think Misha Pushkin is one of everybody's."

"Could be. I never liked the guy much. But what's the connection?"

"Pushkin gave me the rifle. As a present. He sent me to train at Neustadt. You can check this. He told me about the General. He pushed me into all this."

"Why?"

Lucky we can't read each other's minds. I can't tell him the truth. I was one step away from becoming a paid assassin. Or was it just the Russian's attempt to manipulate me? I feel more and more like a sucker.

"I don't know exactly. The General fought in the '89 revolution, then kept getting government posts. There were all sorts of stories about his involvement. Pushkin wanted to provoke something. To kill him and accuse me."

"Why would he do that? You seemed to be in the same boat. Isn't he the one who saved all of you that time in France? That's what I heard."

I am sure Steiner knows exactly what happened then. But he's testing the ground.

"Can you help me with something?"

"I can try."

"Can you find out whether Misha Pushkin is in Austria? I am certain that he is."

"How would his presence here help?"

"Nothing. But I would like to know how closely he was following me. You could trace his telephones. I am convinced he hired a marksman to shoot the General."

Steiner laughs.

"Because you do not want to admit that you were hired to kill the General, and because all the evidence against you is indisputable, you believe that this man, Pushkin, knew that you wouldn't do it, and employed another hitman. Isn't it all a little crazy?"

I don't know what to reply.

"Mister Munteanu, I will look with close attention for traces of another marksman. However, the spent cartridge comes from your weapon. I can't see how anyone else could have fired it with you being there as well. Unless you were working as a team…"

Does he want to trap me? He's played the friendship card and now he tries to get a confession? I don't get his game.

"Nobody fired my rifle until something past 7 in the morning when I left room 106. The weapon was in the case, dismantled and unloaded. There's something dubious here!

Please look for Pushkin. You have my mobile. His number is in the contact list. Please call him. We need to clarify this."

He purses his lips, gnashes his teeth, and massages his jaw with the fingers of his left hand.

"Yes, I will tell them to call. To check."

He rubs his temples; it is clear to me that he is tired. I try to catch a glimpse of his eyes but I can't. I start to suspect Steiner also knows more that he lets on. And from here to suspecting him as an accomplice of Misha's is just a step. A small step for such a big conspiracy. It seems like Sci-Fi![112] What *the mother of the mother* was the General hiding?

"I'll leave you, Mister Munteanu. I have other matters to deal with. I was glad to see you again. I am convinced everything will be sorted out."

"You are convinced? You mean you have information I don't?"

"Mister Munteanu, it is obvious I have more information than you and that I have a more complete picture of the whole story. Don't be afraid, it will be fine."

That's what the General said, too – he was a captain then – when they woke us all up one night for an alert and handed us live ammunition. Yes, and it was fine. Nothing happened. We soon went back to sleep. Is it a coincidence that he used the same expression? Probably yes.

"Can I ask you something else?"

"Of course, Mister Munteanu."

"Chief Commissar, did you know General Gheorghe Simionescu?"

He hesitates for a moment, as if he's thinking deeply.

"I am not sure. I think not, I can't remember well. I did visit your country two years ago, after the NATO Summit.

112   *Pare SF*, in Romanian – an expression denoting incredulity, when something is very strange.

I remember you were involved in a story on that occasion, as well. Something about a possible assassination attempt in the autumn of 2007, while they were preparing the summit. Again with this man, Pushkin."

What does he want to prove? Is he changing the subject, or is he telling me that he knows everything?

"You are well informed."

"Yes, I have to be. I met many superior officers, active or retired, at that time. It is possible that he was there as well. It was a friendly meeting in a superb building in your capital. In the centre. An army building."

He's bullshitting me. He is lying. I think he knew the General. Just as I am convinced he's met Misha again. Maybe they even work together. Who the devil are all these people working for? Do I have to start believing in a worldwide conspiracy?

"Yes, probably the National Military Circle. What about Pushkin?"

"I promise we'll look into it. Good day. We'll probably meet again."

We shake hands firmly. Steiner goes out without looking at me. Why did he come? What did he want from me? The discussion was almost aimless. Or maybe I didn't realise what the aim was.

I am alone again. The policeman comes and takes the phone from me. He mumbles in approximate English something like "Battery off."

It doesn't matter any more. I don't trust anyone. I sit and wait. In the end, somebody will come and explain to me what is going on here.

Chapter 20

Vienna, August 2010

I AM LEFT GAZING AT THE BARE WALLS. Then at the mirror, feeling more and more inclined to pull a face at the people behind it. Then at the opaque window. I think of Lulu – it would have been better if, at least, I had called her. I also think of Sofia – who I would have frightened by calling from detention.

After a while, the policeman came back with some of my things. The phone was missing. Of course, the gun was also missing. And he brought some more food. A salad with vegetables and chicken, a bread roll, and a half-litre bottle of still water.

My watch is on my wrist now – a Festina, the twin of Sofia's, bought together in Malta last June, when we both went on the run for several days, thanks to my bosses at the magazine. It was a short holiday but we totally enjoyed the hot days, the little excursions in boats, a bit of sunbathing and swimming in the Mediterranean, as well as the old buildings of La Valletta. We then returned to our respective jobs, her in London and me in Bucharest. The watches now tell us how time passes, and it passes damned slow.

5 in the afternoon and the policeman returns, the same grumbling sourpuss, bringing back my BlackBerry. He puts it on the table and leaves. I look at the screen carefully. No calls have been made or received, and the battery is full, meaning that somebody has charged it up.

I wonder if they expect me to start making calls

everywhere while they are watching and recording me. I leave it on the table, do nothing and wait for the next meal. Maybe dinner.

At 18.22 I hear the lock again. Isn't it a bit early? The door opens and, from the doorway, Toni looks at me, with an amused and cheerful air.

"I hope you haven't been waiting for me too long, old boy?"

I have to admit this is an unexpected surprise. I have known Toni for some years. I met him during the same summer that I had met Steiner, in the course of the same investigation. He was a sort of sidekick of mine during that period – only a short time – when I was spokesman for the Romanian police.

"Always happy to see a friend. The old gang's coming back together – have you seen Steiner?"

"Yes, I'm coming from him now. I was summoned from Bucharest this morning. It seems as if this fuss about the General's murder is creating waves in all the government palaces[113] back home. The press conferences are going on back to back. At all the palaces. The association of revolutionaries[114] has jumped on the bandwagon as well. The press is already over the top. You can imagine what's going to be on tonight's talk shows."

"I can. It's summer, anyway; they were short of topics."

"Stelică, I came to take you home."

"Just like that, straight and simple?"

"Yes, it seems the affair has been discussed at the highest levels. These are my orders. I execute."

"Anton Demetriade, I don't like the look of this! What the mother are their covering up?"

---

113   The author refers to Palace Cotroceni, seat of the President, Palace Victoria, seat of the Government, and the Palace of the Parliament.
114   The Association of the Fighters in the 1989 Revolution.

"You mean Commissar Demetriade!"

"Congratulations, Commissar. Time flies… And, as I was saying: what the mother of the mother are they covering up?"

"I have no idea what they're covering up, Stelică. We'll disentangle the threads in Bucharest. Or, as usual with us, they'll stay as tangled as they are now. That is if they don't get even more snarled up. Permanently."

"You've started to talk in parables."

"Like on TV."

We laugh and shake hands. Of course he's talking in parables, because the Austrians will certainly be listening. I feel more relaxed about the prospects. In Bucharest I have my own circle of friends, and enemies, too.

They found tickets for Toni and myself in a hurry, on an Austrian Airlines flight leaving late from Vienna. I didn't ask any more questions. They took me out of that room and led me outside. Into the street. No handcuffs, no goodbyes. I was ushered out by the sourfaced policeman. I signed some papers written in German. Toni signed others. Klein and Steiner didn't make an appearance. Total mystery. I said nothing. I didn't act surprised. I didn't show any reaction. A taxi was waiting for us in front of the police station. It went straight to the airport. I wondered who had paid for it. I ask myself the question in my own thoughts, not out loud. That would not have been political common sense.

We are drinking whisky in the airport bar. I paid with the card which had been charged up with money from the… I don't even want to think about it. Neither of us feels much like talking. I actually do want to talk, in fact, but I don't know how to start. I don't know either how sensitive matters are back home.

I keep worrying about the question of who might have told Diana, and about whether Sofia knows anything. As for Lulu, let's not talk about that…

Uffff – I sigh deeply, and Toni Demetriade gives me a long hard look over the brim of the glass from which he was just draining the last drops of liquid. Then he lowers his eyes.

"You are sighing."

"Yes."

"Tired?"

"No, not really."

All that's left is a conversation about the weather.

"You know, Toni, I'd like to ask you…"

He raises his head and looks at me.

"I am listening."

"I wondered if you know about..."

"The handgun? Yes, they handed it over to me. It's in the hold, in its box. You'll get it back in Bucharest."

"No, it wasn't the gun that was puzzling me."

He says nothing but looks at me attentively. I watch his face, which bears the marks of his worries. A few years ago he was a mocking, carefree youngster.

"I don't know what will happen to me."

"The investigation will go on."

"But what about me?"

"You will be free. I don't know what forces are at play here. I was informed that in Bucharest we would receive all the evidence collected by the Austrian police. Including the rifle."

"And the cartridge?"

"Yes. I have a full list."

"And the General?"

"The body?"

179

"Yes. Was he released from the morgue?"

"In a lead coffin that will be sent to Bucharest. In a day or two."

"Have you seen him?"

"No."

"Who made the identification, then?"

"I don't know."

"What about the death certificate? The ballistics report? Other papers?"

"I haven't seen anything. They told me they'll be sent to Bucharest."

"Toni, this just doesn't feel right. I'd like another small one. Would you like one too?"

"I won't refuse."

We toast each other again. There are still one and a half hours to go to wait until boarding begins.

"Toni, I don't believe he was shot. He could not have been shot – I was there, in that building, the Saturn, and I was looking at him. He was not shot at half past four. I saw him breathing, through the telescopic lens. Maybe later…"

"I believe you."

"The hell you do. You don't believe me."

"Stelian, I don't have too many answers either. I was sent to bring you back to Bucharest. In one piece."

"You don't think a sniper is waiting for me in Bucharest?"

"Why? Do you think you're Lee Harvey Oswald? This is not America. Do you have anything to hide?"

"No, that's precisely why. I want to prove it's been a set-up. Who can I trust? Misha stopped answering my calls. Steiner's chatter went round and round, till it made my head spin, a diversion in which he claimed not to be sure that he knew the General. And you – you don't trust me."

"Stelian, I don't know what you lot have done here. What do you think things look like from my end? A gang which includes you and Misha, allies on many occasions. Let's not forget Somalia. It's clear they wanted to eliminate the General. That you two wanted…"

"But, Toni, it was not me! I was a dupe caught up in these events. What does the media say?"

"That this is the hand of the Securitate and the KGB."

"The usual story."

"Believe me, it is the most logical version."

"And about me?"

"Nothing, your name hasn't been mentioned. They talked about the publishing house. Everybody has found out the book will be published. By Trident."

"I said nothing about this. Who blabbed?"

"Diana Simionescu is telling everyone that he was killed because he wanted to publish his book, that he had signed with Trident to launch it this autumn at the Gaudeamus book fair."

"She shouldn't have made such statements. It means we'll be targeted as well. I wonder where the manuscript is."

"Have you talked to your people in Bucharest?"

"No. I'm the only one who knows where it could be. On a memory stick dumped among the papers on my desk."

"It could easily have been found. Anyone could have taken it."

"Yes, but nobody knows the book is on that particular memory stick."

"Nobody?"

"I told no-one. Only Diana and the General knew. I don't understand what the point of this set-up is. Why involve me? What was so incriminating in the manuscript?"

He is silent, watching me with cold, sharp eyes. For a

moment. Then the expression on his face changes and switches back to amiability.

"What if you were the one who put yourself in it?"

It's my turn not to reply. I sigh again and search for a way of communicating with him.

"Toni... You know, I need to trust somebody. Otherwise, everything is useless. I can't take it any more. You and I have experienced moments in which we could count only on each other. I would like... I want you to trust me. And vice versa."

"So I'm listening."

"OK, I will start. I was hired to kill the General. Misha was trying to convince me to change my profession. He gave me the rifle as a present. He paid for my training sessions. I told Steiner the same."

"You were training to become a professional assassin?"

"I don't know. I still can't work out what was going on. What is still going on. I was unsettled. I didn't have enough money. Everything was crashing."

"And Sofia? And your daughter?"

"Both of them were always far away. I was somewhat tempted. No, not somewhat, I was very much tempted. Misha Pushkin followed me for months. He pressured me. He almost had me convinced."

"To kill a man?!"

"I couldn't have done it. I had known the General for many years. It's an old story. Strange that Diana Simionescu approached Trident to publish the book. I don't know if the Russian knew that."

"I am sure he knew everything. I am sure he knew Simionescu as well. Who knows the kind of secrets they shared."

"Toni, I did not kill the man. There was someone else. No

one fired a weapon from the outside, there would have been traces left. The broken window. It would have been heard. The hotel was quiet. No siren, no alarm, no disturbance. This means they killed him in the room. The body was discovered later. I was arrested after a few hours, two or three, I am not sure. And this means they want to direct the investigation onto a false trail. That's why they let me go, so that they can say to the press the killer was delivered to the Romanian police, who could do what they like with him… they want to cover up for somebody. Maybe the threads, as you say, should have been disentangled right here in Vienna."

"Stelică, I had no choice, I obey orders."

"I know that, it's the regular thing to do. And it would be entirely normal if you had misgivings in regard to me."

"It certainly is normal for me to have misgivings. You agreed to cross over to the other side."

"No. I wanted to. I thought I could. I thought that was what I wanted."

"Tell it to your mama, Munteanu. You had a weapon in your hands pointing at the General. Yes or no?"

"Yes."

"So, then? I am a policeman, how would you want me to react?"

"It's not that simple."

"The hell it's not that simple. You were going to shoot the General."

"But I didn't do it."

"Let me tell you something. I had a case in Bucharest, and I had been working on it for two weeks. They called me this morning to fly to Vienna and bring back a prisoner. I only found out it was you when I arrived here. They sent me because they knew that we know each other. I tried to piece together the way things developed, and I discovered that I was called within minutes. Actually, less than ten minutes after your arrest. They wanted to make sure that I would get to Vienna and take you away, today."

"But why? I'm worried about what's waiting for us in Bucharest."

"They assigned the case to me. We are going to work together. Well, that's a manner of speaking – you are the suspect."

"Toni, I am convinced these people are hiding something. I am almost sure there are snipers waiting. They'll try and shoot me. Then you'll have another incomplete investigation."

"That's not how it is…"

"Toni, twenty years have passed since the revolution. I talked to Simionescu some time ago, and I told him to make changes in the text, to spice it up, to make it stronger. He promised he would do it. The manuscript is with me. I think we should both read it. Who knows what we'll find."

He gives a sad, tired smile.

"Listen, Boss," he says ironically, the way he used to, "whatever you say. You have a curse hanging over you… all these manuscripts. You remember when we read the diary of that man in 2007, the manuscript with the curse on it. And, once again, it was Misha pulling the strings."

"The KGB never gives up. Toni, I am very frightened. They will try everything. Bucharest is not Vienna. For us everything is possible. I am frightened. It's a big, beautiful plan. See what you can do. Otherwise I'll be going to join the General. Up there…"

"Or down there, old boy. Or down there!"

Chapter 21

Vienna-Bucharest, August 2010

I ALWAYS WANTED TO CHANGE THE WORLD. Either the world around me, or the whole thing. I don't remember what I wanted to be when I grew up. Something silly, like all children: rubbish collector, aviator, fireman, tram driver. In any case, something that was part of my surroundings. When I was slightly older and starting to play with letters, reading and sometimes even writing – longer, more epic compositions – I wanted to be an explorer like Jacques Yves Cousteau. There was this scientific series on television – Captain Cousteau and his research vessel (whose name I can't remember) – in black and white, with travels and adventures and much moralising. I can't remember the details. Only the thin, long and lined face of the captain, and his pleasant French language, like a teacher's. During my sixth year in school I was operated on for appendicitis and I stayed for some five days in the CFR 2 Hospital[115], which even nowadays stands across the road from the former Sofitel Hotel. I got bored sitting in bed, although everyone spoiled me: it was a hospital for grown-ups and I was the only child on my floor. Everybody talked to me and brought me treats. So, I started writing a novel, in a school notebook with red plastic covers. How is it I remember the colour of the covers?

The novel was called *Alone on the Seas*. It was about

115   CFR Hospital – CFR stands for *Căile Ferate Române*, the Romanian Railways. Some hospitals in Romania were supported by state institutions, like the Army or, in this case, the Romanian Railways.

explorers, and, because I was patriotic, they were Romanian. My parents encouraged me to continue writing. It wasn't enough. I gave up somewhere along the road. I don't know exactly where. Perhaps it was around the time I started doing target shooting, or taking photographs. In any case, I had tried to save our planet.

I always believed that people were virtuous, and this was an attitude which led to my being taken for a sucker. With the passing of years and the accumulation of unpleasant, unhappy or unlucky experiences, I came to the conclusion that not everyone was good. I also understood that most people were thick-skinned and uninterested in anything. They could also be completely bad. In spite of knowing all this, I was still a sucker. Easy to influence and incapable of saying no. I think I stayed an idealist on the inside, although my outward behaviour displays, with the utmost naturalness, a cynical and blasé attitude. Some people still laugh in my face – in a friendly manner, I am told – declaring that I am still a child. I should be glad of this, but I am not.

I always believed that everything I do is in good faith. Many people have tried to convince me of the opposite. Some have almost succeeded. Nowadays I believe I don't know exactly what universal values are, and whether they are still embedded in our consciousness, hidden in one shape or another. That is, if universal values still exist. And if anyone still needs them.

We boarded the plane in silence, after our discussion had got nowhere, without me having the first idea whether Toni believed me or not, whether he trusted me, and, especially, what he was going to do once we got to Bucharest. The flight from Vienna is short enough to allow you to remain silent for the whole trip without the appearance of sulking. It is also too short to allow for a long and healthy nap.

I kept on thinking during the flight. No conclusion. The impossibility of concentrating gave me the sensation that my brain had turned into a muddy and putrid mush. A nauseating sensation, and throughout the flight I was cold and afraid. Afraid of what I might find in Bucharest.

There was nobody waiting for us. Except for an official car with a driver. A white Dacia Logan carrying a policeman whose rank I couldn't work out because he was in plainclothes. They dropped me at home and went on their way. I had a sensation of déjà vu: a few years ago Toni had picked me up from the airport in an old wreck of a Dacia. I was coming from Rome, on the trail of a murder that had taken place in Greece... I didn't ask Toni if anyone was watching the flat for my protection. I didn't ask anything. Just "good night", a handshake, and "see you tomorrow", without fixing a time. Then I found myself in my own shower and, afterwards, in my own bed. I was exhausted, but, somehow, I fell asleep.

It's early in the morning. The air in the room is stuffy and it's very hot. The window is closed. My throat is dry and I am drenched in sweat. There is a lot of light, although it's only just past 6. I throw the balcony window wide open, and take another look at the bustle on the street. The fact that I am home gives me a feeling of safety. Then I remember the snipers and Lee Harvey Oswald, so I take a look at the surrounding roofs. I imagine myself in the crosshairs of a sniper and, in spite of myself, I look at my chest, where the heart should be. For the time being, I am not marked by laser dots and nobody shoots me. It is August and the city is on holiday. Fewer cars. The snipers are probably on holiday, too. I turn the tap on in the bathtub for an early bath, to cool down. I see, en passant, the red light of the BlackBerry. Who could it be? It's been more than 24 hours since I talked to Sofia… while Pushkin didn't reply at all, although I called him dozens of times.

"Call me when you wake up – Toni," and after the signature, his mobile number.

It's not even 7 o'clock. I call him. He picks up on the second ring.

"Yes, Stelian."

"Morning. You weren't sleeping?"

"I've been waking up at 6 o'clock for years. Especially during the summer. I am doing my exercises."

"Right. I'm calling you – as you wrote and asked."

"Yes, we need to meet. So… how long does it take you to get ready?"

"Half an hour."

"OK, I'll be there to pick you up."

"I'll be waiting for you upstairs with some good coffee."

"Perfect. I'll bring all I have."

He hangs up. I have to hurry. It's too early in London. I'll call her about lunchtime. Lulu has school… My eyes are fixed on the travel bag in the hallway but I don't have the time to unpack now. I take a look all around me: armchairs, sofa, desk, books. Everything seems to be in order. The bath, intended to cool and calm, is postponed. A short hot and cold shower, then a look in the fridge, where I find a few lost slices of ham and a lump of cheese. I have good coffee that Sofia gave me, from Venezuela, with a name I can't pronounce. And a French coffee press – that she'd also given me.

When Toni rings on the intercom, I have everything ready. I buzz him in. By the time he rings on the door of my flat, I have already poured coffee into two fat cups. He comes holding a white plastic bag, not by the handles, but by the object inside.

"Look – I brought your weapon."

"Do I need to sign anywhere?"

"*Sictir!*"

He sits on the stool at the end of the table and picks up one of the cups. He smells it and then tastes it.

"Good."

"Sugar, milk?"

"No, nothing."

He's dressed very informally in pre-stressed jeans and a Metallica T-shirt. From his shoulder bag he takes out a not very thick file with covers of translucent plastic.

"Everything is in here."

"Meaning?"

"Everything I could collect in connection with the General, and the investigation in Vienna. All the documents which have come by e-mail and by fax. I didn't sleep last night – well, only about three hours. I read them twice."

"And?"

"I will leave them with you for a day. But, in two words, things look like this: we don't know anything detailed about the General. His CV has been made public several times. Missions from the Ministry of Defence – nothing special. NATO training. Bursary in America, in San Diego. Studies in international relations. No PhD – which is rather strange[116]. He ascended to the post of undersecretary of state. Foreign travel, delegation member negotiating Romania joining NATO, military attaché in London, and that's..."

"Attaché in London? When?"

"Er... look: '97-'98. Why?

"I wonder where Misha was at the time."

"Do you think they know each other?"

"I am convinced of it. But we won't find a biography of

116   A comment on the recent fashion, among the higher strata of Romanian society, of having a doctoral degree.

Mikhail Sergeyevich Pushkin anywhere. This man doesn't exist. You know that. We've looked him up before."

"To hell with it!"

"Try looking him up on the internet and you'll find all kinds of petty actors or painters. There is nothing about him. In fact, I've never seen any of his documents, so I don't even know what name he goes under."

"Well. Let's return to our business. On the surface, Simionescu had no reason to publish any big secrets in his memoirs. So…"

"But you don't know what he did in '89."

"This is irrelevant."

"Bullshit, Toni! Everything is relevant. Every Romanian intelligence agency was fighting with the others during those months. The maps were being re-drawn. They must have had infiltrations, agents uncovered or reactivated. That was the case with Popescu."

"All right, all right. Wait till you see what he's been doing lately. There are several matters which are not in his CV. For example, the room in the Haydn Hotel was not booked for the period following his murder."

"How was the booking paid for? With a card?"

"No – in cash at the reception desk. He paid himself. He stayed only three days. What kind of a holiday is that? You said he was there on holiday."

"That's what Diana told me. Diana made the booking."

"Yes, Stelică, but in the reservation she didn't mention the number of nights. The minimum stay was three nights, payment at the reception desk on arrival, with the possibility of extension."

"And what does this mean?"

"I think he was due to have an appointment the day he got killed."

"And?"

"Using your reasoning of yesterday – no broken window, no noise – and if I trust your statement that the General was alive when you left, around 5 o'clock, I can only reach two conclusions. One: the person you saw sleeping was not the General, because he had already been murdered in the room and the body hidden…"

"Wait, wait a little! So if I had fired, would I have killed anyone?"

Toni grins from ear to ear, and he slurps from the cup of coffee which had already gone cold.

"Well, I suppose they were certain you were not going to shoot. What do you say about this? They needed a false trail."

"Toni, that's exactly what I told you yesterday. And conclusion number two?"

"Number two is simpler. The General was shot after half past 5, and the medical examiner made an error – conscious or not – in estimating the time of death."

"It can't be an error. He couldn't overestimate by an hour."

"Then, it was no error – he lied deliberately. Or was made to lie."

"But that means the Vienna police is mixed up in this."

"The police or some persons in the police department. Like the medical examiner."

"When did they discover the body?"

"The documents don't give a precise time. After 8 o'clock."

"There is something I don't get. How come they found me? Unless somebody had sent them they couldn't have got to room 106. It is quite far from the General's. They had a tip-off. Why did they tell me to leave everything the way it was? Plus the spent cartridge from my weapon. It's strange."

"What did you do while in room 106?"

"I changed clothes and took a shower."

"For how long?"

"Shit, I don't know. 15 minutes or more. I was in a state of shock and I couldn't regain my equilibrium."

He suddenly puffs his breath out, drinks the last drops of coffee and holds the cup up to me.

"Do you have more?"

"You're drinking too much. No, but I can pour you some of mine," and I pour him half of mine. Untouched.

"15 minutes? An assassin wouldn't need more than 5 to go in and out with the weapon in the case, assemble it in another room, get into the General's room, kill him and then do all of this in reverse. I exaggerate – not 5, but 7 minutes would have been enough. The rooms are not more than 40 metres apart. If he had the key…"

"What about the risk of getting caught by me?"

"I don't think they were risking too much. There must have been two of them. If they were convinced you were not going to shoot, they expected you to be pretty shattered."

I slap my forehead.

"You know – now I get it! They did not know I was not going to shoot. They just had a plan B. They also had me followed. Maybe there was a video camera in room 106. When they saw that I wasn't doing anything and that I was out for the count, they liquidated him themselves. That was it. They had to blame it on me, somehow."

"It seems logical. But who was it that kept silent when you were arrested and when you were so furtively released? And why? Stelian, we are back to the involvement of the Viennese police. There's some sort of conspiracy going on here."

"Toni, leave me the file. I'll try to read it over in peace. I propose we go to Trident now, I'd like to read the manuscript.

I'm very curious about what we might find."

"We'll both read it. Let's go."

"Listen, Toni – is the press saying anything about me, about the book?"

"No. Diana appears on various TV channels, tearstained, accusing the system and the unsolved mysteries of the revolution, but it looks to me she's taking advantage of this misfortune to advertise herself."

"Frankly, I don't have the strength to see her."

"She doesn't suspect a thing. Nobody suspects anything. You're mentioned only as the editor. Nobody knows you had the weapon or that you were in Vienna."

"You know, my car is still there, at the Anna Pension."

"Not any more. It's on a trailer, covered with a tarpaulin. The Austrians sent it over. Tomorrow it will be parked in front of your building. The Manlicher will also arrive here."

"Oh, my God. What organisation! But, since nobody is mentioning me in connection with the murder, why was I set up?"

"I don't know yet. We'll see. However, I think you will have to meet up with Diana. It would be unusual if you didn't."

"True. After all I'm Simionescu's editor."

I give Toni the other half of the coffee in my mug. He drinks it in one go. I take the Colt out of the white bag, check the ammunition clip and insert it in the gun. I cock the hammer and put on the safety catch. I attach the holster to my belt and pull on a thin khaki jacket.

"You'll die of heat. Are you still afraid of snipers, Mister Oswald?"

"I don't know. You said we'll see – I wouldn't want to see it blowing a hole in my own skin."

He laughs carelessly, taking his bag from the peg. Given

how heavy it appears, I imagine that's where he hides his gun. I don't really feel like laughing. There is something I can't put my finger on in this maze, and I don't know what it is.

Chapter 22

Buzău, May 1986

I HAVE ONLY ONCE BEEN THE SUBJECT of a deliberate and targeted observation. Not by a sniper, and not while I was in action. Not now, but then. In another world, a previous life.

I was about a month and a half short of my release from the army, and I had already started to count the AMR. We were engaged in shooting exercises. At night. The training grounds belonged to the paratroopers, and their officers were monitoring us from an observation tower. Our unit was supposed to obtain a FB[117] qualification, as part of one contest or the other. This might have been "Socialist Competition" or "Praise to Romania" or "First Class Military"[118], some shit like that... Our men had to get the *foarte bine* qualification because, if we didn't, we would have lost the number 1 slot in the competition and, with it, the bonuses and promotions and congratulations from the Number 1 HQ. This meant next to nothing to us. Maybe some permits for time off, but, apart from that, it was just a lot of fuss and headaches.

Even though they had actually stationed me at HQ to paint titles with ink and nibs, they had previously read my file and knew about the target shooting. The Quarter Master

---

117 *Foarte bine* – very good.
118 Having "comradely" competitions was part of the official state propaganda in all communist countries. In Romania, there was of course an accent on Romanian prowess. *Cântarea României (*Praise to Romania) was a national competition comprising of all sort of activities. It encompassed factories, the army, the schools, cultural houses etc. In the 1980s, it had become almost exclusively a Praise to Ceaușescu, with songs, dance, plays, and music, all praising the country's leadership and their "grandiose achievements".

in charge of the unit's weapons was a skinny, withered old man, a warrant officer who was just a small step away from his pension. He used to take me with him to the firing range when he was checking the weapons, fine tuning them. I'm not referring here to my fellow soldiers' weapons, Romanian-made sub-machine guns patterned after the famous AK 47, the ones that were dropped in puddles and mud while training… No – I am talking about the weapons in the arsenal, the weapons for real fighting, God forbid we should ever need them. I am also referring to the handguns of the officers, the TT 33s. They were heavy and robust, invented by the Soviet designer Tokarev, and looked exactly like the more famous American-made M1911. Perhaps the design had been stolen some time during the interwar period, or perhaps not, and it was just a similar idea. It had been invented by John Browning, produced both by Colt and Browning, and then spread around the world in millions of copies. I was fascinated by that huge, manly gun. I fired it with passion from 25 and 50 metres, positioning myself the way they did in the movies – arms held straight out, left index finger curled round the trigger and the right hand supporting the butt of the weapon.

That night however I was not carrying a pistol. I had, instead, my special target weapon: a calibrated, shiny sub-machine gun, with a 30-bullet clip, which was probably forbidden. An officer had been allocated to supervise me. He had a big, heavy, old radio unit, maybe you know the kind of unit: the militiamen used to carry them back in those days.

The officer was supposed to whisper to me the detail about which firing line I should use in order to compensate for the shots that my colleagues missed, when their bullets went astray, towards the sky or the ground.

I felt like some kind of Superman. I wasn't nervous. I had done this many times before.

On the other hand, it was night, and I was shooting at a chest-high target in front of which there was a flicker of light, simulating the flash of an enemy's rifle, firing at us. These flickers came, obviously, from electric light bulbs, but, before we could start, the electricity cut out and all the lights went off everywhere in the training ground.

They had two possible courses of action: to postpone the shooting exercises, or to wait for the electricity to come back. They chose a third. Strange and very unsafe. Candles. Using flashlights would have been another possible solution, but there were no batteries.

The weather wasn't bad. It had been sunny all day. No wind. In theory, the candles should not have gone out. In theory. Because, in practice, from time to time, a gentle puff of cool breeze blew out half the candles.

My colleagues had eight cartridges per clip. Every second cartridge held a tracer bullet which allowed them to correct their aim. Candles or no candles, they would have missed a lot of shots, but, as things were, we were definitely heading for disaster.

I sat and waited. For orders.

Simionescu came and sat close behind me, and whispered in my ear.

"You know what you have to do, don't you?"

"Yes, *să trăiți!*"

"Position yourself on the central range and wait for my order. I'll tell you the precise target in the series, to the left or to the right, then the number of shots. Is that clear?"

"I understood, *să trăiți!*"

I lay down in the firing trench, armed the weapon and lowered the trigger into single-shot mode. Simionescu was wearing the radio unit on his chest. He placed himself on one knee.

"Won't the people in the tower see us, comrade Captain?"

"No, there is too much confusion. Some of ours are there as well."

"I understood."

"Pay attention. Now: second from the left, two slugs."

I fired twice, the second one was a tracer.

"Fourth from the right, two."

I pulled the trigger twice. A tracer.

"Third from the right, three slugs."

Three shots. The second and the third were tracers.

Now I was getting worried that the supervisors in the tower would all too easily spot the fact that there was a marksman compensating for the unit's errors.

"Comrade captain, I have too many tracers, they'll see them from the tower."

"Get on with your job."

They did see us, though, after about a quarter of an hour. The tracers showed them the strange directions in which I was firing. A quarrel probably broke out up there in the tower, because I heard on Simionescu's radio the very loud voice of one of the bosses:

"Get out of there immediately! Immediately!"

The captain gave me a quick look and spat out:

"Put the safety catch on, jump to your feet and follow me, on the double – now!"

I was scared. I couldn't imagine what might happen if we were caught. So I obeyed the order – as usual in the army – precisely and on time, running through the rows of soldiers who were waiting for their turn, through vehicles and equipment, to a whitish car in which we hid ourselves.

It was a Dacia model 1300, the captain's car.

Half an hour later, we were told that everything had been covered up. My fright vanished immediately, especially since Simionescu had a small bottle with a "Carmol" liniment label, which was filled with *țuică*. In two slurps, one each, we emptied it. And I think I started to nod off.

With a push and a pull, our unit took a *foarte bine*.

Chapter 23

Bucharest, August 2010

HE PARKS IN FRONT OF THE OFFICE. He's driving a white Dacia Logan, probably the same car as last night. I pet my German shepherd dog through the railings and then go inside the building. I exchange quick greetings with my colleagues and climb up to my own office, with Demetriade following me. I take a quick look at the table, and my supposition becomes certainty.

There is no memory stick there.

"What happened?" the commissar asks, seeing the look on my face.

"The manuscript's no longer here! What a mother cunt life! I had a premonition. I should have called..."

Involuntarily, I throw myself on my swivel chair, and I bang my fist on the table. Once again I have been taken for a sucker. In a useless gesture, I call Misha again. He doesn't answer. Obviously. Toni sits on the sofa. I try, breathing deeply, to calm myself down.

"And?" he says.

"Let's have a coffee. I am trying to concentrate." I stand up and go out into the hallway.

"Aunty Gica, could you please bring two coffees?"

Marius comes out of the kitchen, chewing. We shake hands.

"Welcome. She is not here today, she's taken a day off. We've brewed coffee, I can bring you some."

"Do you know anything about a memory stick on my desk?"

"No. What stick? The one brought by that lady, some ten days or two weeks ago?"

"*Exact.*"

"I don't know anything about it. It was there where she left it. Nobody disturbed your desk. Maybe Aunty Gica, if she went in to dust, but she doesn't go through things. Are you sure you didn't take it?"

"I didn't have the opportunity. I haven't been here."

"I swear to God I don't know. I'll go pour the coffee. I'll ask the others as well. Is it something nasty?"

"It was the General's manuscript."

"I know. Haven't you got it on e-mail?"

"I didn't want the document on the net. It is safer."

"Sorry…"

Toni watches from the sofa. Then he stands up suddenly.

"Apologies. Didn't anyone else pass through here in the meantime?" he asks Marius.

"Anyone – yes, various people passed through. What do you mean, exactly?"

"Were there any other people using this particular office?"

"Yes. There were three translators, a bookstore manager… and that lady. She came again, wanting to talk to you, by hook or by crook, and you were not answering your mobile."

"What lady?"

"The General's daughter, Diana Simionescu. She was here with a TV crew, they wanted to film you and your office. I helped them."

"Aha. Was that all?"

"Yes, I think so…" He thinks hard. "There was this other fellow. He stayed only three or four minutes. I invited him into your office so he could get off his feet. He wanted to buy books, a lot of books."

"What fellow?"

"You know him – that nice old boy with the air of an Englishman, although he's a Russian. The pensioner spy."

Both Toni and I give a start and exclaim:

"Misha?!"

"He was here?!"

"It's clear now."

Marius looks at us as if we were from Mars. He leaves to get the coffee without commenting any further. It is certain that, in his eyes, we appear to be either mad or idiots.

"It's clear, Toni! Misha is orchestrating it all, as usual. He dropped in under the pretext that he was looking for me. He didn't find me. He was the one who had sent me round the world, so he knew I wasn't here. Instead he said he wanted to buy books, and while in my office he had all the time in the world to take the memory stick. And that's the end of it."

Fine, but the manuscript is also on the General's computer. In *Telega* or Bucharest."

"I hope it's still there. What now?"

"We should check the General's correspondence. We'll need his daughter's permission. I already asked for Simionescu's bank accounts and properties to be monitored."

I suddenly remember my own account. I stay silent. Demetriade must know of the two recent payments: and if he knows and he keeps silent, it means that I have no call to open my trap.

"This means that…"

My phone rings. I look at the screen.

"It's Diana, his daughter."

"Perfect."

"What shall I do?"

"Talk, arrange a meeting – fast."

"Yes, but… in what capacity do I speak to her?"

Commissar Anton Demetriade gives me a cheeky smile and winks.

"As a partner in the investigation. It wouldn't be the first time."

"OK, but the authority? After all, I am the suspect."

"Stelică, nobody knows who you are. We've worked together before. And you're the editor – answer!"

"OK."

I push the button.

"Hello?"

"Hello? Stelian? Can you hear me?"

Her voice is hoarse and frightened, the rhythm is slower than usual. I can feel exhaustion running through it. I don't know how to start.

"Yes, I hear you. I found out about… I am so sorry, I don't know what to say. My sympathies… Believe me, I am as shocked as…"

"Forget about it. Where the hell have you been? I needed you! The funeral takes place tomorrow. Do you know, they've brought him in a lead coffin. And I have nobody to help me. All he had was me."

"Diana, wait a moment."

"I didn't know what to do. With all the documents. Locating him a place of rest, and everything else…"

I hear her bursting into tears. Toni looks at me patiently from the sofa. I cover the receiver and ask him:

"What should I do?"

The commissar smiles sardonically.

"You go and you console her. You should also talk to her about getting the authorisation. We should move fast. If it concerns Misha, I think it might already be too late."

"OK. Diana? Diana... can you hear me?"

She is breathing heavily and I hear her crying. She stops for a moment.

"Yes, I hear you."

"Where are you? I am coming over right away."

"I am at home. No. 17, *Aviator Petre Mircea Street*, near the Romanian-American University. Do you know it?"

"I'll manage. Do you need anything?"

"No. I don't know. I need someone to help me, to advise me, to keep me from losing my mind! Do you understand? I am... I lost my... I don't have a compass to guide me anymore. My father was so fond of you. Help me. Please."

"I'm coming. Soon."

I hang up.

"My God. What was that all about?"

Toni shrugs his shoulders and purses his lips. He sighs. Me too. Marius had put the coffee on the tables, but neither of us had touched the cups. I swallow a big mouthful. Toni drinks his in one go, scalds his mouth and chews out a curse through his teeth.

"Come on, let's go, I'll drive and drop you off there. I know the street."

I am descending the stairs to the courtyard. My BlackBerry vibrates – a text message. From Sofia.

"Are you well? What's going on? I heard the news. Call me when possible. What's going on with you? Love you, S."

I feel nauseous, as if I'm trapped in a whirlpool. Events - fast, illogical, incoherent. I cannot concentrate and, somewhere in the middle of my brain, a silent pain springs up. I wish I had taken my anti-depressant hawthorn-berry pills this morning. But I forgot. And that's not very good; this day will be bad.

Aviator Petre Mircea Street is a tranquil area. I knew it myself because close to one end, near *Expoziției Boulevard*, is the headquarters of *Flacăra*, a magazine where I was a contributor when I had time.

Number 17 is a small bungalow, the walls covered in pebble-dash, painted beige-orange with brown window frames, an uninspired combination. You can see the house hasn't been painted or repaired in a long time. The wrought iron fence is a little rusty, but the roses in the little garden in front of the house are in bloom. Their strong, brilliant pink calms the stress I have been imposing on myself because of the forthcoming meeting. At the door, there's a long-stemmed candle holder. There is also a black scarf[119] draped over the threshold. The yellow candles are burning slowly, almost spent, and, as cynical as this might sound, I have the feeling that a bunch of professional mourners will suddenly emerge, weeping, out of the door. But nobody appears. I get out of the Logan. Toni shakes my hand and wishes me best of luck. He drives off, leaving me in front of the gate. It's hard to take my courage in both hands and make the final step. A neighbour's dog growls at me and then starts barking aggressively. I pay no attention to it. The door opens and Diana looks at me from inside.

"I came."

She takes one step outside, leans on the door frame, and looks at me. I am not a fan of dark colours on women, least of all the colour black, especially when it's a question of mourning. However, Diana looks very impressive. A knee-length dress on her curvaceous shape, simple high-heeled shoes, slightly ruffled hair, dark, smudged make-up... It's hard for me to work out whether or not she is acting a part. Isn't this the plum role of the abandoned daughter? I

119 The candles and black scarf tied at the door are a traditional sign of mourning.

can almost see the headlines in the tabloids: *"The General's Daughter at the Funeral: Sexier than Ever"* or *"She Should Wear Black More Often: It Becomes Her"*.

I wonder why there's no TV crew around. I am being cynical: and unfair. How would I have looked her in the eye if it was I who had pulled the trigger? I prefer not to think about it any longer. I go through the gate and reach her in four steps. At close quarters, her face is marked by the traces of tears and sleeplessness.

"*Sărut mâna*. I came…"

"Come in."

She moves over so I can squeeze past.

The house is filled with candles and flowers, wreaths and bouquets, letters of sympathy and photos of the General. In the living room, on the table, there is a larger image in black and white, from his younger days. He's dressed in the uniform of a second lieutenant. It is framed in black velvet and it's guarded by two candlesticks with tall, white candles burning in them.

"What am I to do now, Stelian?"

"I wish I could answer."

"Do you want anything? Water, juice, wine? Something to eat? I have some in the kitchen."

"What can I do to help? Are you alone?"

"I am. He had few relatives. They are at the chapel, in the cemetery. I couldn't bear it any longer."

She sits down in an armchair, crosses her legs, and begins crying quietly, tiny tears trickling down onto her cheeks.

"You know, I was always afraid of this."

"Afraid of what?"

"Afraid they would kill him."

"But we don't anything for certain yet."

"How can you say that? They shot him!"

"Do you have the strength to discuss other problems?"

"Other problems? Now? I am burying him tomorrow. Do you want to stay with me for a while? Until later on in the evening. Until the others return. I am afraid to stay here alone. It feels as if there are ghosts in the house."

"Of course, I will stay with you. I wanted to ask you about his e-mail address. The police would like to check on…"

She slams her small fist on the coffee table; an empty glass teeters and, in the silence of the house, falls and is pulverised on the slate tiles, in thousands of small fragments, making a noise like a bomb.

"I don't feel like talking to the police now!"

"We want to find out what happened as soon as possible."

"We want? Are you working with the police? You? You are the editor!"

"Diana, there is another problem."

"Another? That's why you're here, to torture me?"

She looks a little theatrical – maybe this is the nature of the situation – but I feel her reactions are a little exaggerated, as if she's all the time in front of the TV cameras.

"Diana, I apologise, but we do have to talk a little. The manuscript was stolen."

"What?! How was this possible?"

"From my office, from my desk. The memory stick."

"How was this possible?"

"Have you ever heard your father talk about a man called Pushkin? A Russian, Mikhail Sergeyevich Pushkin."

She thinks for a moment then answers:

"No, never."

"I have worked with this man on several occasions. I have reason to believe he knew your father. For a long time. This man used to work for the KGB."

"Are you insinuating my father was a Securitate man?"

"No, in no way. But I think he had some special missions. On special occasions."

"I don't understand."

"Well. I have reason to believe this man is behind your father's assassination. And it was also he who stole the memory stick from Trident's offices."

"That's terrible. What can I do?"

"I would like for you agree to allow the police to check all your computers, to check your father's office – to find clues which could lead to some conclusions."

"I don't understand your connection with the police."

"The commissar leading the investigation is a friend of mine. We have known each other for a long time."

"Everybody knows everybody in this country."

"Diana, where else are the files with the manuscript to be found?"

"In *Telega*. That's where he worked on the book. On the computer up there."

"Have you managed to read the last version of the manuscript?"

"No, papa sent me the actual memory stick."

"I think some serious stuff came up in it for which the General got… I mean, he wrote about dangerous things."

"But it's your fault. You made him do it, you bastard. You told him the manuscript was too boring. It's your fault! He's dead because of you."

And the storm of sobbing chokes her. I look for a glass of water; I think this is what you do in these situations. Oh, my God, what a situation to get mixed up in!

The telephone vibrates – a text message from Sofia.

"I see you forgot me. Hope at least you're fine. Love you to desperation, S."

I sigh deeply. I am embraced by despair.

Chapter 24

Bucharest, August 2010

THE RELATIVES ARRIVED TOWARDS EVENING. Two old aunts and their chatterbox husbands, spouting venom against everyone in the world, politicians, mayors, peasants, urban dwellers, newspapermen, NATO, the EU. There was also a youngish cousin, thin and frail-looking, a student of political science. Then there was a massive man, with drooping shoulders and completely bald. This one wasn't a relative, but the last driver the General had before his retirement. I asked him for his mobile number. Without commenting, he wrote it on the back of my business card. I left with Diana's promise that, from the next day, after everyone had left for the cemetery, Demetriade's boys could install themselves and check everything. I didn't mention anything about the house at *Telega*, but I asked Toni to send a patrol to watch it day and night. It was probably already too late...

I got home around midnight because I stopped to eat a pizza in the district. I also had a beer, two... trying to put my thoughts in order. My own fatigue was growing and I couldn't concentrate at all. The sensation of being on an eternal merry-go-round had overwhelmed me. Every attempt I made to escape had been useless. My destiny seemed inexorable, as if playing itself out in a casino against the destinies of others. Today it might be your turn, tomorrow it might be mine. The croupier with the scythe in his hand will decide... I was delirious, and trying to restore my equilibrium.

I finally spoke to Sofia on the telephone. She'd sensed

that I was not all right, but she hadn't insisted. Instead she encouraged me by saying that everything would be fine. She said that her day had been rather quiet, with only two meetings which had not even been boring.

I throw myself in one of the armchairs. Uncharacteristically, I am not sleepy.

I have a bottle of whisky somewhere. I know though that the alcohol won't do me any good. I pour a finger into the round glass and add three ice-cubes. I turn the television on and stare into space. Only idiocies. Endless talk-shows, and two of them are discussing the General's death. I get annoyed and switch off. I look around for an unread book – on the table, on the shelves, on my desk. The old desk, bought by my parents when I was in my fourth year of school, when they felt I could not learn forever on the table of the living room through which everyone passed: too much homework, too many books, too many notebooks, too many writing implements – I had to have a space of my own. Back in those days it had been a magnificent piece of furniture, big, brown, lacquered, a huge item for an 11-year-old like me, built of solid wood, not of laminated boards like the desks of today. I had kept it and moved it every time I moved house, either with my family or on my own. And my eyes fix on a small object sitting in the middle of it: a memory stick.

Could this be it? But how? Am I starting to believe in magic? It could be the lost stick. But how did it... with whom? Somebody had broken into my house. I try to remember if it had also been there last evening when I got home. I can't say. Last evening I was dead tired.

I take the laptop from its bag with spasmodic movements. I turn it on and the unmistakeable Windows sound comes on like a loud creak in the silence of the night. It is already late and the noises from outside had quieted down. I insert the stick and open it. A single Word file, with the name *My Revolution*. I find myself giving a long whistle.

I start reading.

"Instead of a foreword.

I started to write this long text because I have had many moments in my life when I did things which I regretted afterwards. My regrets were in vain, obviously.

I learnt eventually that regrets are useless and that all you can change refers to the future. And then I tried, as best I could, and in all good faith, to act for the future, but the ideas that seemed logical and beneficial to me have been interpreted by those around me as being outmoded or dictatorial. Although I always wanted to do good, people perceived me as an exponent of the old regime, interested in fortune and positions in the apparatus, a cynical man lacking any scruples, a kind of little Ceaușescu.

After a while, I started to tire of fighting a system that has left so deep a mark in the psychology of my fellow citizens, and I decided to withdraw, away from the internecine struggles, to the mountainside, to Telega. But I had been accustomed all my life to being on the front line, and it was hard for me to get used to gardening and to the lack of challenge.

My daughter Diana listened many times, in the long evenings, in the solitude of our small family, to part of my stories. One day, she asked me why I wasn't setting them down on paper. I tried to explain to her that they were now of no interest to anyone. She insisted. She didn't manage to convince me. Another day, she talked to me about Stelian Munteanu from the Trident publishing house, who she'd just had as a guest on a TV show. I suspected that it was the same Stelian Munteanu who I had met while he was going through the reduced term of his military training in Buzău, during the 1980s. I did some research and found out that he was the one. Diana convinced me to offer him these pages for publication. Munteanu accepted. Diana and Stelian are the two persons who I must thank first of all.

I then have to spare a thought for those who are no longer with us: my parents, my wife Adela, gone all too soon from this world, and also to many comrades who have been beside me in numerous difficult, delicate situations. They too have left for a world we hope will be better than this one.

Thank you all."

This is where I stop. My eyes are hurting and automatically I rub them with my fingers. They start to burn. My old allergy to dust and dirt. When exasperated by the itchiness and the reddened, ulcerated look of my eyes I went to a doctor, who ran all kinds of tests. He asked my profession, because I should try to avoid working with paper. For a moment I thought he was joking and I gave him a puzzled look. Then I started smiling.

I replied "I'm a book editor, so..." – and I started to laugh as if it were a good joke. He didn't react at all, probably because he had no sense of humour or just didn't care.

He gave me a prescription for an ointment and said, shrugging his shoulders "It is up to you how you preserve your health and, most of all, your eyesight, Mister Munteanu. I offered a medical solution. It's your choice to apply it or not."

My good humour vanished, and I left. The ointment was good for a while, then I finished it and forgot to buy another pot from the pharmacy. I started wearing sunglasses and washing my hands as often as I could.

I go to the bathroom to splash my face. I probably shed some tears, too. I look at myself in the mirror above the sink. My eyes are half open and very red on the rims of my eyelids but also further in, where the small capillaries invaded the whites of the eyes. They still itch.

The whisky tumbler is empty. I am looking for red wine and the corkscrew. Very carefully, I open a bottle of Shiraz Jidvei from 2007. This is all I have in the house. I pour myself a long stemmed glass full, and then pick up my BlackBerry. I search for Demetriade's number and send him a short text, although, in the corner of my eye, I notice that it's gone 1 a.m.

"Found the manuscript. Am reading it. SM."

The phone starts ringing in less than five minutes, showing that the network is not very busy and the commissar was not sleeping. I answer immediately.

"Yes, Toni!"

"How the hell did you find it? Was it lost in your pockets?"

"I have no explanation. I'll search for one in the morning. The stick was on my desk at home."

"Since when?"

"I didn't see it when I came back from the airport."

"Magic? Or an intruder? Anything missing?"

"Toni, people who break in generally take something, rather than brining it."

"This is not a normal situation. What are you up to now?"

"I wrote to you – I am reading."

"So am I. I am reviewing all the elements in the file. I also started to receive information from colleagues in the army. I hope to receive something from the *happy boys*[120] soon."

"Can't you make a quick dash here? Like the good old days."

---

120 Euphemism for the intelligence agencies. At the time of writing, Romania had five secret services: external intelligence, internal intelligence, police secret intelligence, special communications, and official protection.

"Why not, it's a good idea. I'll grab my stuff and come. Do you have any food?"

"I'll look around and make something."

"OK. Coming in forty minutes."

"We'll have some wine[121]. Red."

"Are you in a strange mood? Or what the hell is going on, Stelian? This was not your type of joke."

"I don't know. I am tired. I've had enough. Or I drank too much."

"OK, you take it easy. I'll be there soon."

He hangs up. I take another wineglass from the wall cupboard and put in on the table. Then I search the fridge-freezer for snacks. Two tins of fish, some wilted salad, four rather old tomatoes. Not enough. The almost empty freezer displays the ice-cube trays and, at the bottom of it all, a pack wrapped in plastic. I'm in luck: several pairs of chicken frankfurters. They have probably been there for a long time, saved up for when I returned from one of my endless trips. I throw them in a little pan to boil and pour a bit of wine – not more than a finger, in the bottom of the glass. I really don't feel like drinking too much. We have work to do. I look for a coffee pot and start brewing coffee.

Toni joins me in less than thirty minutes, and he brings a loaf of sliced bread, a bar of chocolate - 75% cocoa content – and a shoulder bag bursting with his laptop and the files.

We start eating in peace, frankfurters with a little mustard I also discovered in the fridge, hiding behind two jars of black cherry confiture which nobody had yet dug into. We gobble up two pairs of frankfurters each, give up on the fish and tomatoes, and drink our health with a glass of wine, our eyes on the very hot coffee.

"So have you found something?" I ask Toni in the end,

121 *Vin* in Romanian means both 'I come' and 'wine', so this constitutes a pun – Tony says 'vin' to drink some 'vin'.

my mouth full of dark chocolate.

"Nothing, absolutely nothing. His file is clean," Toni says, sipping from his coffee. "I am convinced it's been cleansed. No financial manoeuvres, no nothing. That story about General Milea cannot be proved. It's true Simionescu was in Bucharest on 21 December 1989, but he was on official business at the Ministry. He needed an approval for the extension of the army vehicle pool in *Mărăcineni*. Absolutely innocent."

"And he stayed in Bucharest?"

"Yes, until the 25th. He then returned to *Buzău*, but got permanently transferred from January, and then moved to the Ministry."

"There is something strange here."

"Could be, but there is no evidence. There are papers, there are documents... We have no way of finding out anything else."

"What about the secret services?"

"They had no business with him."

"Bullshit. I don't believe that."

"Stelian, believe what you want. Out of intelligent reflection or stupidity, many files, reports, and dossiers have been destroyed or lost."

"And you haven't managed to find his name anywhere? Anywhere which has a nasty aura?"

"Nasty aura? No. Normal business."

"Anything from *Buzău*?"

"The former Army HQ lost many records when they moved. There was no order left. They told me to take a look myself if I felt like it. Obviously I felt like it, but didn't have the people."

"And the City Hall?"

"Nothing special. He comes up at some point in an

adoption file."

"Adoption?"

"Yes, in 1989, in May, Simionescu received approval for the adoption of Diana Simona Popescu."

"Diana was adopted? I'm surprised, she doesn't look adopted."

"She was young, born in 1985, so less than four years old."

"And the wife?"

"I don't know, I haven't considered looking. At the time of the adoption they are both there, Adela and Gheorghe Simionescu. It seems it was complicated. It took more than two years. The first request was filed in 1987."

"For Diana?"

"Yes, it looks like they knew her. Maybe they had visited the orphanage."

"What about the girl's parents?"

"Nothing on them. With the exception of the names. The file is incomplete."

"Or somebody is hiding something again."

"Stelică, you suffer from conspiracy theory syndrome."

"Toni, you forget where we are. We have an assassination without a killer or a clear motive. Of course I suffer from conspiracy theories, mother cunt. It pisses me off!"

"Calm down, amigo! Cheers!"

And he raises his glass of red wine. In the poor yellow light of the living room lamp, the liquid has the colour of old blood…

Chapter 25

Buzău, June 1986

I AM CALLED TO THE DUTY OFFICER'S DESK. He is a major with an agreeable demeanour. Well, a major who wants to appear agreeable, at least with me. He doesn't know whose man I am and doesn't want to take any risks. Furthermore, there are only two weeks left until our escape. He had adopted a crow. Well, a raven. Jet black and a thief.

The major is from Engineers' Corps, our section. A dark haired man with a little paunch. I can't remember his name but he had baptised the raven with the name Relu. The bird sits all day long on the window sill, cawing from time to time. He flies off rarely, and when he does, it is only to steal something from the kitchens or from the alleys. Not necessarily food. Anything he finds: a cigarette, a fork, a bonnet, without discernment or logic. Of course, he is just a bird.

It is immediately after lunch, close to 2 p.m. and I wonder what the hell he wants from me. I knock on the door.

"Come in, Munteanu."

"*Să trăiţi*. You called me."

"I have a request. Our doctor procured some medicine for Simionescu, injections. He has a bit of a cold and somebody should take them to him in town."

"Understood, but…"

"You are his emergency runner, here's your service sheet. The commander knows. All is approved."

"Understood."

"It's this *pungă*[122] you have to take to him." While he holds the *pungă* out to me – the famous 1 Leu plastic bag – the raven is flapping his wings and threatening us with his angry cawing. I think I am startled, since I hadn't noticed him on the corner of the desk, among the papers.

"Shut it, Relu! Sit nicely."

If I were a religious person, I would have made the sign of the cross. But I am not religious enough, and it is not a good thing to use this kind of gesture in public. Therefore, I content myself with swearing at the bird in my mind, and I go out after saluting with one hand to my bonnet.

We were a society whose individuals were alienated and looking for salvation in all kinds of sedative bolt holes. Generalised dementia, a country whose people were scared and sad, without vision or optimism… Bullshit.

It is a long way to the town, two or three kilometres. It's sunny and hot, almost scorching hot, and I wonder how Simionescu caught a cold, a cold so bad that he needed injections in this weather. At the gate, they look at my papers and let me go out. The guard commander is a young and bored sub-officer, and the on-duty guards were my colleagues. I exit the metal gate which got a new coat of green paint every spring to hide the traces of rust from the previous winter. I start out with short steps towards the metal bridge that seems to separate the civilised, urbane world from the poor and dusty air of Mărăcineni village. I walk slowly, dragging the huge, black and one-size-bigger boots after me. They had been excellent during the winter, I had put three pairs of socks on my feet, but they are now chafing me and my feet are sweating. The burst blisters sting

---

122 The ubiquitous white plastic bag by which you could tell whether someone had managed to buy goods of any kind after standing on a queue. The *pungă* therefore, which cost 1 Leu, was more or less symbolic of the deprivation and drab uniformity of the society

and I try to step with great attention.

One week before, they had taken us out on a march. A two-day exercise, 60 kilometres on foot with overnight camping under the open sky. I didn't do too well. During the first day I had carried the whole lot – weapon, knapsack, equipment – with enough dignity and heroism, but at night I was knackered and a little dizzy. While lying on my back in the grass, covered by a tent sheet, I had asked my colleagues in a loud and angry voice to turn off the light bulb shining in my eyes. My mates in the platoon laughed their heads off for almost an hour, and they weren't even sure I wasn't making jokes because the light bulb was in fact a big, beautiful, yellow moon. I'd had baked beans cooked in the huge pot of a mobile kitchen. It had been delicious, although there was no bacon in it. We had also drunk quite a lot of homemade wine from our cans which had been filled by merciful peasants from the roadside, scared by the thought of some new world war. Things were even more shitty on the second day. I had climbed into a military truck – a Czechoslovak Tatra with four wheel drive – trying to unload some boxes of marmalade for the 10 o'clock break, and other boxes with ammunition for the manoeuvres.

Getting off the truck, I miscalculated the distance to the ground, and landed brutally, twisting my left ankle. That ankle had already been wrecked two years previously in *Titan Park* in *Balta Albă* neighbourhood when I had lunged to catch a tennis ball which hit the corner of the ground on the line, raising white chalk dust. I had saved the ball and won the game and set. I had lost the match because of my injury – my ankle didn't allow me to stand up. I had curled myself up in pain on the clay, hitting it with my Soviet-made metal racquet. My opponent carried me with great difficulty to a clinic where we found a doctor. I should have had an x-ray. The ankle didn't look broken, but that would have been safer. I didn't have an x-ray and the injury healed itself gradually, although it stayed swollen.

So, landing on the ground from the truck, I heard a dull crack, and I was sure that I'd broken my ankle. There was no doctor around. An airheaded paramedic with no experience bandaged my foot and told me to tie the boot as tight as possible, so as to not feel the pain. I tried to protest but nobody cared. I would have liked to complain to Simionescu, but he wasn't with us. I continued to carry the equipment, marching for some twenty kilometres until the evening, when we reached the compound. We were all dead tired and that was the only time in my life that I fell asleep while walking. I wasn't aware of it, but when the platoon commander called a left turn to pass through the gates of the unit, those of us who were still awake turned, while the rest of us went straight ahead. A huge pile-up ensued and I think we were lucky not to have poked each other's eyes out with the barrels of the guns. I called my parents in Bucharest as soon as I was able, and they sent me packs of Burow's solution[123]. With my connections in the kitchens, I also got ice for compresses. Then I returned to the HQ, to my calligraphy, and my left ankle got a little better. The unit doctor told me he didn't believe it was broken, but that I should drop in from time to time until my discharge, then go and see a doctor at home, because it wasn't a game, and it would be a shame to take risks with my health. Exactly what my parents kept telling me.

Now I am treading even more slowly. I cross the bridge and then there are only a few blocks in front of me until the

---

123   Burow's solution is a pharmacological preparation made of aluminium acetate dissolved in water. It has astringent and antibacterial properties. It is used on skin conditions and also on swellings and bruises. It is normally applied in cold compresses over the affected area.

captain's place. He lives in a four-storey building of the kind that looks like a cardboard box, built with no spirit of artistry from prefab panels, cheap and ugly – a new achievement of our grandiose economy of the Golden Era, on the highway to the construction of a multilaterally developed socialist society, to the advancement towards communism[124]. Bla, bla… I can't remember the rest of it.

I have the address, I know it well – I had been there before. During the night alerts. I climb to the first floor, flat no. 6, signposted by a plastic number glued to the door, below which there is a small plate inscribed in italics "*Simionescu Family*". I give a long buzz on the doorbell.

The door is opened by his wife – I had seen her only once before – a petite woman, a little bent in the back from work, but nicely dressed, even elegant. I don't know too much about her, besides the fact she is an educator in a kindergarten. She has a smile on her lips and she asks me inside.

"Come in, my husband is lying down in the bedroom. He ran a fever last night but he's well now."

"There are the medicines."

"Come in, let me give you something to eat. And a glass of wine. I have a homemade red – with the strength of the bear[125], as they say. It's so red, it sticks to the glass."

"No… I ate in the unit. I don't want to disturb you."

"You're not disturbing us, come. And he likes to chat. You know that. I also have salted cheese pie. It is hot, come on."

I like my food, so I can't refuse. And I know Simionescu

---

124 Stock propaganda phrase from the times of the communist regime. Note that communism as a goal had not been reached yet – society was building communism out of worker-led socialism.

125 Usually this is a risqué expression implying the beverage would confer strength to the penis. But it is unlikely that the captain's wife would have used it in this way to a stranger. "Put hair on your chest" might be the best rendering of the phrase.

likes to chat, especially at home. The flat is small. Two rooms, I think. But it is pleasant. The captain is wrapped in an old cherry-coloured robe which looked as if it had been stolen from a hospital. He shakes my hand and invites me to sit down at the table in the living room. He sits down too.

"I am glad to see you. Adela will bring you something to eat. And some wine."

"Thank you. I brought your medicine. How did you catch a cold?"

"I don't know. I was on duty, I sweated… I don't know. It's so stupid to catch a cold in this weather."

The living room had old furnishing, a table and six chairs, a chest of drawers, and a sofa on the wider side of the room. On top of a shelving unit, in a corner, was enthroned a black and white Diamant television set, draped in a lacy, cream-coloured, crocheted cover. I am surprised not to see the eternal glass fish decorating the top[126], but I don't comment. The walls are plastered in beige pebble dash and the room is very dark. Maybe because the laundry is hanging out to dry on the balcony, stopping the light from getting inside.

It is cool and pleasant, and Adela Simionescu puts a plate with four generous portions of cheese pie on the table. I can't stop myself wondering how they got the cheese. Probably from the countryside, from some of her relatives. She also brings a green mineral water bottle filled with wine, and two big glasses, and she returns to the kitchen. Simionescu pulled out the cork – recycled from another bottle he had bought at the store – and fills the glasses to the top.

"*Noroc*, Munteanu."

"*Noroc,* comrade captain."

126   Stelian describes a more or less old-style Romanian living room with all the trappings. Diamant (Diamond) was a popular black and white TV set relying on tubes, some more easily replaceable than others. Everything about Simionescu's home and his behaviour in it is meant to echo a classic and unsophisticated village and peasant culture.

"Leave the damn comrade out. At least at home I want to forget."

He stops in the middle of his phrase, and we toast, clinking the glasses very loudly. I put the glass to my lips and sip prudently. The wine is strong and dry, a little acid; and although it was red, it had been chilled. The captain put the glass down, untouched.

"Aren't you drinking?"

"I'm on antibiotics, I am not allowed to drink."

"I am sorry."

"It's fine. You drink. Eat."

"I am not very hungry."

"Eat," he says, almost ordering me. "It's fresh sheep cheese. From the countryside. The eggs are from the countryside too. It's a pity not to eat. Adela baked them, she's just taken them out of the oven. They called from the regiment to say you were on your way."

"Did you bake them for me?"

"Adela did. Yes…"

And he stops again, suddenly, with his head bowed. He is frowning. He then sighs, looking through me with empty, feverish eyes.

"Is anything wrong? Are you feeling unwell?"

"No, I was thinking. You know, we wanted to have children. But… well, Adela cannot… she has some problems. They told us there would be some treatments but it's expensive and you can't really find them here." And he stresses the word "here."

"In *Buzău*?"

"No. In this country."

I have nothing to say. So I keep quiet.

"We really wanted to have a child, Munteanu. We don't have too many relatives in town either. She has a sister and a brother in the countryside. They have two children each. *Noroc.*"

We toast again. I drink, he puts the glass back on the table. I had already emptied half a bottle and I am enveloped by a strange, euphoric warmth. I start to feel in the mood for conversation myself.

"Did you try to adopt?"

"We wanted to adopt one of her nephews, but they said it's out of the question, their children are not for sale. Although they live in harsh conditions. It's an isolated mountain village, they still don't have electricity up there."

"I didn't know there were any villages with no electricity in Romania."

"There are, but they go unreported."

"Why don't they connect them?"

He smiles a little irritated, as if the answer was obvious.

"It's simple, Munteanu. Since they were not reported in the beginning, it means that the whole country is electrified. Now they can't declare that this is not how it is, so they can't add it to the master-plan. It's too late. They got tangled in their own lies."

"Will they stay like this?"

"To the devil with the lot of them! Until these bastards disappear, they'll stay like they are."

"But…"

And I stop myself because the discussion had become too political. He looks me straight in the eye. And he smiles, a bitter smile this time, and he sighs. Each time, the lines on his forehead get deeper, and he seems very dour and severe.

"You are afraid, aren't you? You are afraid to talk."

"No, it's not fear. Let's call it prudence."

"Do you think I'm an informer?" asks the captain, irritated, and nervously stroking the top of his head, where the remaining hairs were sticking up.

"No, but you never know who's listening."

"I'll stick all the listeners up their mothers' cunts," he shouts.

The door opens and Adela comes in.

"Gigi, don't get angry. You are feverish. Take care, the neighbours will hear you. Here, I brought you a tea. I talked with our neighbour, the nurse, to arrange for her to give you the injections later in the evening. You didn't eat. Ufff, I'll bring something else."

"I am sorry, Munteanu. I should not have lost my temper. Sometimes I can't stand it anymore. I would have loved for us to have boy. Or at least a little girl…"

"Have you tried the orphanages?"

"We wrote to the City Hall, and got a mystifying reply. They will take it into consideration. Believe me, I have the feeling that I am living for nothing. This place is the arsehole of the world, and nobody cares about us. Look what's going on in the USSR… Whereas here…[127]"

I want to hide somewhere because I am starting to be scared out of my wits. I say nothing. I cannot trust Simionescu. I cannot trust anyone. I take another mouthful of wine. I don't know what to say. My thoughts are the same as his. That was why I want to do civil engineering and then escape. It was lucky the Securitate guys could not read minds. Otherwise they'd have to arrest the whole country.

I stayed at the captain's for a long time. My memories are not very clear. I drank a lot, the whole bottle, I think. I left late, towards the evening. It was still light outside when I reached the bridge and I felt the earth spinning. I had not noticed it until then. I was walking very slowly, in order to keep myself from falling over or vomiting. The guards at

127   A reference to the new policies of Perestroika and Glasnost brought by Gorbachev.

the gate felt I was tipsy and saluted me like accomplices, winking at me. They believed that I had also done some banging. As far as I was concerned, they could believe anything they liked. I hadn't managed to make many female acquaintances in town, so whatever they supposed was a salve to my male honour. I made it to the dorm after lights out. Not everybody was sleeping; some were still listening to music on battery powered transistor radios. Two colleagues were spreading out their socks to dry, while another guy was using a flashlight to read a copy of *The Sport* newspaper, probably stolen from HQ. I went to bed and as soon as I lay flat the earth started spinning like a propeller. I raised up to a sitting position. It stopped. I lay back again, and the spinning restarted. I was not drunk, but the red wine had been too strong.

"You hit the bottle, cousin, didn't you?" I heard the growling voice of Paul, my colleague in the top bunk.

"Not too much, but it was strong."

"Is it spinning?"

"Yes, it is. And I can't sleep."

"You need to puke. Go to the loo and stick a finger down your throat. Otherwise you won't escape."

"You sure?"

"Don't tell me you haven't done this before."

"I haven't."

"All the nicer for you. But it's not something to boast about. Go and sort yourself out, otherwise you won't sleep at all and you'll puke in your bed."

I listened to his advice. Then I poured water – there was only cold water, as usual – on my head and on my face. The earth somehow stopped spinning for a while and I fell asleep dreaming about everything ending faster and my return home, to Bucharest.

Chapter 26

Bucharest-Buzău, August 2010

THE MYSTERY OF THE MEMORY STICK was disarmingly simple: Mrs Gica, the caretaker, had swapped them. She took the one in the office and, thinking there was something important on it – which there was! – brought it to my home, so that it wouldn't get lost, and left it on my desk. So what did Misha find? What of Diana's visit? Around the room with green furniture where I worked at Trident there were certainly other memory sticks, pretty similar to this white one branded with the initials of some important pharmaceutical company. I suspect that, in my absence, everyone had taken from my office whatever they found, just to make sure that nothing was lost, exactly like a Caragiale[128] farce adapted for the digitalised 21st century. Misha probably stole the manuscript of a yet unpublished novel, an unedited translation, or God-knows what advertising materials. Or perhaps he didn't steal a thing and my suspicions are gratuitous. The General's manuscript didn't seem to contain any compromising material, so all the agitation had been pointless. It had only been a smokescreen thrown over the investigation in order to send us all in the wrong direction. Misha was still not to be found – I tried to call him early

---

128   Ion Luca Caragiale (1852–1912) is considered the greatest Romanian playwright. A prolific short story writer and journalist, he was also a theatre manager and political commentator. His comedies (among which *A Lost Letter* is referred to in the passage above) present clear insights into Romanian fin de siècle society, and are widely seen as visionary: many of the attitudes exposed in them can still be observed in the contemporary social and political landscape.

in the morning at least ten times. As for Diana, the difficult day of the burial was about to begin.

I was shocked by the news that she had been adopted, but thinking about the Simionescu family, Adela and Gheorghe, it was obvious that Diana didn't look like either of them. However, a simple resemblance could not be regarded as evidence.

I called somebody I knew in *Buzău*. He had trained as a mechanical engineer, and had become a library director, who, in the '90s, was working as a journalist. I bumped into him now and then, making enquiries and writing reports during those years – the first decade after the revolution. Before the last elections, he made a quick swerve and went into politics. He didn't get very far – he was only a member of the municipal council – but through a stroke of luck and political algorithm he was elected deputy mayor. I found his old mobile number. We hadn't talked for about five years, while he was still at the library, before the grand crisis killed culture and books in Romania. He answered my call.

"What can I help you with, old man? I can't imagine you are calling after all this time just to say hello."

"You are right. I am calling because I need something."

"What's the problem? You know I can't help with the library, the County has cut all the funds."

"It's not about books. I am sending you an e-mail right now. I would like to know more about an adoption from the old days. May '89."

"Is it something serious? Personal?"

"Not really, just a small investigation."

"Gossip column?"

"You know me. Do you imagine I'd be dealing with such things? No. It's about General Simionescu's daughter, Diana…"

"Right, the assassination in Vienna. What's with the girl?"

"I found out she was adopted. I wanted to know more about her birth parents. Simionescu wanted to have a child back in the '80s. He applied for an adoption. And they did not approve it. Then, in '89, it gets approved. I'd like to know what happened."

"OK, old man. I'll look into it. When do you need it?"

"Tomorrow morning? I can drive up to you. We can have a coffee."

"Fine, old man, I'll try. See you tomorrow."

"See you tomorrow."

I have to take part in the funeral, although funerals make me physically sick. This time it's even worse. Plenty of military people, important politicians, TV crews, cameramen and newswomen with microphones in their hands, women with tear-stained faces, men with grave expressions, the curious, the opportunists, children… Above all, Diana, with a black veil on top of the dress I saw her wearing the previous day, like a fairy in mourning, talking to everyone, switching between condolences and declarations for the TV stations, and mingling tears with the outdoor make-up.

An ugly sensation of nausea overwhelms me because it is only at the point when I see the General's sealed coffin that I realise I'll never see him again, and, even worse, that we have not managed during all these years to have a quiet discussion, which might have cleared some things up. Maybe I didn't understand his wish for us to become closer in a normal and sincere friendship. Maybe I didn't want this. Somewhere in my subconscious he always remained an *APVist*.

I can't explain to myself why I rejected or distrusted him. Maybe I was rejecting the military type of those years, when a semi-literate *tablagiu* could wipe the floor with us, almost literally; when another one could make us run an extra fifteen times around the administration building because we had been half a minute late in getting into line, or because the bedding wasn't tight enough for a 25 Bani[129] coin to bounce off it. Idiocies! Not all of them were like this. Simionescu was never one of those who punished us gratuitously. But he always seemed to be the exception that confirmed the rule. Later on I met many outstanding people in uniform, but I never wanted to be in the ranks, among them. I never was, and I am still not, a man of order and orders, and, when I look at the American films featuring ferocious marines or SEALs, I always tell myself that things are like this only in the movies. It's a pity that I only saw a uniform in Simionescu, not a man. It's a little late now. God forgive him.

I greet people by glancing at them. My acquaintances have already heard that the book will be published by Trident. I refuse to give statements and interviews and remain in the background, withdrawn in a narrow alleyway, and it's only just before the exact moment when the church service was due to begin that I see Toni Demetriade in a corner, staring at me. Gradually, I move towards him.

"Did you hear the news?"

"What news?"

"It's on the agency wires and especially on the blogs. Diana has prepared a big talk show for tomorrow night, on Star TV. Loads of guests, including you."

"Me? I haven't been told."

"She forgot. Or it's premeditated."

"It wouldn't be the first time she has invited me at the last minute."

---

129 25 Bani, meaning a quarter of 1 Leu.

"Stelică, bear in mind that the theme of the show is 'The truth about the assassination of General Simionescu'. The intention is certain to be about raising the curtain on new revelations."

"So?"

"I'm afraid Diana Simionescu sniffed out something in connection with you and what happened in Vienna. I think she will attack you live on air."

"No, I don't believe it."

"Take care."

"I promise. Did you find anything in her house?"

"Nothing. Thousands of e-mails, but none of them compromising. I found the death threats, on e-mail and on paper. We are still looking into it. They seem rather childish."

"Angry revolutionaries?"

"I don't know. For the moment we are lost in a fog. Nothing concrete. We're analysing the texts. I'd like to know how many people sent them, but it is difficult and it will be irrelevant…"

"Toni, I am off to *Buzău* tomorrow morning. I have a contact there and I want to find out more about Diana's adoption. I want to know where her birth parents are."

"Be very careful. Delicate and dangerous things can come up all the time. You might be tailed. I don't have any men to cover you. Remember you were complaining about snipers."

"I promise to be careful; you have my word as a pioneer[130]!"

"This is no laughing matter. And we're at a funeral, after all, Stelică."

---

130   The pioneer's word, or honour, was an expression used in the politicised Scouts-type children movement of the Pioneers. Equivalent to the expression "Scout's Honour".

He's right. I shut up. I see Diana again, dressed in black and orchestrating the event. I can't see her face clearly, she is far from me, and I can't say whether or not she has cried some more. Cynical to think like this, but I have suddenly started to miss the General. And I think I am missing my carefree childhood. Without wanting it, I remember the joke beginning with "During Stalin's times…" Everything was fine because we were young. Damn, was it all fine during Ceauşescu's times because I was young? Have I started forgetting all the terrible things? Is my memory failing me? Have I become nostalgic for the past?

I haven't driven car Q since my trip to Vienna. It had been brought to the parking space in front of my building and the keys had been posted to my office at Trident. It was dusty, but not excessively so. The drive to *Buzău* is not too long, a little over one hundred kilometres, and there is not much traffic, so I arrive quickly, without getting tired. I am even in a good mood. I park the car at the meeting point we'd chosen on e-mail, at the Mac.

Oliviu is waiting for me with a coffee in front of him, yawning for all he's worth and reading a local newspaper I don't know. We shake hands and embrace. A manly gesture, maybe a little exaggerated. We are not such good friends.

"I am glad to see you again, Stelică."

"Same here. How are things?"

"Eh, you know how things are with people relying on state budgets. It's hard. To be precise, we're crawling. We're waiting for better times. You?"

"Just like you. Who's reading books nowadays? Or if they're reading, it doesn't mean they're buying."

"Are people passing them from one to another? Off the internet?"

"In all sort of ways. You know how it works, you've been in the system."

"That's life. Want a drink, something to eat?"

"I'll get a juice. And a coffee. Do you want something else?"

"No, thank you."

The conversation is a little dry, tentative. We haven't met for a long time, and he represents the public authority.

I return with the drinks. I attack directly.

"Did you find anything?"

"I did. But not all the news is good."

"I am listening."

"Diana Simionescu's birth parents died in a traffic accident. In 1987."

"Is that all?"

"I don't know more. What would you be interested in?"

"Who were they? How did they die? Where?"

"The file doesn't say much about them. I can make enquiries but I don't know if it's any use to you. They died on the pedestrian crossing at the entrance to the town of *Râmnicu Sărat*, as you drive in from *Buzău*. I think you can find out more from the *Râmnic* police. If they still keep the old archives."

"Is that all?"

"I sincerely don't know what else you expected me to say."

"Thanks a lot."

I stand up without having touched the juice or the coffee.

Adopted. Natural parents dead. I am in a dead end. Nobody ever mentioned Diana was not the General's daughter. Everything was well hidden. Could there be blackmail involved? Could Diana be in danger? I don't understand. But

I'm the fool, because in the summer of '86, when I was at the General's house and we talked about children, there was no Diana present. They didn't prepare any papers, either, for adopting a child of this name. How did Diana appear in '87, and why didn't they ever talk about it? I wonder what is hidden behind the story of the birth parents.

"I'm going. To Bucharest. It was good seeing you."

"Wait a little, my friend, don't run away like that. I have another piece of information."

"I am listening."

"I found out from City Hall, the Child Protection Agency, that a journalist lady came about six months ago to make an investigation about adopted children. Something like orphans who survived car accidents and were then reintegrated into society."

"It sounds strange."

"Yes, maybe I got it wrong. Write down this phone number."

I get my BlackBerry ready.

"0872 098 234."

"Noted. Name?"

"Liliana Petruş."

"Lili?"

"You know her?"

"She's my colleague at *Flacăra* Magazine."

"Right. That's what she said, that she was from *Flacăra*."

"Super. Thank you very much."

I embrace him for real this time. I climb in the car and drive straight for *Aviator Petre Mircea Street*, in Bucharest. I hope she's still in the office. In the evening, there will be the talk show to which Diana has not yet invited me. But that's fine. I can wait.

Chapter 27

Bucharest, August 2010

I DROP IN AT MY PLACE IN A HURRY to pick up a black pinstriped suit and a light blue shirt. I hesitate when it comes to the tie. Yes or no? In the end I choose a navy blue tie, a narrow one. I hang everything on the clothes hook in the car and start driving down *Mihai Bravu* and then *Ştefan cel Mare*, towards *Dorobanţi*[131]. The city is almost free of traffic but the remaining drivers are belting around chaotically and I have to be more careful than usual. The heat is oppressive and, in cars without air conditioning, windows wide open, the atmosphere is like an oven. The unlucky drivers of these cars are the most nervous and undisciplined. I have no reason to hurry, I am within the graph[132].

I reach *Aviator Petre Mircea Street* at half past three. I drive slowly past the General's house. A black BMW X3 is parked close to the pavement, in front of the house. Its registration number is B 85 SIM. It's too much of a coincidence. The car must definitely belong to one of the Simionescu family. It is empty, so is the courtyard. Through the windows there is nothing to be seen. I drive on.

I find a narrow parking space immediately after a carwash which, in the middle of August, has almost no clients. I take my laptop and the bag full of papers, half of which there is no point in carrying around, and I pass through the metal gate of the *Flacăra* Publications building.

131   Major thoroughfares in Bucharest.
132   An expression from the old times meaning everything is as planned (reference being made to the graphs of statistics).

I drop in at least once a month, bringing a new article and collecting an envelope with some money in payment for the previous story. Naturally, I could send the text by e-mail and receive the money by card, but I would deprive myself of the pleasure of chatting to colleagues in the newsroom. I would, especially, miss the pleasure of drinking the coffee brewed by Lili. Liliana, the editor-in-chief of *Flacăra* Magazine.

The phone rings. I'm at the bottom of the stairs, so there is no space in which to put down the bags. I drop them, and take out the BlackBerry. Diana. I am certain I know why she's looking for me.

"*Sărut mâna*, Diana."

"Hello, Stelian." Her voice has an official tone and she sounds exhausted. I can't whether she's playacting or whether she really is. "I have a big request. You have to help me."

"Of course. I am listening."

"I have been invited to organise a talk-show about my father. Nicuşor Tătărescu is coming as well, and the policeman, Commissar Anton Demetriade, and we'll probably have a journalist from Vienna."

"When?"

"We'll be on air tonight at 20.00."

"You are asking me at the last minute again," I reply, although Toni had told me this was going to happen.

I suspect Diana had first assured herself of his presence. I don't know much about Nicuşor Tătărescu, I've only seen him on a few shows. He's a journalist-analyst, a former celebrity politician, a sort of Jack of all trades, a small, thin man whose voice turns shrill when he gets angry. I think he's in his thirties. I can't say how intelligent he is, nor if he knows anything about armies or revolutions. I had only seen him on shows with VIPs about scandals generated by legacies and extramarital affairs. Maybe Diana couldn't find anyone else. As for the "journalist from Vienna" it sounds like a phrase thrown in just to make things look good.

"Can you hear me? Are you still there?"

"Yes, I hear you. I was thinking."

"You're not going to tell me your schedule is so full you can't come. It's for my father. You're his editor. And you can publicise the book."

She knows what pedals to push, but it's too direct. I am silent, pretending to think, while a colleague runs down the stairs, almost trips over my bag and laptop, then goes out waving a greeting at me. She's from the monthly *Rebus*[133].

"Yes, I will come."

"Thank you very much."

"I hope I'll have the time to get changed."

I'm making it hard for her, although I already have the suit I'll wear for the show in the car. "What time?"

"19.45 at our TV studio. You still know how to get there?"

"Of course. I'll be there. Any special preparations?"

"No, we'll talk about my father. Each guest from their own angle. It will be a sort of retrospective."

A retrospective?! Strange word. In vogue, dry and cold. I'm saying this to myself.

"Aren't we going to talk about the investigation?" I try to provoke her.

"That too – there is a policeman coming after all. So that's all right?" Diana is pressuring me.

"Yes, it's all right, I'll be there. *Sărut mâna*."

"Good bye."

Our conversation ends. I stay there for a moment gazing into space. This will be a long, hard day. I pick up the bag with the papers and the one with the laptop and throw them

133 'Rebus' means crossword – also the title of a monthly devoted to crossword puzzles.

over my left shoulder. I sigh involuntarily and climb to the first floor.

I throw a greeting towards the reception, poke my head through the chairman's door, and say hello to George Arion[134] who is sitting at his desk, writing. At the opposite end Alexandru is walking around his desk, speaking rapidly on his mobile. I wave my left hand at him and climb two more flights of stairs.

The newsroom of *Flacăra* Magazine is on the third floor. Alice and Tibi the photo reporter are away. Only Lili is there, tapping calmly on the keys of her laptop in the quiet of the room.

"Oh, new blood! New blood!"

"*Sărut mâna.*"

She stands up, frail and thin. We kiss each other on the cheeks. The office smells of good, strong coffee, and Lili is dressed, as always, in a mix of office-wear and *flower-power*. More *flower-power*, as a matter of fact. Every time I see her I am struck with wonder at the chromatically sensitive nature of her outfits.

"How are you, maestro? Did you bring your piece in early?"

"No, no way. I was thinking about a coffee."

"As they say: you want me to make you a coffee."

"May your kindness be repaid in heaven."

I follow her to the kitchen where she prepares the miraculous liquid. I have never checked out her recipe. It's not my business really; the important thing is that the end product will be wonderful. Only Sofia, with her French press which was obviously bought from Starbucks (and,

134   George Arion (b. 1946) is rightly considered the doyen of Romanian crime fiction. His 1983 book Attack in the Library, also published in the Profusion Crime Series, is hailed as a benchmark. His character Andrei Mladin, a reluctant detective, appears in a series of novels. He is the publisher of *Flacăra* Magazine and President of *Flacăra* Publications.

unexpectedly, made in Denmark), brews better coffee than Lili. Apart from these, I am only served various kinds of dark liquids, with some aroma and taste, but without much refinement. Coffee made by automatic machines which buzz and puff very provocatively, but to no effect.

"Listen, Stelică, you're not here for the coffee. What happened?"

"The General's assassination."

"Do you want to do an article?"

"That's what I was thinking, but it's too early, the investigation is still ongoing. This evening I'll be on a talk show about it."

"Did you know him?"

"Yes, from about '85. And Trident was due to publish his memoirs. I mean, it will be published this autumn."

"Aha. Interesting book?"

"Yes, it has all sorts of stories," I answer without much enthusiasm.

Lili senses the nuance in my voice so she says nothing more. She gives me a huge mug of hot coffee, inscribed in italics, on a red background, with the words *"Tommys Brand"*.

"Let's speak in my office," she says. She sits down comfortably, crossing her legs, and she lights up a long, thin cigarette of the kind that we, non-smokers and pretend smokers, call "straws".

"Would you like one?" she asks ritually, although she knows that I will say no.

I smile and shake my head. Besides being straws, the cigarettes she smokes are also mentholated. So, no way I can be tempted.

"What's the trouble?"

Lili is from Transylvania, near *Deva*, but she doesn't

speak with an accent. Too many years in Bucharest. From time to time she throws in a word from back home. Maybe for fun. Or out of nostalgia.

"I need your help."

"Tell me."

"It's about a story you wrote a while ago. About six months. I have a friend at *Buzău* City Hall, and he told me you made an enquiry at the Child Protection Services there. It's about a little girl's adoption."

"Yes, I was there. But I haven't published anything. It was all too sad, especially for the January-February issue. I postponed it. Maybe for an issue in the autumn but I still need to work on it. There were several children. Which one are you talking about?"

"Diana Simona Popescu. She was adopted by Adela and Gheorghe Simionescu. The girl was born in 1985 and the adoption file was finally approved in 1989. The parents apparently died in an accident."

She doesn't reply immediately. She's thinking. Then she starts tapping with her thin fingers on the laptop, faster than I had ever seen her do.

"I have something, but it's more of a rough draft. You know I write things down in my diary and I don't use a tape recorder. Then, if I give up the article..."

"You haven't gone and deleted it?!"

"No, but I haven't finished the article. It's a sad story. Not the only one. There are many children orphaned due to accidents. This particular child lost her parents in a car accident."

"Yes, that's what I've been told: at the entrance to *Râmnicu Sărat*. On a pedestrian crossing."

"Aha, I know. I remember it. I saw the file then, but they didn't want to give it to me. They were afraid, I think. A very strange story."

"Do you have the time?"

"Yes, it's not a long story, but it's very strange, even shocking. Well…" She lights up another straw and takes two drags calmly while I sip from the coffee which is now getting a little cold.

"There were two cars involved. One had lawfully stopped in front of the pedestrian crossing, waiting for the people to cross, and another that had come from behind, speeding. It was like a billiard table. The driver of the stationary car did not have his foot on the brakes – so I was told. I didn't talk to the police in *Râmnic*, but the woman from Child Protection seemed to know the whole story. She was an elderly lady who was around at the time. It seems the accident had created a stir back then."

"I wonder why."

"I'm going to tell you. The stationary car was pushed forward and brutally struck a family of three: mother, father, and a baby in a pushchair. The adults could not be saved – serious cranial fractures and internal bleeding – but the child was strapped into the pushchair and well padded. She was lucky. The pushchair was thrown to the side of the road into a bush. The baby suffered no injury. It was a horrifying accident. The two-year-old girl in the pushchair was Diana Simona Popescu."

"And who was to blame?"

"It appears there was a strange law on the books. It wasn't only the driver from the moving car who was put on trial. Even the man in the car waiting at the pedestrian crossing was accused of murder with intent."

"Why the hell?"

"I don't know. I don't know the laws now, even less the laws back then. In any case, it was a horrifying accident."

"And that Diana ended up in an orphanage?"

"Yes, she had no other close relatives. But the interesting part only starts now: the driver who was waiting at the crossing was convicted, but the punishment was suspended."

"That's stupid, he wasn't guilty."

"I agree. But this was not the problem. The problem was the fact that the driver was in the military, a captain, and he didn't…"

When the penny drops, I slap my forehead. Lili stops, startled, and she looks at me in alarm, her lit cigarette the breadth of a hand away from her mouth, and the other hand on her little coffee cup.

"What? What happened?"

"Now I get it. The captain's name was Simionescu, wasn't it?"

"Exactly, Gheorghe Simionescu. They started a long investigation, and they wanted to discharge him from the army. It seems he fought with them and applied to adopt the little girl. He and his wife wanted a child very much. A rather strange way to adopt one, after killing the parents. It's a strange event, a tragedy with a happy end, if you can call it happy."

"And the girl knows she was adopted?"

"I think so. It's normal. She was two when the accident happened, and almost four when she was adopted. I suspect she has memories. Ugly memories. But I don't know. The records don't show whether she was seen by a child psychiatrist. In those times…"

"But I suspect she doesn't know she was adopted by the man who killed her parents."

"I don't know. It is possible she found out. It wasn't hard for me to do the research. If she had time and patience, she could find out."

"She's a journalist for Star TV."

"In that case... I don't know."

"Did something happen to Simionescu after the accident?"

"I can't find out much more from the Child Protection Agency. But there are rumours and urban legends still circulating in the city and the county of *Buzău*. Some say he had a big connection backing him so that they couldn't throw him out of the army. Others say that it was the army which asked him to adopt the child."

"I don't think so, Simionescu wanted to have children. I talked to him about it."

"You did? When?"

"In '86... I did my military training in *Buzău*, in the unit where he was posted. We met then. Long story."

"I gave up writing the article. Alexandru said it was too downbeat, and even for me it wasn't very pleasant finding out all this. It's best to leave it alone."

"Yes, but the General was killed, his memoirs will be published by Trident, and his daughter has invited me to be on a talk show tonight."

"And? You don't want to talk about all this there. It has no relevance. Diana is Simionescu now, not Popescu. Years have passed. Leave it alone, the story is too sad."

"But, Lili, the General was killed. We should find out why."

"The press is stirring up a storm about it. The complications of the revolution... Leave Diana out of it. I don't know her and I don't want to know her. I saw her once on the television. I didn't even make the connection. She signs her name Diana Simionescu, not Simona. Anyway, I say you leave it alone."

I don't answer immediately. I don't know what to say. This

is a 22-year old story with no connection to the revolution or the army.

"I wonder how it is that they didn't discharge him from the army, though."

"They tried to, I told you, and almost succeeded, but the adoption was approved in May '89, then came the revolution and everything started to change. He was rehabilitated, and the file was cleansed. But this is street corner gossip. People were afraid to talk about it openly."

"I know. No one has found out about this accident until now. I am surprised the press didn't dig around in his past, given the number of scandals…"

"Maybe some are afraid. Or maybe some of the journalists still have a shred of decency left in them and don't drag in the family lives of personalities in the news…"

"I don't believe it. I can't believe it. They wouldn't have missed anything. I am certain they didn't know about it, or they were too afraid to dig so deeply. Simionescu was, after all, an influential person."

"I am sure. Your coffee is cold."

"I like it cold."

I would like to light a cigarette. I would trick myself by puffing on it, without inhaling.

I don't know what to believe or what to do. I have uncovered a new story. Later on Simionescu lost his wife, Adela, and he was left alone with Diana. Adela's disappearance had been a further blow. The girl had lost her adoptive mother as well. The General never married again.

"Thanks a lot, Lili. The coffee was wonderful."

I pour the last drops down my throat and stand up.

"Are you leaving?"

"I don't know. Not yet. I'll visit the lower levels, the bosses…"

"You can't settle down, can you?"

"No, I am going to this TV thing this evening, and I don't feel too comfortable."

"You? I always thought that you never freeze up in front of the cameras."

"I don't, but this occasion is a little more special. I'll tell you all about it when it's all finished."

Liliana doesn't pursue the matter. She gives me a cheeky smile.

"Another coffee on the slate. You owe me about twenty cups. They keep on adding up."

"I will gladly repay the debt one day. Kisses."

And I leave, dragging my bags. I don't know where to go. I have several good hours until the talk show, but, right now, I am too dizzy, and I start searching for a place where I can be alone.

Chapter 28

Bucharest, August 2010

I HID MYSELF IN AN EMPTY OFFICE. I found one on the ground floor, near a storage room for old magazines, packs of returns tied crosswise with plastic tape. The room seems chilly, but for mid-August it's perfect. I have also brought the suit from the car.

There is a rickety table and white walls. No posters, no papers – just the light of the sun coming in through a narrow barred window, throwing long shadows on the dusty surfaces. It's just like Vienna, when I was waiting for my fate to be decided.

I start waiting now, thinking of everything that has happened during the last few months. A succession of mad events, some of them illogical, some of them predictable, a toboggan run of news and actions which kept me on the go, but which gave me no sense of direction or finality.

Sofia is far away and I seldom see her, Lulu is now near and I still don't have time for her. A shudder of futility, of inexorable destiny, of despair, embraces me like a cold November wind and I feel the shivers pass through my body again. I cross my hands on my chest and yawn, eyes half-open. I feel alone and without direction.

I don't feel like opening the laptop again, and I look at the BlackBerry hoping somebody will call. I need a stranger's voice to take me out of this uncomfortable state of mind. But the bell is silent. I pass my finger over the command button and scroll through the contacts list, stopping at

D. Demetriade. But I don't have anything additional to communicate. We'll meet tonight. He warned me I would be attacked. He will be there as well, and I am sure he'll take my side. I continue to scroll down. I reach P. Pushkin. I push the button without any hope. The Russian's phone is not off. It rings. This is incredible, but I hear his voice after the fourth ring.

"Hello, Stelian."

I am caught on the wrong foot: I hadn't expected him to answer, so I have lost the initiative.

"Can you hear me? I am glad you called. I hope you will be on that talk show tonight, won't you?"

Maybe I should swear at him or hang up the phone, but I do neither and reply calmly after giving a long sigh:

"Of course, Misha, I will go. I, too, am glad to hear you again."

"I heard you are doing fine."

"Yes, I am fine."

I never doubted that Pushkin knows everything that is happening. I give up on trying to call him to account for the events in Vienna. It's pointless now. It is too late and, at the same time, too soon. Somewhere deep in my mind I hope to pay him back one day. I don't know how or when… I console myself with the idea that I will do it, and that it will make me feel happier. Thinking about this calms me down.

"In that case, Stelică, soon. See you soon."

And he hangs up, leaving me holding the phone to my ear. I feel tired and I my eyes are half open, my eyesight is blurred, my head is heavy and my thoughts are murky. I feel like weeping with self pity.

A buzz – text message from Sofia.

"Love you. Take care of yourself. Break a leg! Call me after you're done. Kisses, S"

I smile gratefully at the screen.

I look at my watch. Hours have gone by. I go to the toilet and throw some water on my face and eyes. I rinse them thoroughly. The battle approaches. I change my clothes and, once into the suit and tie, I feel more certain of myself, as if I'm wearing armour. The tourney approaches. The only problem is that don't know for what I am fighting!

There's still light outside when I reach the headquarters of Star TV, and the communist architecture of the decrepit buildings looks even more ugly, deprived of the protection offered by the night. In between the iron construction rods and prefab panels, the TV studio looks like an alien space ship which has landed in the ruins of an atomic war. The giant letters spelling STAR TV in red, green and blue, are lit up, although it's still daylight. I park car Q, still dusty from the roads I travelled before going to Vienna, and I take my two bags with me, although I know they won't be necessary, and that I could leave them in the trunk. I had received a text message from Toni ten minutes before. "I'll be there at 7.40." I look at my watch. It's 7.45. I made it in time. Demetriade is probably already here.

I pass the security guard without looking in his direction. He doesn't stop me and doesn't ask any questions. We ignore each other. He is watching the news on another TV station. He could be punished for this… I don't care. I enter the green room slowly, feeling my way around. I am the last to arrive. The commissar is also wearing a suit, but no tie. Nicuşor Tătărescu wears a very loud check shirt and bluejeans. Diana dominates us all in her tight black dress. It seems like the same dress that I've seen her wearing in the last couple of days. Or something very similar. I can't help myself from sizing her up from top to bottom, just like every time that I meet her. And she knows it.

When I entered the room, she was standing, talking to the two other guests. Not a trace of the Viennese journalist. It had been a bluff, but I don't say anything. She approaches me and holds out her hand.

"Good evening. Thank you for coming. Let me introduce you to the two other guests. Commissar Anton Demetriade from the police…"

"We know each other."

We shake hands. It seems Diana didn't know that we knew each other, and she seems caught by surprise.

"…and Nicușor Tătărescu, commentator and analyst."

Another handshake, with a silent nod of the head.

"We have six or seven minutes to go until the show starts. Please step into the studio so we can fit you with microphones."

The studio is the same that I was in for the cultural show back in the spring. It seems a little more crowded now. There are four chairs around a curved table and four cameras are getting ready to focus on us. The spot lights are turned on and, although the buzz of the air conditioning is obtrusive, the temperature is not exactly comfortable. I look for a pack of paper tissues in my pockets and I calm down on finding them. We are not taken to a make-up room, but a young lady with a huge make-up box comes around and dabs foundation on our faces. Diana is heavily made up, trying to conceal the black rings around her eyes produced by the last few days. I have the sense that she has such a thick coat of make-up on that her face is armour-plated. Or that she's wearing a helmet with the visor down. This really seems to be a tourney.

The stage director calls us to attention:

"One minute. Attention!"

Silence.

"30… 20… 10… Now!"

The show's titles start running on the monitors. For the first time I now see the title of the show - "The Mystery of General Simionescu's Assassination."

"Good evening, ladies and gentlemen," Diana begins. "This is Star TV, and we are live from our studio with our guests. They are…"

The sound starts to fade and I fall into a gently hypnotic state. I am tired and dizzy.

"… and Stelian Munteanu, editor of Trident publishing house and old friend of Gheorghe Simionescu…"

I wake up abruptly on hearing these words. "Old friend" – since when? I mumble a stupid, stereotypical phrase:

"Good evening and thank you for the invitation."

"Thank you all for agreeing to be part of this show. It might look out of proportion and unchristian for us to debate these matters only one day after the burial of Lieutenant General Gheorghe Simionescu, but it is in our interest, the interest of public opinion as a whole, to try and clear up the mystery which surrounded the passing away of…"

I see her shedding a tear at the right moment. If she's playacting, she's doing it very well.

"… of my father."

She stops for a moment.

"Mister Commissar, what can the police tell us?"

"Not too much, for the moment. We are waiting for all the details to arrive from our colleagues in Vienna. We have only received a part of the file. I can say we should be able to present the first conclusions in a maximum of ten days. It is too early to say anything definite until then. We do not want to launch any speculative hypotheses."

"But still – the rumour has it that we are dealing with a

sniper. What is your opinion?"

"I repeat, I would not like to give birth to any speculations. The Vienna Police have already sent a ballistics report which mentions a cartridge fired by a SSG 08 Steyr-Manlicher, an Austrian-made rifle for long-distance shooting. However, it is too early to be able to draw any conclusions."

"The General's body arrived in Romania in a lead coffin. Were the Romanian authorities allowed to perform their own autopsy?"

I hold back a reaction. The question is stupid, and Toni answers precisely.

"No, the coffin was sealed. The conclusions of the autopsy will arrive from Vienna. It was conducted by the Austrian coroners."

Diana Simionescu turns to Tătărescu.

"What do you think about this issue?"

The man looks as if he's been caught unprepared. The questions are not consistent and it is evident that Diana is trying to create a following by throwing words around.

"I can't have an opinion. Of course, the Romanian police will decide if the Austrian report is enough. I am not a coroner. I think one autopsy should be enough. And the Austrians are trustworthy, are they not?"

"But still, gentlemen, can we be certain of what happened there?"

"What do you mean, madam?" Tătărescu intervenes. "Do you have information which the rest of us are not aware of?"

"There are certain rumours about the involvement of some Romanian citizens in the assassination."

"What is the basis for these statements?" Toni asks, throwing a brief glance at me.

"We have launched our own inquiries and we found out

there was a Romanian sniper stationed in a department store close to the hotel."

"A Romanian sniper?!" intervenes Nicușor, caressing his beard. "Are these not stories like those with the terrorists during the revolution? Let's be serious, there are no clear evidence that Simionescu had anything to hide. At least not up to now. And I can't see where new evidence could come from. Maybe only from you, madam. Have you checked his notes?"

Diana ignores him. I think she didn't expect to be attacked. She turns to me.

"What do you think, Mister Munteanu? You have read my father's manuscript. Did it contain information that could generate such a reaction from a group of former Securitate members?"

She looks deep into my eyes, and I can see her malice. Is she paying old debts because I turned her down, because I didn't accept her advances? Does she want high ratings? Or does she know more? Did Misha bring her in on this plot?

"No... I don't think so. To me, it seemed the text presents only events from the General's life. Nothing secret."

"How is the revolution presented in the manuscript? Are there any facts about people who are still under the scrutiny of the press?"

I don't know what she wants from me. I can't understand what she is after. Toni also looks at me attentively.

"Esteemed viewers, if you would like to talk live on air with our guests, please dial the numbers shown in the lower part of the screen. So, Mister Munteanu?"

"Yes, there are public figures mentioned in the text, but I don't think those things are as grave as to..."

"Excuse me," Diana interrupts. "Apart from you, did anyone else read the manuscript?"

"No, not at the publishing house. Only you and your father."

"I have not read this last version you discussed with my father during your last meeting at *Telega*, in his holiday house. Could it be possible that it might have reached the hands of others?"

"Speaking frankly, this is speculation. The book will be published this October. All the readers, journalists or the man in the street, will be able to read everything then."

"Do you mean that you will not censor anything?"

"I do not have the right to censor it. Why would I do that anyway?"

"Even if some things bother you?"

"Why would they bother me?"

I don't understand what she is aiming at. My nervousness increases. Tătărescu looks at us curiously, first at one, then at the other, as if this is a game of tennis, while Toni keeps blinking rapidly.

"There might be things from your past that my father could have known and that shouldn't be known by everyone."

"What things? There is nothing of the sort!"

"But you have known my father since 1985. Can you deny it?"

I suddenly feel she is spinning her spider's web around me. The black widow. She is presenting a picture of herself as the desperate daughter, victim of the Securitate people who murdered her father, and of me, someone who has signed a pact with the murderers…

"I don't deny it. We met in *Buzău*, while I was undergoing military training."

"Have you seen him since then?"

"Yes. Once. During the revolution. But that was it. I don't understand why you are interrogating me."

"Because I have information that, the day my father was killed, you were in Vienna!"

BANG. The missile hits the bull's-eye.

"Can you deny this?"

Where does she know it from? Who betrayed me? Until now, nobody has mentioned my involvement. And then?

"Can you deny you were in Vienna that day? There are people who saw you there."

"I don't deny it. I was in Vienna, but what's that got to do with…"

"Mister Munteanu, can you deny that as a young man you were a top level target shooter?"

The earth starts to spin like the time I drank a full bottle of "bear power" wine at the General's house before I returned to the unit. Everything is spinning too fast.

"No, I don't deny it. This fact is public knowledge."

"Can you deny that you possess, with all legal formalities, an SSG 08 Steyr-Manlicher rifle?

Check mate.

"No."

She turns to the policeman, who also looks disorientated.

"Mister Commissar Demetriade, isn't it true that in the papers you have received from Vienna concerning my father's assassination," Diana says, stressing the last words – my father's assassination – "the name Stelian Munteanu appears in the box for the suspect's name? Isn't it true that all the evidence incriminates Mister Munteanu?"

Toni is left open-mouthed. He was expecting an attack on me, but the strike is extremely precise. Tătărescu moves his head from left to right almost spasmodically. The studio is quiet. I start feeling afraid. Exactly like that time I was shooting at my colleagues' targets during the night manoeuvres.

"We have a caller. A journalist from Vienna."

This is too much! I was sure there was no invited journalist. I start making some room around me and to push the swivel chair little by little towards the back. I am preparing my retreat. I don't know what could happen to me here. Toni is in a state of shock and isn't reacting any more.

"We are listening, Mister Helmuth."

This is strange, but I can see that even Diana is a little surprised as well. It appears this Viennese journalist was not exactly planned.

"Good evening, I will speak in *Rumanian* a little. I know a bit of the language. My name is Helmuth Kepler."

Romanian words with a heavy German accent. The accent is a little too theatrical, a fake. I recognise Misha's voice. No doubts about it.

"We are listening, Mister Kepler."

What is happening here? Is this a trap? I don't think Toni recognised the voice because he is listening with great attention, his elbows planted on the table.

"Madam, in Vienna we had a regrettable incident. But there were many *Rumanians* that day in the capital of Austria. I can say to you that…"

"Excuse me for interrupting. Do you know Mister Munteanu?"

"No, it is only now that I hear of him."

"Then how can you…"

"Fraulein, I want to say that the Austrian police have information that the killers were *Rumanian*. But it was a team of two. And General Simionescu was killed in his room."

"We are aware of this fact, he was staying in the Haydn Hotel."

"I agree. But the General was not killed from a distance,

from the building on the other side diagonally, as you imply. I suspect you mean Saturn Department Store."

"Exactly, the Saturn electronics store."

"The ballistics report mentions a Steyr-Manlicher rifle, but the analysis of projectile impact shows that the General was killed from a short distance of less then two metres."

"Mister Kepler, are you saying that somebody came into the General's room with a sniper rifle and shot him from a distance of two metres? Why would they need a long distance rifle? It is absurd," Tătărescu says. Until that moment he had been fidgeting in his chair, not knowing how to get into the discussion.

"Not at all, my dear sir, if this modus operandi is trying to cover the tracks of the real killers. Not at all. Things are not what they seem at the outset."

Diana seems to be getting into a rage. She is holding a Parker pen in her left hand and she keeps spinning it. I am convinced that the trick with the Austrian journalist has backfired. Misha found out the lie about the "surprise guest" and rushed to play this part from a distance. But I don't understand what he is after.

"But our guest did not answer the question. What's it all about, Mister Commissar? Will you tell us or not? What are the police concealing?"

Demetriade looks at us all, one by one, calmly, either trying to increase the tension or simply looking for a way to avoid answering. He doesn't find it, then he starts speaking slowly:

"Yes, the report we received does mention Stelian's name…"

I don't wait for the end of the sentence. I push the chair back forcefully, rip off the microphone, and run out of the studio without looking at the people standing around. Nobody follows me.

Chapter 29

Bucharest, August 2010

I CALM DOWN ONLY WHEN I GET HOME, storm into the living room and take the Colt 1911 out of the plastic bag in which it has been left since Toni brought it back. I check the clip, I caress the visible cartridge, the top one, then I insert the clip with a rapid movement, arm the first bullet down the barrel and put the safety catch on. I attach the holster to my belt and put the gun in it, with mechanical, automatic gestures. I breathe in, deeply.

What actually happened?

Nobody stopped me at the exit to the TV station. The gatekeeper was in the same position, his eyes on the very small screen. I got in the car, reversed and went out through the rusty gate. I drove carefully through the deserted city, still lit by the sun, low down in the western sky, and about to dip below the horizon. I have no idea how the show continued. I don't even try to imagine.

In Star TV's parking lot, I catch a brief glimpse of the BMW X3 model with the B 85 SIM number plates, with someone sitting at the wheel. Judging by the profile, it was someone familiar to me. It looked like the General's driver, the massive bald headed man. He didn't look at me, not for a second.

I now realise that I am still dressed in my black suit. I take out the holster, gun still in it, and leave it on the table. I throw the clothes on the sofa, and offer myself the luxury of a 5-minute shower. I clear my brain. I will go to

Diana's place. These things must not be left up to a random outcome. I exchange my elegant clothing for a pair of jeans and a short sleeved shirt. Then I reattach the holster, gun still in it, and put on a light khaki jacket.

I stop moving for a moment. To gather my thoughts. I feel just as I did in Vienna, after I refused to shoot, and after changing in room 106, following my shower. I make myself a sandwich in the kitchen and eat it in small mouthfuls, chewing thoroughly in order to force my brain to come up with an idea, with a solution. So, I will go to Diana's house and then what? What will I solve? Why do I have the sensation, lacking any evidence, that she knows more, that she's hiding things, that – just like Misha or Steiner – she had set a devious trap for me?

The red LED light of the phone is not lit up. Nobody is looking for me. Strange. Nobody asking for explanations? Maybe the talk show is not yet over. I wonder…

I refuse to torment myself with all these speculations. I leave my block of flats, taking key to car Q out of my pocket. However, at the last moment, I give up and jump in a yellow taxi.

"*Bună seara.* To *Aviator Petre Mircea Street*, please."

The driver nods his head knowingly. I've seen him before. His pick-up point is on the corner of my block. I think he's driven me a couple of times before. He glances at me quickly and understands that he needs to be quiet. I am glad of it, because I am trying to organise my thoughts. I should have a clear discussion with Diana, to find out exactly what she knows, and from where she knows it. Then, I will be frank with her in my turn, and tell her about Misha Pushkin's game; and then we should try to find out together who the murderers are. It is more than obvious that Toni and the Romanian Police know it's not me. I should convince

Diana of this, as well. I ask myself why I have taken the gun with me. Is it premonition? Am I afraid? Of course I am. Am I once again imagining snipers on the top terraces of apartment buildings? Yes, especially now after the whole story was broadcast on TV and they've seen my face live on air.

We reach Diana's street quickly, and I ask the driver to stop at some distance from the house. I pay and take a few steps. It's already dark and the public lighting is not too generous, the lampposts are sparse, the light bulbs are weak. The street is deserted. A dog growls somewhere in a courtyard, but doesn't start barking.

The BMW is parked in front of the house. There is nobody in the car. I approach the gate and push on the handle – it's locked. An entry phone with the small eye of a video camera built-in. I push the button. After a minute I hear the metal bolt opening. Probably some kind of entry system. I step into the courtyard where there is a rather strong scent of flowers. Probably beds of *Queen of the Night*. There are five or six metres to the door of the house. Above it, a yellow incandescent light bulb goes on, and the hinges squeak like the soundtrack of a bad horror movie.

Through a crack in the door I see Diana's black-clad silhouette. She looks at me, in the dim light, with a face full of hate, with burning eyes and a terrifying expression I have never seen before. In her right hand she is holding a long-barrelled handgun, a big, heavy, black weapon. It could be a Smith & Wesson revolver, or even a Colt. It doesn't matter too much, because she is holding it very firmly, fingers clasped around it, and I am certain there is a bullet in the firing chamber.

"Get inside," she commands. "And no sudden movements."

I take a step and think of my own handgun attached to the belt. Too late. While her revolver is poking in my ribs, her left hand pushes the jacket aside and takes out my Colt 1911.

"Inside the living room. On the sofa. Sit down slowly."

The room looks more or less the same. On the left hand-side, I see that the table on which his photograph was guarded by candles, is in fact a sculpted desk. A chair with a tall backrest behind it and an open laptop on it. The photograph has been moved to one of the shelves of the library on the far side of the room, where there are two armchairs and a coffee table. The sofa is to the right. I move carefully and sit down. Somewhere, off the small entry hall, there are two doors. I don't know where they lead to. She goes to the desk, holding both guns in her hands. She sits down in the chair and leans her elbows on the heavy wooden top. She doesn't take her eyes off me for a moment, both barrels carefully aiming at me.

"Should I ask if you'd like a coffee or is it too late and it might ruin your sleep?" she says ironically, her lips thinning into a malicious smile.

"Diana, what is this masquerade?"

"Are you asking that? You run off from the show and then come to my house, armed! What's the logic of that? You killed my father and I was next in the line, isn't that so?"

"Diana, this is stupid. You know well this is stupid."

"I only know you were in Vienna and that you killed my father."

"Diana, it wasn't me. The police know."

"The police have you down as a suspect."

"Until others should appear. Please, let's calm down. Let's discuss things like human beings."

I see her swollen face, the muscles tense, and I think my phrase about a human discussion sounds absolutely absurd, given the situation in which we find ourselves. This woman's eyes are lost and, out of despair or madness, she might do anything. I try to move as slowly as possible, not to provoke her. I am looking for a solution. My phone is attached to my belt on the right hand-side. I don't think I can reach it without her seeing. And I haven't told anybody where I was going tonight.

"You were saying about coffee. I'd actually like a coffee… and we should talk. I am here to talk."

She leers at me. Her eyes are burning and they are already no longer looking at me, but through me.

"You think I'm yearning for coffee now? When you came to kill me as well. What do you want, really? To cover all your tracks? *Securist nenorocit!*[135] You are just a killer. You are filth!"

My mind is searching desperately for a solution. But I don't find any. She still holds both guns in her hands and it's only now that I notice the gloves which she was also wearing at the funeral. This smells like premeditation. I was invited on the show in order to be provoked… Then I was received here with gloved hands and a loaded gun.

"You came into my house to kill me! To cover all the tracks. You killed my father, assassin!"

She turns my gun toward one of the armchairs in the back of the room and fires a shot. In the calm of the night, the bang echoes like thunder.

"And now, adieu! It was legitimate self defence."

She raises the right hand with her own revolver towards me. And I wait to see and hear the fraction of a second

---

135 An abusive term for former Securitate agents. 'Nenorocit' is literally 'with no luck' but in practice is extremely abusive, equivalent to the way that English uses 'fucking'.

when the bullet will fly in my direction. Like a goalkeeper 11 metres away from the penalty kick, I ask myself on which side I should jump. I ask myself if it makes any sense for me to move. I ask myself if it is destiny, if this is the end.

During this brief interval, it's not life which flashes in front of my eyes, only the black hole of her gun barrel, and I am hoping she'll change the firing line, so that I'll be able to jump, to run, to dematerialise as in Star Trek, teleported; but the moments are long and her arm raises, aiming without hurry towards…

"Stop!"

The shout is so loud that everything seems to freeze. From in front the open door, the General's bald driver is looking at us. He too is holding a gun. Also a huge pistol, maybe Soviet-made, a TT, or maybe even a Glock. I can't see too well in the semi-obscurity of the room, lit only by a lamp with three decorative candle bulbs and a small reading lamp on the coffee table in between the armchairs.

"Nobody shoots!" the man orders.

As if I could.

His weapon is pointing at Diana, who has turned 45 degrees so that she can cover us both. I am on the left, the other man on her right. My own Colt is aiming at me, and her weapon at the driver, her arms, raised almost horizontally, forming a 90-degree angle. I am once again living the sensation of a B movie, one of those featuring tattooed musclemen, tuned up cars, and sexy blondes. Then, all of a sudden, in a second or two, she changes the weapons from one hand to the other, with a set of movements so rapid as to be hallucinatory. In the still rational corner of my mind I realise that it would not be legitimate self defence if I died shot by my own Colt.

"Tudose, stay out of this! Go away, get out!"

"Diana, put the weapons down, this is madness."

"No, he's the man who assassinated my father. Get out, Tudose. It's not your business."

"Diana, put the guns down, nobody has to die."

"He assassinated my father."

"Diana, I can explain. Put down the guns."

But neither of the two makes a gesture to slacken the tension. Only words, volleys of words. I see their fingers tightening on the triggers. My mind refuses to understand the idiotic farce we are living through here. I think again about what I should do. She won't be able to hold her arms straight forever. The weapons are heavy. I see her leering, and her index fingers are curling around each trigger. Instinctively, I jump to the left.

I hear a long explosion. I distinguish three gunshots. I am down, close the sofa, my head near an armchair. I am apparently unhit. A few seconds go by before I regain my hearing, then my eyesight, and then I can take a look around. The driver is down on his back, and, from the region of his belly, waves of blood are pouring onto his grey shirt, mixing with the surreal spiral of his black tie, and flowing down onto the carpet. He groans rhythmically and he shakes, attempting to speak.

I stand up and take a step forward. Diana is also down, fallen behind the desk. The weapons are on the floor, less than a metre around her. The left hand, the one which had been holding my Colt, is wounded; with her right palm she tries to stop the bleeding. Her eyes are open and immobile, fixed in a strange direction, somewhere towards the upper corner of the library shelves. The driver is groaning, while the pool of blood is growing bigger, advancing to the middle of the room and soaking the Persian carpet. Diana is also groaning and her breathing is syncopated, her blood advancing towards the middle of the room as well, mingling in a sinister way with that of Tudose. I look at my shoes and trousers... I notice that they are drenched in the thick dark red liquid that has invaded the entire room. Planet earth suddenly accelerates its rotation, and the world disappears into an immense black hole.

Chapter 30

Bucharest, August 2010

I WAKE UP WITH A FEMALE PRESENCE STARING AT ME, from close up. Dressed in white. A doctor or a nurse. A lot of medical equipment around me. Hospital. My eyes adjust slowly to the environment and the image begins to coalesce. The woman withdraws silently, and Toni appears from behind her.

"First of all, stay calm: you are not hurt. It was just the shock."

"What happened?"

"When the cavalry arrived, you were all on the floor. At first I was terrified. It was a tableau from a horror film. A huge pool of blood in which you had collapsed."

"The others?"

"Tudose is dead. He was hit in the stomach, the flow of blood was rapid, and we got there a little too late. He died in the ambulance, on the way to the hospital."

"Diana?"

"She is wounded in the left hand. A nasty wound, with torn muscles… The doctors stabilised her. But that's not her problem."

"Meaning?"

"She suffered a powerful shock. It seems she'd had some psychiatric problems in the past, and hid them. Her father covered it all up. Now she is no longer in our world."

"What?"

"She is awake but not communicating. It's called a

265

catatonic state or something."

"Traces from her past? The car accident from her childhood? The parents killed by Simionescu on the pedestrian crossing?"

It's the commissar's turn to be surprised. He looks at me, very interested, and passes his fingers through his hair, in a tired, pointless, gesture. It's a reflex. He snorts.

"When did you find this out?"

"Before the talk-show, today. Or is it yesterday? I don't know."

"Yes, it is already yesterday. Meaning tomorrow. You understand, don't you? You should have told me, Stelică. It was stupid of you to go there."

"I didn't have the strength to call you, and talk before the show. I didn't understand anything about Pushkin's game. Or Diana's. I am completely confused."

"Pushkin called me to come with the boys to *Aviator Petre Mircea Street*. I think he followed you. Or he suspected something."

"Strange. He usually makes a forceful intervention. This time he stayed in the background."

"I don't understand too much about Misha's role either. Why did he want to convince you to shoot the General, just to have it proved afterwards that it was the driver who did it?"

"The driver?!"

"That's what we suspect. His last words were 'It must not end this way'. What does it mean?"

"And Misha? Did he turn up?"

"No. A quick phone call to me and that was it."

"He was the one who pretended to be the journalist from Vienna. I recognised his voice."

"I suspected as much. I saw how you reacted when you

heard his voice. What did he want to prove?"

"I don't know. He wanted to defend me."

"Stelică, there are two things which are unclear. First, why would the driver want to kill the General? He's been loyal to him for all these years. And why did he barge in and try to stop Diana shooting you? Did he want to confess, to turn himself in?"

"And the second?"

"The second is your luck. Diana's revolver was loaded with blanks."

"Blanks? How the hell? Who loaded it?"

"We can't tell. Not Diana, that's certain; she wanted to kill you."

"The General? Before he left for Vienna."

"Or the driver, Tudose."

"Toni, I swear I don't understand a thing."

"We'll do a thorough analysis. I do know for sure that you did not kill the General. The great unknown is who ordered and paid for the assassination. Which brings us back to the problems of the revolution."

"In this case, the driver… He was in Vienna, he came and stole the weapon from room 106 and then shot the General from close quarters."

"Very possible, but we don't have a motive."

"Money. Maybe loads of money. Who ordered the hit, and who paid?"

"That's what I was saying. This is the key to the mystery."

"What will happen to Diana now?"

"She will be sectioned. They will do a medical investigation. If she is found responsible for her actions she will be tried for murder."

"Why did she shoot the driver?"

"He killed her father. Or not – Diana could not know. She just wanted to defend herself. In any case, madness was already at work in her."

"But why shoot me?"

"For the same reasons."

"Toni, this is an aberration. You cannot just shoot people. It is crazy."

"Yes, Stelică, I think this is exactly what it is: crazy. And now, enough – go to sleep. Tomorrow is another day."

I jump up, and the wires connecting me to the medical apparatus stretch dangerously.

"Where did you get this expression from?"

Demetriade shrugs his shoulders.

"Easy, brother. It just came to me. It's from a film. *Gone with the Wind*, I think… What don't you like?"

"The General used it when we met. It's strange. Did you know him?"

"Stelian, calm down. You'll start believing that I killed him."

"Commissar, I can believe anything now. Pushkin, Steiner from Vienna, you, Tudose, or Diana… because it wasn't me."

"Drop it, amigo."

He shakes my hand and gets off the side of my bed.

"We'll talk. Have a nice rest."

He salutes me with two fingers raised to his temple, and he leaves my hospital room. I am alone. I search for my phone. It is on the nightstand. The LED light is red but I ignore it, and I write a short text message. For Sofia. "Love you. And I miss you very much. S." I fall asleep waiting for her answer.

Chapter 31

Bucharest, October 2010

NEARLY TWO MONTHS HAVE PASSED. I am still confused. The story is almost Science-Fiction.

Sofia felt I needed her. She turned herself inside out and came to Bucharest for a few days. We spent them together, walking in parks, holding hands, kissing passionately under the shade of a chestnut tree, laughing indecisively in front of ice-cream stalls, drinking hot coffee in bed in the mornings. They went fast, incredibly fast.

This was a crazy year.

But the book appeared. Within just a few days after the publication, we had sold the first print run, and the bookshop owners kept on demanding it. I left everything in the care of my colleagues. Beautiful posters, TV adverts on two niche channels, partner blogs, a men's monthly magazine. *Flacăra* will publish the whole story in the November edition, and there will be interviews with me in two dailies. Many statements. I only did a little PR. I was reserved and mysterious. It was a hit.

I think that, in fact, I still am confused and scared. Two corpses and a commitment to the madhouse – it's all too much for a book, no matter how successful I would have liked it to be, and, even if I should have been happy to be sought out for the screen rights. But I refused to think about it.

The investigation is not closed. But I had lost interest in it. I had other priorities. It was hard to find my equilibrium again. I think I managed to do it. I was not alone. Sofia kept in touch with me several times a day, by phone or e-mail. Lulu had me running, chasing her through the parks. We drank juice in petrol stations, we ate pizza, and we went to cartoon shows.

All I can think about now is Diana's madness, and I am waiting for Toni and his white Dacia Logan. I want to see Diana once more. For the last time I imagine. Although someone should go and look for her from time to time. Then, I'll go to the cemetery, to the General, to leave a flower and a copy of the book on the tombstone.

Demetriade arrives in the parking lot. He looks at me through the windscreen. I am outdoors, standing, dragging from a cigarette. My first for many months. I see him and crush it in a metal bin. I get in the car.

"Are you sure you want to go?"

"Absolutely."

"The doctors told me she's not recovered."

"Toni, I want to see her. For Simionescu's sake, at least. I want to close the book on this story for good."

The policeman starts driving slowly. He knows I am in no mood to talk. I take a copy of the book out of the bag. I show it to him and then put it on the backseat.

"It's for you. I'll invite you to the launch."

"Thank you."

He doesn't say anything else. Neither do I. He turns the radio on, so that the silence shouldn't become embarrassing. We are both thinking of our own problems. I have two more copies of the book in my bag. For Diana and for the cemetery. If they'll allow me to give it to him.

At Hospital No 9[136] they open the gates immediately, a sign that the car was expected. Toni parks near a pavilion.

136 Hospital No 9 – a hospital specialised in clinical psychiatry. The name became synonymous to madhouse, akin to Bedlam in English.

The weather is grey, bleak, and there is a wind blowing. An ugly autumn atmosphere. A man dressed in a white coat flapping around his legs welcomes us at the entrance.

"Mateescu."

"Munteanu."

"Demetriade."

We go inside. A lot of greyish white. He leads us down through a now deserted hallway. He stops in front of a door. A white, metal door with a peephole. Almost a prison door. My heart beats fast, with terror. He opens the door. A small room with one bed, a nightstand, a small table and a desk. Diana is in pyjamas with orange and pink teddy bears, her back turned to us, seated at the desk and looking through the window. The window is barred. She is looking outside, drawing in pencil in sketchbook.

"Diana, you have visitors."

She turns for a moment and takes a look at us. Then she continues to draw. I can't see what – her hand, holding a stub of red pencil, travels over the paper almost chaotically.

"Diana, do you want to talk to us?"

Silence.

"Maybe it helps if you talk to people from the outside. What do you say?"

Silence. Then a barely heard whisper:

"No. I don't want to talk to anybody. Only to my father…"

I quake with terror. And I want to leave as soon as possible. The doctor closes the door.

"Step into my office for a moment."

From the hallway, we climb the stairs leading to the next floor. Another door with a tag reading "Head of Section" and the name Dr Mateescu. He goes straight in. A desk and four chairs. On one of them, his profile turned away from the door, is Mikhail Sergeyevich Pushkin. He doesn't get up. He looks at us and remains silent.

"Sit down," the doctor invites us. "I'll bring coffee."

He goes out, leaving us alone. We have things to say which the doctor does not want to hear. He is shrinking away from it all.

I plant myself in front of the Russian.

"What was that, Misha?"

"What was that? A pile of crap, that's what it was."

"Can you explain it?"

"Yes, I can. I thought they wanted to kill him for the secrets of the revolution. I was trying to help him find out who was attempting to kill him."

"I see... Who was it?"

"You really didn't get it, Stelică? Is it so difficult?"

"The driver?" I guess at random.

"Nonsense. The driver didn't act on his own. Neither did you!"

"You were the head."

"No, I was the transmission belt. Diana was the head."

"Diana?! How come Diana?"

"Diana looked for hired assassins. The boys intercepted the request on the way, passed it on to me, and I sent it to you. But I swear I had no idea where it had started. I didn't even suspect it. Nobody suspected it was her. I was convinced you would not shoot, and, together with Simionescu, we decided to go through to the end, to find out who commissioned it."

"So Diana wanted to kill her father?"

"No, Diana wanted to kill her adoptive father. He killed her birth father in that stupid accident. Simionescu was not guilty, it was the other driver... A driver about whom nothing more is known after 1989. He disappeared. A terrible story."

"Revenge? After all these years? Why?"

"I don't know. The doctors…"

Head of Section Mateescu returned with a tray and four cups of coffee. He feels the need to say something:

"Mister Munteanu, that childhood accident left marks. She wanted revenge but she waited for the right moment."

"And the moment was the publication of the memoirs?"

"We suspect so."

"And she was prepared to accuse me of killing Simionescu. And shoot me in self defence. Was everything premeditated?"

Misha stands up and pats my shoulder.

"I am sorry. I believe this is the case. Everything was premeditated with diabolical calm. Absolutely diabolical."

"And all was in vain… Simionescu died."

"Stelică, his story keeps him alive. The book will sell."

"Stick it up the book's mother!"

"It was his wish. You have to go on…" Misha insists. "Believe me. I talked many times with Gigi… with George Simionescu. He was a special person."

I see Misha is showing emotion. Or maybe for one moment he lost his English sang froid.

"Let's get out of here, Toni."

I stretch out my hand to the doctor and leave. I don't even look at Pushkin. He shouts after me:

"Stelian, you need to find your peace of mind!"

I don't reply. I'd like to run away, somewhere far away, and hide from everyone. Away from people, from books, from troubles. Bullshit. This is not possible. Sofia… Lulu…

"I'll get you out of this, old man," Toni whispers in the car, starting up the engine.

Chapter 32

Bucharest – Copenhagen, December 2010

SUPERB WEATHER. Warm. Too warm. Abnormally so. Just like the weather during the revolution. History is repeating itself. I want to go out and take the rubbish. An envelope wedged in the frame of the door falls on to the dusty doormat. I pick it up. Plain white, nothing inscribed on it. Or written. An A5-size envelope made of thick paper, which looks very fat. Meaning that it's full.

It's obvious what it contains. I open the door and throw it on the kitchen table. I go out again to finish the rubbish removal operation. I return, put the dustbin back, then put in a new bin liner and wash my hands. I take the envelope and sit down on an armchair in the living room. My fingers are burning. I have a premonition. I change my mind and look in the kitchen for a box of matches. With methodical gestures, I light a match and bring it close to the envelope. The small flame flares up suddenly and everything catches fire quickly. I hold the envelope in my hand until the fire almost burns me, then I throw the remains in the stainless steel sink. It continues to burn for a few moments. Only the ashes remain. Then I turn on the cold water tap, the ashes are washed away and the sink is empty. And I was not even curious to learn who the next target was. "What you don't know doesn't kill you." According to Sofia.

It is strange to tramp around Europe with no apparent aim. Toni wants to save me. Sofia cannot escape from

London. Misha keeps on calling me, proposing meetings. The books are selling. The sales reports are good. An author who got killed before the launch of his book. A debut volume.

The airport looks new and, most of all, huge for a country so small. We landed with a short thud and a little skidding. Or so it seemed to me. I run through the hallways towards *Baggage Claim* and towards Toni, who, after taking over his new job, really wants us to have a talk. We'll talk. We'll talk rubbish and what will be the use of that? I have a void in my stomach and in my head. Things pass me by in their own rhythm, independently, with or without making sense. Toni said "I'll wait for you at the *Meeting Point*!" I didn't ask him what that was. I am carried away by the river of people and wake up in an open space, and a huge creature wrapped in overcoats and woollen scarves embraces me and grabs the bag from my shoulder.

"Welcome, my friend."

And he really is happy to see me. He seems strangely warm and close.

"I wasn't sure I'd be able to convince you to run away from the world."

"Hmm… I think I wanted to run away from the world. Too many things happened this year."

"It's all ended now."

"It all ended badly, Toni."

He waves his hand and shows me the sliding door marked Exit.

Outside, I am hit by an icy wind that passes through my clothes and freezes my cheeks.

"The weather's ghastly for pleasure trips, Toni."

"I wanted to get you out of there. You needed a week-end away."

"Yes, I needed it."

The film of the last few months runs again and again in front of my eyes, like a passage on the TV news which runs in a loop, repeating *ad infinitum* for the want of anything better.

I watch the new landscape with vacant eyes. Small buildings, not very tall, in a reserved modern style, then 19th century industrial architecture, warehouses converted into offices, a wide space, a field, the sea. After a while I wake up somewhere else: monumental buildings, a bridge, cars and buses, short flashes from this summer's story, then buildings again.

"We are right in the city centre. I'll park as soon as I find a space. How do you like Copenhagen?"

"I don't understand much of it. What are you doing here?"

"They asked for a Romanian policeman to work with the Danish police. The Romanians have multiplied, and problems appear. You know it, you've heard about it."

"Did they really need a big shot commissar?"

"I asked for the posting. I wanted to run away. To take a break. Just like you. That's why I called you. I knew you like the sea, the sailing ships. I'll take you somewhere nice. They even have a Christmas fair."

He parks the car and I get out. The wind blows and I feel chilled by it. I take small steps in the snow.

"This is Nyhavn. The new port. The Number 1 tourist area."

Old buildings on the left, with restaurants on the ground floor; small wooden houses on the right, in front of the now empty summer terraces. A Christmas Fair with globes, clothes, souvenirs, silly trinkets… I half close my eyes and allow my mind to drift.

"How is Sofia?"

"We'll see each other in between Christmas and New Year's. That's when she has free time."

"Don't miss out on the beautiful moments, Stelică. You don't know when the next ones will show up. Take what is offered to you when it's given, don't leave it for later. Don't hesitate! You might not get a second chance. Aren't you going to buy her something for Christmas?"

"Like what?"

"A souvenir, a gnome, a little angel…"

I look, freezing, at the alley lined with kiosks. Many tourists, a crowd of people, words in Spanish, Russian, or German. Photo cameras, little coloured lights, somewhere far off there's a choir, I can hear voices in Danish singing "Jingle Bells".

"I will buy her a little house. Look!" I say, showing Toni a small object imitating a fisherman's house, with a jetty, fishing net, lifebuoy and a boat which looks like an old primitive row boat, the kind we have back home, all reduced to the size of a one-litre juice carton. It's the first object on which I laid my eyes.

"It's not very symbolic for Christmas."

"But it is for us, Toni."

"A birdhouse? You hang those in the courtyard, in a tree."

"Yes, Toni. That's the metaphor," I say, and burst out in a noisy laugh which scares off a pair of Spanish lovers. "A little house for the lovebirds."

"I hope Sofia understands your metaphors."

"Toni, we need a place of our own."

I take out the wallet and pay in Euros, although their local money is the Danish Kroner. I prefer not to think about the exchange rate and how favourable or not it was to me. Tourists are always guaranteed and innocent victims.

Demetriade smiles and pats my shoulder. We both look like mountains of clothes.

"Let's go in here…. Let us not miss out on the beautiful moments. As I said, we should take advantage of what we have, so as not to lose…"

"You are repeating yourself. Have you become a philosopher, Commissar?"

"I don't know. I wanted to take you out of your routine. To offer you a break. A man to man discussion, a discussion between friends. I think I learned how to be a good friend, Stelică. And I care for my friends. There are few of them, too few. But that's life."

We choose a table with high stools. I order an Irish coffee, Toni gets a regular. I take off my hat and thick overcoat.

"Your hair turned white, Stelică."

"Yes, the white hairs multiplied this year. I could barely see them before. But after all that's happened… You know, I didn't keep in touch with anyone. I just worked on the book. Do you have any news?"

"I've been away for almost one month now. Misha doesn't say anything. But he sent a CD with all the e-mails exchanged by everyone, when Diana was looking for assassins. He gave me everything. Contacts, letters, messages. Everything is very clear. It was her. Her and the driver."

"Sinister. And she ordered Simionescu's killing with his own money?"

"Exactly."

"What about Diana?"

"Still in the hospital. Even if she gets better, she will remain locked up. It's sad."

"You know, I still have the money in my account. I didn't spend anything more. What should I do?"

"You keep it. Spend it with Sofia. Or ask Misha… I don't

know. Was the coffee good? Would you like another one? It's very cold outside, and you're not too used to this. After that, there are several other places to visit with you."

I don't hear him any more. I think of Sofia and I have a mad desire to hug her, to cook spaghetti, to make love to her, to talk platitudes in bed while we sip our coffees. We'll go to Vienna. Right there, at the Haydn. To end this story once and for all. And to have a little house, our little house.

Chapter 33

Vienna, December 2010

I THINK THAT THE STORY behind the General's book should also be written. His story. Grandiose or stupid. It should be written and printed, not just... mentioned... at book launches or in interviews, as a marketing and promotional strategy. I should write it, instead of throwing words at the reading public, manipulating these people into buying the memoirs. Because he is no longer among us, and nobody can write dedications on *My Revolution*. They would ask for autographs from me, saying "you are the editor", but I won't be able to do it. I sigh deeply, or perhaps it just seems like it. The big paperback book pokes me in the ribs. I pick it up and start reading again. Somewhere in the middle, where it has opened, at random.

The red LED light on the BlackBerry winks at me. It's on the nightstand. I stretch out and pick it up. A short e-mail from Bucharest, from the publishing house. We have yet another review, this time in *România Liberă*[137], and the sales are increasing daily. The book has entered the top ten. But of course – a dead author sells better than a living one. Especially a murdered author. From Stieg Larsson onwards... We are negotiating the film rights already. I should get ready for sales outside Romania... There is beautiful money in it. Money – again? Oh, God, what am I into?

"You haven't slept well?"

She looks at me, propped up on one elbow, with

---

137 *România Liberă* – Free Romania – one of the main Romanian dailies.

narrowed eyes and dishevelled hair, and with a restless and sincere smile. She loves me. I love her as well. I love her desperately.

"No, I slept well. I woke up early and I am trying to read. I read from the memoirs."

The room is lit up. She checks her watch. It's the same Festina – a simple one with no second hand and no extra dials, same as mine but smaller in diameter. We bought the pair in Valletta, in a small jewellery store. In a sale.

"What are you thinking?"

"About Malta."

"Malta? Yes, that was beautiful. Aren't we going to eat something? I am rather hungry, and it's a quarter to ten already."

"We go. I'll take a shower and we go."

There is a bit of sun outside. And Maria Hilfer Strasse is almost deserted. Several days left to New Year's Eve. The tourists have not yet arrived. It is windy, but it's not cold. Not December cold. She holds my arm, all wrapped up, with a little hat on her head and gloves on her hands.

"In London it is not so cold."

"But in Bucharest it's a lot worse."

"I will have to go back."

"I know."

"Before New Year's Eve. I have to be on duty on the 1st of January."

"I know, my love."

"I am sorry."

"It's fine, we'll find time for us. More time…"

"Don't you want to you come with me now?"

"I can't. It's the book… In January."

"Yes, the book. The sales!"

"This is no joke!"

We find a café behind the Opera, right opposite the taxi rank. I have no idea what it's called. It doesn't matter and I don't even look. It has worn parquet on the floor, small round tables and wooden chairs, and several clients, probably Austrians, who are languorously reading their newspapers. The waiters wear white aprons, silent and ceremonious. I have the sensation of a jump back in time to the interwar years.

We order Viennese coffee and an espresso lungo. Then two mineral waters. A cold one and one at room temperature.

We are silent. I'd like to have a newspaper to read.

She is smiling at me.

The BlackBerry bug vibrates and buzzes on my belt. And it ruins our moments of peace and quiet. Again!

A text message. I read it: "Stay where you are. I am coming to you. Misha."

I look around me involuntarily. He's following me, and he's finding me, just as always. I show the screen to Sofia. She laughs, trying to suppress her laughter.

"You'll never get rid of him, will you?"

"If you take him in small doses, he's OK."

"This is your life, my love. Stelian Munteanu must assume responsibility for it. I did the same with my life."

"Our life."

"Yes, our life."

I order another espresso lungo, with milk.

Misha Pushkin enters silently, leans towards Sofia and plants a kiss on her left cheek, then puts a hand on my shoulder and takes a seat. All as if in one single fluid, sliding and elegant movement.

The waiter is already near him.

"A Schnapps."

He then turns to us.

"How are the lovebirds?"

"Fine," answers Sofia.

I am silent. And I am looking in another direction.

"I am happy for you, my dears."

"What more do you want from us, Misha?"

"Nothing, Stelică. Nothing from Sofia. She has her own business. You…"

"I?"

"You are kind of unemployed."

"It's the crisis."

"Bullshit."

"Misha, what do you want from me?"

He lights up a Dunhill languidly. He asks for a coffee. Espresso.

"I would like you back. Back to work."

"Another dubious proposal?"

"No, nothing dubious. It never was anything dubious."

"You lie, Misha. You got me in this game with the General."

"I wanted to prove a point. I was right."

"But you toyed with me."

"Now you're starting up again from the beginning. I knew you would not shoot. I based my plan on that. I had to find the truth. For George."

"And now he's dead."

He smokes with pleasure, a cloud of tobacco smoke floating around his head.

"Yes…"

He takes another sip from his coffee, and one from his schnapps.

"You've sent me another envelope. I burnt it. And you know it."

"I know it."

"Why did you do it?"

"I wanted to test you. The envelope had newspaper cuttings inside."

"You are so full of shit, Misha."

"No..."

And he stares into vacancy again.

"I would like you to go to St. Stephen's Cathedral Square. To meet somebody."

"When?"

"Right now."

"Not in your dreams."

"Please."

"Who is it?"

"He'll come to you. Please. We'll wait for you here."

"OK, but..."

"It won't take long. I promise."

"Another one of your crazy plans?"

"No, Stelian. You'll see. No crazy plan. You need this meeting."

"So you say."

"Please."

"Tell me who it is."

"No. You'll find out."

I have no chance with Misha. And I give up. I sip the last drop of coffee.

"I am going. Wait for me."

Sofia looks at me with her lustful expression. She'd like to be in the hotel, in our warm room. Misha smokes a second cigarette absentmindedly.

St. Stephen's Cathedral Square is the best known and busiest place in Vienna. It's hard for me to believe somebody can find me, even if there are fewer tourists now. A cold, wintry wind blows. I start to feel it through my clothes. I position myself near the kiosk where they sell sausages and I wait. No customers there, and the sausage seller asks me with his eyes if I want anything.

The minutes pass slowly and, without realising it, I start looking at the people passing by. People with paper bags from famous brands, photo cameras, maps and tourist guides. I am trying to guess the nationality of those passing by.

"Morning, Stelian Munteanu."

I am tremendously startled because I recognise the voice. I turn, shaking.

From the left, a little more than two metres away from me, a man in a hat and an overcoat with an upturned collar is looking at me. Even with his sunglasses on, I know precisely who he is.

"So everything was a trick, General?"

He takes another step towards me.

"No. There was no trick. I did find who wanted me dead."

Another step. And he holds his hand out to me.

"You found out… Yes. What about Tudose? Didn't he kill you? What did Tudose do? What was he supposed to do? Did he die in vain?"

"Yes, he did…."

I shake his hand firmly. He shakes mine in the same way.

"I am glad to see you again, Stelian."

"So am I. The surprise is a little too… It's like we are in a bad American movie, with a predictable ending. But a man did die, and another person is in the madhouse."

"I didn't know the finale. Until recently. I was in the hospital."

"In the hospital? So you did get hurt?"

"No. I was in Vienna for something different… I wasn't running away from responsibility or from the revolutionaries, as people thought. I was ill. Cancer, Stelian. A tumour of the prostate. I was admitted into the AKH hospital. You know it… I suppose."

"Yes, the famous hospital-city for the wealthy."

"For everybody. It was a good pretext for my disappearance. Apparently murdered. Everybody helped me disappear: Misha, Steiner, old acquaintances, Tudose. I was operated on."

"And now?"

"I am well, the operation was successful. I am undergoing treatment."

"Yes, I am glad you are well," but I have a cynical, insinuating tone in my voice. "In this case, what happened in the house on *Aviator Petre Mircea Street*? All the shootings?"

"Tudose wanted to stop Diana. Things got out of control. Diana's revolver was loaded with blanks. Tudose had loaded it like that. He wanted to unmask her in front of you. But you came armed. It seems nobody took this into account. Not even Misha."

"And it all ended badly. A man died. Does it mean I am to blame for it?"

"No. Nobody is to blame. It was destiny, fate. Tudose was a trustworthy comrade. He, too, wanted to protect me. He also wanted to protect Diana, as well. And you. Things got out of control."

"Playing God is dangerous."

"Yes, Munteanu, we forget humility."

"And now? I mean…"

"The book? My reappearance? No. I think the Stieg Larsson model is more successful."

"So you want to stay hidden?"

"Yes – low profile! I can finally enjoy life in peace. And you can sell your books better. There are many TV recordings of me. And from the radio, and photographs. You have enough material for the advertising. You don't even have author rights to pay. I am dead and Diana is in the madhouse. Tudose is no more…"

He stops. He is disturbed. Sad. I seem to see a trace of tears under the sunglasses that have slid down his nose. I can see he is no longer in top form. Shoulders are slightly drooping, movements seem to be heavier, the skin of his hands is aging.

"I am sorry, General. I really am sorry."

"This is life. I wanted to offer everything to her… That was fate. That damned accident… Would you like a sausage? Aren't you hungry? I am."

"I am too. A sausage and beer."

"OK, my treat."

We eat in silence. The sausage is juicy and hot. The beer too cold for this season. The sausage seller is looking at me in a way that seems to say "thank you". Then the General looks at his watch. So do I. It's been not more than 15 minutes.

"It's time for me to go."

"Yes?"

We shake hands again. I don't know what to say.

"I will write a postcard. Probably. From somewhere… Give my regards to Misha and Sofia. You know, I would have liked to meet her. Please go and visit Diana from time to time. Maybe she will understand, eventually. Maybe she will be forgiven. I already have forgiven her. If…"

"I will take care, I promise."

"Farewell, Stelian Munteanu."

"Farewell, General. And a happy new…" But I stop, the

words freezing on my lips. He smiles bitterly.

"You wanted to say happy new year. Hmm… Yes. Have a good year. As for me, I'll get by."

He turns and leaves. I return to the café near the Opera. That was it. It is all finished. Am I happy? I don't know. I am glad it's all over. A sort of happy ending.

Epilogue

London, February 2011

IT IS QUIET IN ST JAMES'S SQUARE. The offices of the British branch of Grimaldi agencies are here. Only a few office workers. Same for the clients. It's the crisis. Sofia works here. I walk around London. In the middle of the square there is a park. A little park inside a bigger park, St James's Square Gardens. The gate of the little park is locked. I wonder who might have the keys, and why they keep it locked. What building administrator is responsible for the key? In the five days since my arrival I wasn't able to find out. There are plenty of parks here, finding out is not a necessity, it's more an ambition of mine.

My mission is accomplished. My mission? Duty is more like it. I brought the book to the top of the major booksellers' charts. A super campaign to promote it, online and offline, adverts and outdoor advertising. We sold 3,850 copies in December alone. In January, we remained at the top although the sales were lower, only 1,780[138]. For Trident, this was a mouthful of oxygen. It looks like February will be good too.

After a bonus served in envelopes, together with a beer and cakes for St John's Feast[139], timid smiles began to appear on the faces of my colleagues. We drank to the second year

---

138   The figures are important for the Romanian book market, even if they don't seem to be very high in comparison to the British market.

139   The Feast of St John the Baptist, on 7 January. It marks the end of the traditional winter feasts. In Romania, a majority Christian Orthodox country, the celebrations held on the feasts of various important saints are taken very seriously, some people putting on a bigger party than for their birthday.

of crisis and maybe the last, to a better year, and to our friends, to our enemies and so on and so forth. The fact that I mentioned friends and enemies does not mean that we listened to *Manele*[140] music. We listened to no music at all. Marius told jokes and Sorin told us how he is going to modify our website in order to make it more accessible. The girls ate and were quiet. We talked about new books and about our respective families. I told them about Lulu. They asked me about Sofia and then I suddenly started missing her.

Now I am here next to her. And I am as timid as a virgin. I should make things clear. To make the decision. I am sitting on a bench and I'm looking at the buildings. I am thinking of a good coffee. A long coffee with milk, cooling slightly. I would drink it calmly, reading the papers. Any papers.

My BlackBerry vibrates and rings. A text message. "Don't you want to visit me? Misha." That's the last thing I need. The pink building in Crystal Palace. I haven't been there in a long time. I didn't even think Pushkin had kept the place. He received me there back when I was looking for that manuscript, some two years ago. Time has passed.

Buzz – another text message. "Love you. What do we do this evening? You taking me out? S. Family name still Matei!" I smile looking at the screen. Sofia is still waiting to settle the date of the wedding. When? Where? After this mad year we've had. I take a big breath of air and reply "Love you too. We will go walking on Oxford St this evening. You book your time off, I'll book the wedding. S."

I then call Misha.

"Hello. What do you want?"

---

140 *Manele* is a style of urban-Gypsy music with Balkan influences. In Romania, this style of music is generally associated with a lack of good taste, based on the so-called "aspiration lyrics" that make reference to giving loads of money to one's friends, all enemies dying of envy, being "Number 1", and enjoying "living it large".

"Morning. You are a little rude."

"Every time you contact me, Misha, you want something from me."

I hear him laughing.

"You are right. But this time I want to offer you a good cup of coffee. What do you say?"

He's read my mind. As always. And all resentments come back.

"Misha, what was all this bullshit? Why did you convince me to become a killer? What did you want from me?"

"This is not the kind of thing one discusses over the phone."

"I don't want to see you again, Pushkin."

"You have no choice, Munteanu."

"That's what you say. I didn't deserve any of these things."

"No, you did not. You do believe in friendship, don't you?"

"Bullshit. A question coming from the script of B-movies. A cliché, and you know it."

"Then it is simple, my dear. I told you when we met in Vienna last. You were either not paying attention or did not understand. You are not stupid, but you certainly are rash. Before you went to meet him. There was a price..."

"A price?!"

"Yes. Simionescu suspected they would try to kill him. He was receiving threats. From everywhere. He was afraid. He had to find out who the people were that wanted to kill him. To see what forces he had to confront. He asked for my help."

"Of course he did – and you found me."

"You are wrong. He found you. He had to trust somebody from outside the system. From outside the old system! He thought about you and called me. Stelian, I stood guarantee for you. As a friend – if you are not ashamed of this friendship. Simionescu wanted to escape and to disappear. And to leave the book to you. As a sort of compensation for what you went through. Everything has to be paid for."

"Yes, one has to pay for everything. Somehow. And you never know how. But a man died."

"Tudose, poor man… Yes, he died because you were stupid and took the Colt with you. Diana's weapon was firing blanks. Tudose had loaded it himself, but you mixed things up. We already suspected Diana. Nobody would have died if you didn't have the weapon on you."

"Are you accusing me? After all you've done to me?"

"Will you calm down now?"

"What about Diana?"

"Nobody thought Diana could be behind it, at first. Not for one moment. We realised it only towards the end. A tragedy from a childhood that left such scars… You have to understand we were talking about extremely grave secrets, problems connected with the revolution. We all suspected that big interests were at stake, that somebody wanted to silence him for what he knew about… It doesn't matter anymore. You concentrate on the book and forget about the past. Come on, I am waiting for you, Sofia is working now and I don't think you've much to do."

I don't reply. I hear him breathe. It sounds more laboured than in the previous years. Must be the age. The running around. Is he really my friend? What does it mean, though? Having shared memories? Shit. Life is too complicated. 2 Lei philosophy… I am laughing inside – it's true that I have nothing to do.

"OK, I'm coming. But you promise we are not going to talk about investigations and spies?"

It's his turn to be quiet.

"Misha, can you hear me?"

"I can't promise a thing, you know very well. Come, let's have a good coffee and then we'll see."

"Misha, I want to get married. Now."

"May your house be built of stone[141]."

"You're annoying me."

"And you're acting like a spoiled brat."

"I am going to swear at you."

"That wouldn't be the first time."

"Misha, another question."

"Leave it for now. We'll talk here."

"No. I have got to know. Tell me – the lead coffin was empty, wasn't it?"

He stays quiet.

"Misha, answer!"

I can hear his slow breathing. Then his voice:

"Well, not exactly empty. But we're not going to discuss this."

I hang up on him. I hail a black cab and jump in. For once, he can reimburse my travel expenses. On the streets, there are still decorations saying "A Happy 2011."

Buzz – text message: "I can hardly wait to be Mrs Munteanu." I smile with a dumb and melancholic expression. The driver looks at me through the glass partition without interest. I reply: "See you this evening, Mrs Munteanu!" I take another deep breath. A new year has started. Buzz – another text message: "I know about a good offer for wedding rings on Oxford St. Coffee is hot. Calm down. MP."

The rays of sunshine have broken through the compact mass of clouds. I feel like whistling. I feel freer and calmer.

141   A traditional wish for young married couples is *casă de piatră*, literally meaning a house made of stone. By extension, a lasting, stable marriage.

Suddenly, I realise that I have got rid of the pressure. The years from before, from the old days, are not haunting me any longer. A pleasant holiday, General, wherever you are. And thank you!

The End